THE DUKE OF DARING

The Untouchables

DARCY BURKE

Copyright

The Duke of Daring

ISBN: 1944576037
ISBN-13: 9781944576035

This is a work of fiction. Names, characters, places, and incidents are the product of the author's imagination or are used fictitiously. Any resemblance to actual events, locales, or persons, living or dead, is purely coincidental.

Book design © Darcy Burke.
Cover design © Carrie Divine/Seductive Designs.
Photo copyright: Couple © Novelstock.com
Photo copyright: Background © FairytaleDesign (Małgorzata Patrzyk)/Depositphotos.com.
Editing: Linda Ingmanson.

For Steve
Thank you for being my Duke of Everything
for 25 years and counting.

Chapter One

London, 1816

"HELLFIRE, THAT ONE'S got the luck of the devil tonight," Andrew Wentworth, fourth Earl of Dartford, remarked to one of his companions. Andrew didn't know the gentleman currently scooping up his winnings, but he was causing a stir.

His friend, Edgar Charles, nodded. "Never seen him before. You?"

Andrew shook his head. The gentleman looked young, his fresh face framed with dark sideburns that cloaked the upper edge of his jaw.

The banker, one of the fairer as far as gaming hells went, nodded toward the young man as he finished paying out his winnings.

The lad's gloved fingers, slender and long—almost graceful—swept the bounty across the table and scooped it up. He stashed the profit inside his coat, perhaps in a pocket sewn into the lining. Everyone in the room would know exactly where to find it, should they wish to rob him outside.

Andrew glanced around at tonight's visitors—young bucks and rakes, a few working men. He didn't think anyone would accost the man, but he also doubted the fellow's ability to defend himself. He was on the shorter side and a bit thick. His legs were long, however, so perhaps he could outrun trouble if necessity required.

Charles gestured toward the table. "Again?"

Andrew was more interested in this mysterious gentleman than in continuing his own play. But then gambling was not his favorite pastime, as it was Charles's.

The banker called for the next round, and the unknown gentleman went in again, placing his bets on the various cards. It was a game of chance, yet the man looked as though he had a strategy. That alone was enough to pique Andrew's curiosity. He watched as the round started up. Immediately, Charles began to lose heavily. The unknown gentleman, however, continued to have incredible luck.

By the end of the round, Charles was lamenting his misfortune. "Do save me from myself," he said to Andrew and the rest of their group.

It was a commonplace plea from their friend, and one of the reasons they ventured forth as a group. Each had their vice and relied on the others to keep them in check. Except for Andrew. His only vice was that he'd rather be out, be *doing*…anything but staying home alone.

Was that really a vice?

Of course it wasn't. For Andrew, though, it might be termed a compulsion.

The portly young gentleman appeared to be without company, which was odd, and not just because Andrew would never dream of spending an evening thus. Again, he scooped up his winnings, but Andrew noted he stashed them in a different pocket within his coat.

Horace, the banker, looked up at the young man. "You finished?"

The man nodded. "Thank you, sir." His voice was surprisingly deep, with a hint of gravel.

Horace grinned, revealing a gold tooth. "Come back

soon. I need a chance to win my money back."

The stranger's mouth tugged into a half smile, but he quickly masked it. Though not before a flash of awareness curled up Andrew's spine. There was something about him…

The lad turned and left the salon. Charles was still bemoaning his losses, but their friends had rallied around him. It was time to go. Knowing they would be right behind him, Andrew quickly departed.

He strode to the entry hall, where the burly footman was just showing the unknown gentleman out. Andrew nodded at the footman as he moved outside and followed the man down the short flight of stairs to the pavement. The man moved at a sprightly pace, differently than Andrew would've thought given his girth.

"'Evening," Andrew said. "I'm Dartford."

The man turned, but his features were shadowed by the brim of his hat and the fact that the streetlamp was behind him. "'Evening." His low, almost steely voice caught Andrew off guard even more than it had inside. There was something…off.

Curiosity burned through Andrew. "It would be polite of you to introduce yourself as I've done."

"Ah, of course." He coughed. "Smith."

Andrew moved so that the man had to turn, which brought him into the splash of light from the lamp. "Indeed?"

He gave Andrew a furtive glance, his long, dark lashes sweeping down over his eyes. "Davis Smith."

"Pleased to meet you. Come, meet the others."

Smith tipped his head up, and his eyes widened briefly. "Others?" He looked down at the street and tugged at the brim of his hat.

Andrew nodded toward his small group of friends as they joined them on the pavement. "Gentlemen, meet my new acquaintance, Smitty."

Pleasantries were exchanged, and then Roderick Beaumont, a young viscount whose preferred vice was that of the flesh, looked around at everyone. "Another hell, or is it time for Mrs. Longley's? I'm sure you know my vote." He grinned, and there was no doubt he would end up at his favorite brothel—either now or at some point later.

"Longley's," Charles said. "I can't afford another hell tonight."

The group consensus was quickly made—Longley's was their destination.

As they started along the street, Andrew looked at Smith. "You should come along with us."

"To a brothel?" His deep voice had climbed a bit on that last word.

Andrew laughed. "Why, Smitty, are you a virgin?"

"No." The answer came too swiftly to be believed.

"Then you should definitely…come." Andrew looked at the young man's face to see whether he registered the double entendre, but there was no indication.

"I don't think so. I need to get home." Smith turned from him and started to walk away.

Andrew caught the shadowed movement near the hell they'd just left. He reached out and snagged Smith's arm, drawing him back. What he felt beneath the sleeve was soft but not fleshy. And the gentleman was not as heavy as he looked, for though Andrew hardly exerted any effort, the man came crashing into Andrew's side. His head tipped back, and the full illumination of the lamp spilled over his features.

Those ink-black lashes curled away from moss-laden hazel eyes, and the gasp that leapt from the too-supple lips gave the man away completely.

"Damn me," Andrew breathed. He kept his hand firmly clasped around the *woman's* elbow and tugged her along with him as he followed his group of friends.

"I'm not going with you." Her voice had gone low again as she yanked the brim of her hat down.

"You've no choice."

She tried to pull free of his grip. "You can't force me."

Andrew stopped, and she nearly tripped. He held her upright. "Should I let you wander off alone? There's a man—perhaps more than one—waiting for you back by the hell. He's probably going to rob you, and when he finds out you're a woman, I daresay he'll do far more."

She gasped again, and this time when she looked up at him, her face was scrunched into a scowl. "How did you know?"

"I'm very observant."

"Damn." She brushed her fingertips against what had to be fake sideburns glued to her face. "I worked so hard."

She probably would've succeeded too, if Andrew hadn't taken an interest in her. But he was glad he had, or she might find herself in dire straits indeed. "Come on." He pulled her along again, but she tried to resist.

"I am *not* going to a brothel." She didn't bother lowering her voice anymore, but it was still deeper than most women's. It possessed a dark, raspy quality that stirred Andrew's interest. The curiosity he'd felt at the hell intensified.

"What the devil were you doing in a hell?"

She looked up at him, blinking, with a saucy curve to her mouth. "Winning."

He laughed, loud and boisterous. He liked her instantly, even if she was as foolish as she was alluring. Alluring? Yes, because any woman who would dare to venture into a gaming hell alone was a mystery Andrew wanted to unravel.

The small group of men stopped at the street corner. Charles called back, "Dart, you coming?"

Andrew started forward, but she dug in her heels. He backed up and looked at her. "We aren't going to the brothel, but I need to part ways with them. Just follow my lead."

This time when he moved ahead, she went with him. Still, he sensed her reluctance. He let go of her as they approached his friends.

He gave them all a jovial grin. "Smitty and I've decided to find another game. Perhaps his luck will rub off on me."

Beaumont snorted. "As if you need it. You're one of the luckiest bastards I know."

Not always and not when it mattered, but Andrew wouldn't illuminate them. "See you tomorrow."

"I've got quite a wager on you," Charles said, his dark gaze piercing him. "Don't let me down."

Andrew grinned. "When's the last time I lost?"

Charles smiled in return. "Never. But there's a first time for everything."

"Do me a favor." Beaumont dug around in his coat and beckoned for Andrew to come forward. "Have your friend there place a bet for me. I want some of his luck too." He tossed a few guineas into Andrew's hand.

Andrew tucked the coins into his coat. "Now do *me* a favor and don't allow the fair Mrs. Longley to abuse you overmuch."

Beaumont flashed a toothy smile. "But I like that."

Andrew rolled his eyes as he turned back to Smith, or whatever her name was. Only she wasn't there.

He turned his head to look up and down the streets. They were at an intersection, so she could've departed any number of ways. *Silly chit.*

One of his friends pointed down the street they'd just come to. "He went that way. Looked like he was in a hurry. Maybe he'd rather be alone. Just come with us, Dart."

Not a chance. He looked back toward the hell, trying to discern if the man in the shadows was still there or if he was even now tracking down the enigmatic and excessively foolish young woman. "Thank you, but I must catch up to Smitty. Beaumont's counting on us." He tossed them a careless grin in the hope that they would just continue on their way.

Thankfully they did just that, and Andrew turned in the direction she'd gone. He walked quickly, his gait devouring the pavement in his haste. He scanned both sides of the street, reasoning that she had to have ducked in somewhere or turned a corner, because he couldn't see her.

He detected something moving across the street and craned his neck to see if he could make it out in the shadows. Then he heard the cock of a pistol behind him, and he froze.

Very slowly, he turned, his hands outstretched. He carried a blade in his boot when they visited the hells. He'd whisk it out if necessary…

He exhaled because it wasn't necessary. Smith—the young woman—glared at him from the alleyway he'd neglected to check while he'd studied the opposite side of the street.

"Stop following me." Her words came out in a near growl. He was impressed with just how dark and fierce she could sound.

He inclined his head toward the pocket pistol in her hand. "Do you know how to use that?" He was surprised to find that she was armed, but at least she hadn't been quite as foolish as he'd thought.

"Of course I do. And if I had a sword, I'd know how to use that too."

He appreciated her bravado but wondered if she was exaggerating her abilities. "So you're a gentleman in every way but the most"—his gaze dipped down her body—"fundamental."

She scowled at him again. "Just turn around and go on your way. Catch up to your friends. It sounded as if you have quite an evening planned."

Andrew dropped his hands to his sides and took a step toward her. He froze again as she aimed the gun at his chest. "I only want to help you, see you home at the very least. I mean you absolutely no harm. Wouldn't I have taken advantage by now?"

She lifted a shoulder. "Rather difficult when I'm the one with the deadly weapon."

He let a smile open his lips. "Just so." He tried another tack. "Where are you going now?"

"None of your business."

"I'd still like to offer my assistance—wherever you're going. Please, I don't know that I'd forgive myself if I let you go off alone into the night, even with a pistol at the ready. You can trust me. Will you?"

Her gaze was shrewd, skeptical.

A movement down the street lured Andrew's attention. He couldn't know if it was whomever he'd seen lurking outside the hell, but he wanted to get her away from this area. "Come on." He grabbed the arm that wasn't holding the pistol and turned her away from the man down the street. "We need to go."

She wrenched her elbow free. "Don't touch me. I could've shot you."

"Doubtful. You'll need to work on your reflexes as well as your distance. You were much too close. I could've overpowered you at any moment."

She made a deep sound in her throat—somewhere between a dark laugh and a cough. He found it oddly enticing. "Then why didn't you?"

"I'm not that sort of man." He glanced over his shoulder and saw that the man was coming toward them, but not quickly enough to seem like a pursuit. Still, Andrew wanted to quit the street. "Let's move. Where are you going?"

She started walking, straightening her spine as she moved. "I'm not telling you."

He groaned. "I hope you aren't married. If you are, I'll need to have words with your husband, and then I shall extend my extreme condolences on his choice of wife."

"Of course I'm not married, you imbecile." She said this with such heat and vigor that he was sure he'd struck a nerve. Curiosity assailed him once more, but he didn't pursue the topic.

"Are you going to tell me where we're going? I'd like to move away from this neighborhood." He glanced behind him once more and saw that the man had crossed the street and seemingly had no interested in them. Andrew relaxed slightly, but—noting that she hadn't answered him—began to weary of her stubbornness.

He pulled her into the nearest alley, where he disarmed her. He turned so that she backed up against the brick wall. He loomed over her, frowning, and drawing a breathy gasp from her. "Confound it, woman. I'm helping you whether you like it or not."

"I don't like it one bit."

He pressed the pistol back into her gloved hand and leaned forward, catching the barest hint of her fragrance. It was soft, and tellingly feminine with floral tones. How had he missed that before? Because he hadn't been this close. "Will you trust me?"

He nearly laughed at the sudden ridiculousness of the question. For in that moment, with her body so near and the sound of her agitated breathing filling his senses, he wasn't entirely certain he trusted himself.

⁂

WITH EACH BREATH, Lucinda Parnell inhaled the strong, powerful, and inconveniently seductive scent of Man. But then she expected nothing less from the Earl of Dartford, who was presently pressing her up against the wall in some alleyway as if she were a common harlot. A harlot, ahem, dressed as a man.

She was being terribly overdramatic. Her friend Aquilla would approve.

The weight of Lucy's pistol was a familiar comfort in her hand. She considered bringing it up hard against his head—she was far stronger than anyone ever gave her credit for—but he really wasn't a threat. After all, he *had* returned her weapon, and it did seem as if he only wanted to see her safe. Still, she didn't need him. She didn't need anyone.

She employed her haughtiest tone, irritated that he'd

found her out in the first place. "I appreciate your concern. However, I am quite capable of seeing myself home. This is not my first foray into this neighborhood."

He didn't budge, but his eyes widened briefly. "Hell and damnation, you're joking."

She kept her gaze pinned to his, which actually meant she had to look up at him since he was rather taller than she. But she was determined to show him she was made of stern stuff. Just as she determined not to be drawn into the velvety sable of his eyes. "I am not."

"I frequent this area, yet I have never seen you."

Because this was, in fact, just her second outing. And if she continued to do as well as she had, she'd be able to stop after only a couple of weeks. All she needed was a small nest egg.

She raised her chin. "Then I am succeeding in my endeavor."

He snorted. "Except I discovered your identity tonight—or at least, your sex. I still don't know who you are…*Smitty*."

"You may keep calling me that."

"I'd rather call you by your given name."

It was her turn to scoff. "That will never happen, my lord."

He shook his head, momentarily breaking eye contact. When his gaze found hers once more, she pressed back against the wall under its dark intensity. "Back to the matter at hand. You are not succeeding at…whatever you're doing." She opened her mouth to refute him once more, but he cut her off. "No. You're not. I don't care if you *are* winning. Anyone with half a brain wins on their first time at a hell. And you clearly have a full, well-functioning brain. Who taught you to play faro?"

She couldn't help but feel flattered by him. She'd never been one to receive compliments, especially about her beauty, but those didn't matter to her anyway. To be noticed and appreciated for her intelligence was a dream she'd long since abandoned. "My father."

"And where is he?"

"Cold in his grave." For what, seven years? Goodness, she barely tracked the time. Not like she did for her mother.

His lips clamped together briefly. "I see. It's no wonder you're running about unsupervised. Have you no mother or brothers either?"

She cocked her head to the side, tiring of his meddling. "None of this is any of your concern. If you'd permit me, I should like to go home."

"Oh, I'll permit you. With my escort."

She pursed her lips. "I don't need your escort."

His brows pitched together as his features descended into a scowl. "We're back to this?"

In another situation, she might've laughed at his consternation. "We never left it."

A determined glint stole into his gaze. She didn't like it one bit. "You're a cheeky woman, whoever you are. But let me tell you how this is going to proceed. I am not leaving your side until I see you home. You may have escaped danger so far, but it's only a matter of time until luck deserts you."

She blinked at him. Then she *did* laugh, and his expression changed to one of bemusement. "This is rich coming from you—the Duke of Daring. Your exploits are legend—and fraught with risk."

"The…*what*?" A light of understanding, and perhaps

appreciation, stole into his dark eyes. "You know me."

She gritted her teeth, annoyed with herself for loosening her tongue. "I know *of* you. That's quite a different thing."

"Never mind that. You're out in Society. Who are you?"

"Never mind *that.*" She took great pleasure in throwing his words back at him. "However, since it seems you will not leave me be, let us walk." She shoved at his chest, which was hard and unforgiving, but in the most unnervingly *spectacular* way.

She half expected him to crowd her against the wall again, but he didn't. He held out his arm for her to precede him from the alley.

She tucked her pistol back inside her jacket, where she was covered in several layers of padding to make her appear larger than she really was. She'd had pockets sewn in various places for stashing her pistol and her money.

"Where are we going?" he asked.

"I'm not saying. You can just follow along, since you insist upon being a nuisance." She'd stop in front of a house near hers and hopefully convince him to leave her there.

He fell into step beside her as they strode toward Jermyn Street. "Why did you call me the Duke of Daring?"

She cast him a sideways look. "It fits, doesn't it?"

He chuckled, surprising her. "I suppose it does. Makes me sound rather dashing."

"As if Dartford does not. What kind of name is that anyway?"

"It's a village in Kent. My family seat is there."

She knew that, of course. For some reason, she

wanted to provoke him. He seemed up for the challenge. Her mother had always said she should've had younger siblings to taunt—and to love. But the only other time Mama had been able to carry a child, she'd died, leaving Lucy to rely on her father and, thankfully, her grandmother, who was now her sole remaining family.

"You didn't answer my question," he prompted. "Have I earned a nickname? I've never heard anyone say that before."

"Yes, well, it's employed by a…select group." Lucy and her two best friends, precisely.

"I see. May I ask which group?"

It wasn't as if they were a formal organization, but perhaps they should be. Yes, they needed a name, just as they'd recently adopted a designation for Dartford and his like—The Untouchables. They'd actually borrowed it from their surprising new friend, the Duchess of Kendal, a former spinster as Lucy was destined to be.

Lucy turned onto Jermyn Street, and Dartford followed her. "It doesn't signify," she said. "Anyway, you undertake a number of exploits—racing, gambling, a variety of sporting events. I hear you're quite good at bowls."

"Indeed I am."

"And that you sometimes play in Hyde Park very early in the morning." A somewhat scandalous situation, according to Society.

"I do." His lips curved into a captivating smile, and Lucy had the sense he could charm anyone. She would have to be on her guard.

She decided this was the only opportunity she'd ever have to confirm one of Society's most outrageous rumors. She turned her head toward him for a few steps. "Is it true you've swum nude in the Thames?"

He tripped slightly, and Lucy smiled.

"We, ah, shouldn't discuss that." He coughed.

"We shouldn't be walking alone together either, but that's not stopping us. Furthermore, as someone who doesn't seem to care about Society's rules, I'm surprised you'd hesitate to brag about your endeavors."

"Gads, am I a braggart too? The Duke of Gloat, perchance?" He looked askance at her. "You do realize that I'm not even a duke."

She appreciated him poking fun at himself, but didn't say so. It made him seem less of an Untouchable, which was preposterous. They might be alone together at night on a London street, but he was as unattainable to her as any earl or duke or other nobleman. "Yes, well, it hardly matters to those of us in the lower echelon."

She expected another quick rejoinder, but he was quiet for several steps. To the corner of Jermyn Street.

"I suppose we're going to walk on St. James's, despite the fact that you're a woman?" he asked, pausing.

She peered up at him from beneath the brim of her hat. "I'm Davis Smith, remember?"

"Just so."

They turned onto St. James's and walked toward Piccadilly.

"Why are you dressed up as a man and gambling in hells?" He threw her a beleaguered glance. "And please don't say it's none of my affair. Of course it isn't, but I should like to know just the same. Perhaps you have other options."

She laughed, but the sound was hollow. "I'm an

unwed woman with no marriage prospects. My options are all but nonexistent. I require funds, and unless you're prepared to make me your countess, *mind your own business*." She quickened her pace and looked both ways up and down St. James's before dashing across the street.

He crossed right behind and came up alongside her. "If you're hoping to evade me, I should think I've made it quite clear, I won't allow it."

"Just like an Untouchable," she muttered. "Of all the arrogant, insufferable—"

"You flatter me."

She rolled her eyes toward the heavens.

"Why do you need money?" he asked, keeping easy pace with her stride. When she said nothing, he tried to come up with an answer. "Debts? You wish to buy something? You said you had no father, do you need a dowry?"

A dowry. Ha! Grandmama had told her last week that there was no dowry. They'd slowly bled through it over the past few years while funding Lucy's pointless Seasons.

Lucy frowned at the pavement as she continued along the thoroughfare, which was still somewhat busy, despite the lateness of the hour. "I need to cross the street."

"Allow me." He grazed his hand along her arm, as if he meant to take it, but didn't. He must have realized it would look strange for him to escort another gentleman across the street. "There's a break here. Let's go now." He gestured for her to cross. "Quickly." His hand brushed against her lower back, sending a brisk spark of awareness up her spine. She moved faster—to elude his touch as much as to reach the opposite side of the road.

She continued on toward Bolton Street, intending to part ways with him at the corner. When she reached the junction, she stopped and turned to face him. "I hope you won't take offense when I don't thank you for your escort."

He chuckled. "I wish you'd tell me who you are. I might like to seek you out at the next ball."

That would be highly unlikely. Her invitations were dwindling, though the Duchess of Kendal seemed to think she could singlehandedly elevate her and Aquilla's statuses. However, even if Grandmama could afford another Season, Lucy wasn't sure there'd be a reason to go to the expense. She wasn't Marriage Mart material. She wasn't traditionally beautiful, and she was far too brash with her speech. "Unladylike," was how Grandmama phrased it, but not cruelly. She wished Lucy were different but understood she couldn't change who she was—that she liked to play cards and shoot and ride and partake in any number of gentlemanly pursuits. How she longed to visit Hyde Park some morning to play bowls with Dartford and his ilk. Ah well. Once she retired to the country with Grandmama, she could do many things she couldn't here in London. But first, she needed to be able to afford that retirement.

Lucy straightened and gave Dartford a perfunctory nod. "I doubt you will see me again, my lord. As it should be."

He leaned toward her. "Does that mean you won't be frequenting any more hells?"

"Good evening." She turned and started slowly toward her Grandmama's small house, which was the third on the right.

After several steps, she looked back over her shoulder. He was watching her. "Do you really live on this street?" he called.

"Yes. You've done your infernal duty."

"Not unless you promise not to repeat this activity."

She whirled around and glared at him, planting her fists on her hips. "As I mentioned earlier, unless you'd care to make me your countess—an offer I would likely refuse given your autocratic demeanor—mind your own business."

He stalked toward her. "You seem an intelligent woman, but if you continue on this path, I am clearly mistaken. It's only a matter of time before someone else sees through your charade—and they will likely not be as much of a gentleman as I am."

"Then I shall take pains to improve my disguise. If you truly wanted to be helpful, you'd provide me with some assistance."

He gaped at her. "You want me to help you look more like a man?"

She would appreciate that a great deal, actually, but clearly he wasn't going to do *that*. Instead, she asked, "What gave me away?"

He looked a bit surprised by her question. Then his gaze dipped over her. The perusal was slow, purposeful, as if he were collecting his thoughts. When he looked at her again, heat suffused her body, and she regretted her query.

"It wasn't just one thing." Had his voice dropped a bit? Or was her hearing impaired by the blood suddenly roaring in her ears? "But I suppose it was the feel of you when I took your arm. I could tell you were padded. That alone wouldn't have been enough. It was just something…different. Perhaps the way you moved or the gracefulness of your hands."

She considered how she might improve her disguise. Perhaps her maid, Judith, would have some ideas. She'd been instrumental thus far, obtaining the faux sideburns from a friend who knew someone who worked in a theater.

She looked up at him. "Thank you. I'm leaving now."

"I still wish you'd tell me your name."

She felt a bit like Cinderella then, except she was leaving her prince with nothing, not even a glass slipper. Which was as it should be. He wasn't her prince, and she was never going to be a princess.

She turned and dashed away, slipping between her grandmother's house and the neighbor's, knowing he might yet discover who she really was. Even if he did, she doubted he'd expose her. If he was that sort of gentleman, he likely would've insisted on dragging her to her house and pounding on the front door until Grandmama was jolted from her bed. No, the Duke of Daring would keep her secret. Of that, she felt surprisingly certain.

After waiting several minutes, she went back to the street, moving slowly and peering around the corner to make sure he'd gone. Satisfied that he'd departed, she sprinted to the stairwell leading down to the servants' entry, where Judith was waiting to let her in.

She rapped lightly on the frame, and her maid opened the door. Lucy pushed inside, and Judith closed the door behind her.

"Fruitful evening?" Judith asked.

Lucy pulled off her hat. "Not as much as the other night." Because she'd been foiled by Dartford from going to one more hell.

Judith took the accessory from Lucy. "Sorry to hear."

"Someone saw through my disguise." Lucy tried not to think of the way she'd reacted when Dartford had recounted how he'd detected her secret. He'd made her feel…attractive. And that probably hadn't even been his intent.

Judith sucked in a breath. "What happened?"

Lucy preceded her up the servants' stairs. "Nothing untoward. I need to ensure no one gets too close."

"Let me talk to my friend again. Mayhap he has another idea."

Her friend worked in the household across the street and had provided them with the men's clothing Lucy was wearing, as well as the facial hair from his friend at the theater. He'd also suggested the padding they'd used. It made for some discomfort, but Lucy had to admit she felt somewhat protected by the extra layers. Even so, she'd endeavor to keep everyone at arm's length from now on. Perhaps she could develop a nasty cough that would discourage people from moving too close to her.

Lucy looked over her shoulder at Judith. "Be sure he doesn't know why you want to know."

"Don't worry. I'm very discreet." Judith flashed her a smile.

Lucy trusted Judith—she'd been with her for a decade. They'd practically grown up together. Lucy confided in and relied on her more than she ought, given her station, but Lucy didn't care. She had so few people of substance in her life. She'd take what she could.

"Thank you."

They went to her chamber, where Judith helped unwrap her from the disguise. Removing the facial hair was her least favorite part, and when they were finished, Lucy's skin was red and a bit raw.

As Lucy pulled on her night rail, Judith asked when she planned to go out in her disguise again.

Lucy hadn't thought to go out on subsequent nights—she seemed to need to recuperate after each foray—however, she wanted to go again tomorrow since tonight had been cut short. "Tomorrow night. I'm disappointed that I didn't earn more tonight."

Judith nodded. "I understand. The sooner you reach your goal, the better."

"And the sooner you can settle your future as well." Lucy wanted to take Judith with them, and Judith was keen to go.

Lucy hadn't undertaken this endeavor lightly. Grandmama was out of money. She planned to retire to a small cottage near Bath as soon as the Season concluded. She could no longer, however, afford to support Lucy. It was her fondest hope that Lucy would finally attain a marriage proposal this Season. Lucy saw that as an impossibility, which had led her to come up with this scheme. She'd make a terrible wife, but she was an excellent card player and gambler. If only she could find a game of whist, which required strategy instead of dumb luck as with faro.

And she'd been quite lucky so far. Until tonight. Dartford made her question her plans, but she couldn't afford to do that. If she kept her wits about her, and her pistol at the ready, she'd be fine. Still, she'd be relieved when she was finished. "No one wants everything settled more than I do."

Settled.

That described Lucy's aspirations perfectly. She would *settle* for a quiet spinsterhood. It was preferable to any number of alternatives, including a stifling marriage where her freedom was curtailed and her boisterous nature crushed. No, this was her only avenue, and she was determined to succeed.

Chapter Two

ANDREW CHECKED HIS cravat in the glass. His valet had done an excellent job. It was a pity that Andrew would have to let him go at the end of the Season, but that would mark two and a half years of service—longer than any valet he'd had before. It was too long. Things were too…comfortable.

"Thank you, Tindall."

The valet nodded. "Just so, my lord. The coach is waiting."

Damn, he'd neglected to inform his staff that he would be deviating from his normal routine. He typically rendezvoused with his friends at their club, and they determined their evening entertainments from there. Tonight, however, he would venture out as he never did—alone. Only, he wouldn't be alone for long. The question was where his night would go from there.

"I don't require the coach this evening. Sorry for the trouble." He took his hat and gloves from Tindall before quitting his chamber and donned them as he hurried downstairs. He hoped he wasn't leaving too late.

A footman held the door for him as he left, and he saw that the coach was already being driven back to the mews. Damn, if his staff wasn't efficient. But then he supposed they worked doubly hard for fear of getting sacked, since he was known to let people go seemingly on a whim. It wasn't a whim to him, of course, but a calculated effort to maintain a household that was pleasantly detached. Sometimes he felt bad, but it was necessary. Furthermore, he always provided an excellent reference and ensured they landed in an equal or better position.

It was a cool spring evening as he departed Audley Square and cut down to Curzon Street. He moved briskly, concerned that he was going to miss his window of opportunity.

Less than ten minutes later, he arrived at his destination on Bolton Street. He slipped behind the corner of the house on the end of the street and took up a surveillance position. People came and went, but not from the house he watched. He shifted his stance countless times and more than once considered abandoning his post. But he couldn't. After what seemed an eternity, he wondered if she just wasn't going out tonight.

Stifling a yawn, he finally saw movement across the street. A figure emerged from the servants' stairs. He—no, he was a she—looked furtively from side to side before stepping onto the pavement and hurrying toward Piccadilly.

Andrew took a deep breath and dashed across the street, intercepting her at the corner. "Good evening, Miss Parnell. Where are we off to this evening?"

She stopped upon seeing him and now glared up at him, her jaw clenched. "You were waiting for me."

"I was. Couldn't let you venture out alone again. I'm sure you understand."

"I understand you're a nuisance."

He straightened his coat. "So you like to say, but I prefer to think of myself as an assistant. Or maybe even a *guide*."

She opened her mouth, then snapped it shut again. Then she turned but didn't move away. She spun back around, her gaze a glorious blaze of outraged affront. "How did you find out who I am?"

He'd felt beholden to learn her identity and to do whatever he could to prevent her from behaving recklessly. "I watched where you went last night, ascertained who lived at that address, and the rest was quite simple."

"Well, good for you, but that changes nothing." Her gaze turned wary. "Unless you plan to expose me."

"I do not. I'm the Duke of Daring, not the Duke of Gossip." He decided he liked the nickname she'd given him.

She frowned. It seemed she still didn't trust him.

"Does your grandmother know what you're about?" he asked.

For the first time, she looked worried. "No, and you mustn't tell her." She glanced away. "I don't wish to concern her. She has enough weighing on her mind."

He moved closer and spoke softly. "I won't tell her, but you must agree to my terms."

She went back to glaring at him, and he realized he'd tensed at her reaction to his question about her grandmother. It was much easier to deal with her anger than her distress. "I should've known you meant to extort me, but I still don't understand why."

"I'm a gentleman, Miss Parnell, and a gentleman does not allow a lady to continue as you are. I would never forgive myself. Daring exploits are fine and good for me, but not for you."

Her eyes widened, and her lips curled into a snarl. "Is that what you think this is? Some sort of escapade I've undertaken for a bit of excitement? How nice it must be to live for such nonsense."

He ignored her insults, realizing he'd hit another

nerve—like the comment she'd made about being unmarried the night before. He'd learned very little about her today, just that her grandmother was the widow of a baronet and that Miss Parnell was as good as on the shelf. He might not be the Duke of Gossip, but he knew how to obtain information when he needed it.

He crossed his arms over his chest, undaunted. "Then tell me why you're forced to do this. I truly wish to help. Is my solicitude that shocking?"

She stared at him, clearly disbelieving. "Yes, actually. No one pays me any mind. Or at least, they never have." She glanced down at herself. "I suppose it took me dressing up as a man." When she looked at him again, she seemed resigned. "You're incredibly pompous."

"Call me the Duke of Arrogance, then. I've been called worse." He uncrossed his arms. "You have two choices. You can tell me what you're about and allow me to help you, or you can go home, where we will inform your grandmother of your transgression."

"This is not a *transgression.* It's a necessity. I merely need funds, you half-wit." Her cheeks flushed a pretty pink, and she'd never looked less like a man. He longed to see her without her costume. He thought she must be quite lovely.

He didn't bother tamping down his exasperation. "I ascertained that all on my own, thank you. But then any *half-wit* would, since you've been *gambling.* Why do you need money?" He held up his hand. "And before you think to evade me again, let me remind you that it's only a matter of time until you find trouble with this scheme." He hadn't expected her to be this stubborn. He decided it was time for a new tack. "Let me prove that you can trust me. I will take you to some hells this evening. You can gamble to your heart's content, and I will ensure your safety."

She gave him a mutinous glower. "I do not gamble to content my heart."

"There's no need to be defensive. Do we have an accord?"

She tipped her head to the side, and it was somehow a feminine action.

"Don't do that," he said. "You look too much like a woman."

She instantly straightened.

"See how helpful I am?"

Her eyes narrowed. "You could be lying."

He threw his hands up. "You are the most frustrating woman I've ever encountered. Come, let's just go speak with Lady Parnell."

She stepped in front of him as he started forward. "No. You can…come with me tonight."

He breathed a sigh, feeling inordinately relieved. He truly had no wish to visit her grandmother and explain how his accompanying her granddaughter without a chaperone would *not* necessitate a proposal of marriage. That was one daring exploit he had no plans to pursue. "Excellent, and at the end of the evening, after I've demonstrated both my honesty and my worth, you'll share your secrets."

She pressed her lips together. "We'll see."

"Do that often."

"What?"

"Scrunch your mouth up like that so your lips don't look so—" He'd been about to say kissable, but damn if he had any idea where that word had come from. And it could go right back from whence it came.

"Womanly," he said. "Come, we'll start on Jermyn Street and then head to my favorite spot on King Street." Both hells were fair and enjoyed a clientele where she would fit in as a young buck.

Buck?

He looked at her rounded, somewhat lumpy form and again wondered at what the disguise hid beneath. Perhaps she wasn't as fetching as he suspected. Maybe he was basing his expectations of her physical form on that of her mental acuity—for all that she was stubborn, she possessed a fine intelligence and a keen wit. "Why *aren't* you married?" he asked.

She chuckled, and the sound was low and provocative. "You clearly did some research about me today, but you didn't learn everything, did you?" She peered at him askance as they walked.

"Let's cross here," he said, waiting for a break in the traffic before gesturing for her to accompany him. When they reached the other side of the street, he said, "No, I didn't learn everything, and since I'm to be your, er, partner, I thought we might establish a friendship."

She stopped cold and turned on him. "You are not my partner. Not in any way. Is that understood?" It was as close to a verbal slap as he'd ever received.

"Quite." They continued on to Duke Street, when he indicated they should turn. He tried a different line of conversation. "Where do you hide that pistol?" He raked her form, trying to detect its location amidst the padding.

"I have a pocket sewn into the inside of my coat." She patted her lapel. "Tell me, did you win today?"

He coaxed his thoughts back to the present. "What?"

"One of your friends said he'd wagered on you

winning today. Did you win?"

Andrew recalled the phaeton race that morning and smiled. "I did."

"And what was the contest?"

He led her onto Jermyn Street. The hell was just ahead on the left. "Should I tell you? It seems I should be at least half as stingy with my information as you are with yours."

She rolled her eyes at him. "I'm not married because no one has ever asked. Does that satisfy your curiosity?"

"Not by a fraction," he murmured. "We're here." He leaned down and whispered near her ear. "It was a phaeton race, and I won by several lengths. Incredibly exhilarating."

She gave him a look that was nothing short of rapturous. "How I should love to do that."

In that moment, he wanted to take her. Next time he raced, she could come in her costume… He jolted himself out of such nonsense and coughed.

He walked up the steps with her. "This is faro and hazard. I assumed that would be acceptable."

"Yes, but I should love to play whist." She glanced over at him, her gaze uncertain. "I understand there are games where wagers are placed on any number of things—from the card that leads to the number of tricks each pair takes in the round."

He looked at her in surprise, not that she knew how to play whist—this surprised him not at all. No, he was surprised she knew of these whist games. They weren't typical in most hells. In fact, he knew of only one such game, and it required an invitation. Which he possessed. "As it happens, I have access to a whist game. I'll take you there next, but you'll have to let me partner you." He grinned, anticipating the evening more than he'd thought possible. "But not as your *partner*."

She smiled, and he *knew* she was pretty, even with the sideburns marring her face.

"Don't do that," he murmured. "No smiling."

"Then don't provoke me," she muttered back.

Andrew stifled the urge to laugh just as the footman opened the door. He greeted Andrew, who introduced his friend Davis Smith. They sat through a few rounds of faro, and Andrew offered whispered advice on how to behave.

"Make your movements more blunt," he said quietly, leaning toward her. "And faster. Especially with your hands. You can't disguise them with padding, so you'll need to keep them from drawing attention."

She heeded his advice and by the end of the third round had completely transformed her movements. She turned toward him, her eyes sparkling with excitement. He could tell she was enjoying herself, but then so was he.

"I'm ready for whist if you are," she said.

"Let's go." He made their excuses and thanked the banker, who encouraged them to come again.

Once they were outside, he said, "You did very well."

She ran her hand down her jacket, as if she could smooth the lumpy padding beneath it, but of course she couldn't. "I was hoping to do better. I lost more than usual."

"That's going to happen, particularly with a game of pure chance like faro."

She glanced over at him, her gaze eager. "Which is why I want to play whist."

"And so we shall. Come, we're headed to Cleveland

Row." He led her down Duke Street. "You did very well with your movements. You make a better gentleman than most of my acquaintances."

She laughed, the low and throaty sound bringing a smile to his lips. "I'm not sure that's a compliment."

"Then how about this one: you're an excellent gambler. Your wagers are smart—not excessive, but with just the right amount of boldness."

"Thank you. My father was an inveterate gambler. He was incredibly knowledgeable but lacked the ability to stop when he was winning. Or losing." She frowned and shook her head. "He just couldn't stop, and he nearly bankrupted us."

He heard the disgust in her tone, but it was laced with sadness. If she'd been nearly bankrupted, that likely explained why she needed money now. A woman with no marriage prospects and no income had, as she had told him, few options. "How long ago did he pass?"

She was quiet a moment. "Seven years? Yes, I think that's right."

Andrew thought back to a decade ago, when he'd been new to London. He didn't recall Lord Parnell, but then he hadn't begun to frequent gaming hells until a few years ago, when he'd taken up with Charles and their crowd.

"You don't miss him, I take it?"

She scoffed. "Goodness, no. Grandmama does, but she tends to remember her innocent son, not the dissolute man he became in his middle age."

On an intellectual level, Andrew understood why she felt as she did, but emotionally… Andrew missed his family terribly, and he would do anything to bring them back. Time to change the subject.

As it happened, he didn't have to. They reached St. James's and ran into Charles and Beaumont and the rest of their lot.

"There you are, Dart!" Beaumont called. "We waited for you at the club."

"My apologies. I've met up with our new friend, Smitty." He indicated Miss Parnell, who'd twisted her mouth into that nearly lipless expression he'd encouraged.

"Evening, Smitty," Charles said. He looked at Andrew. "Where are you headed?"

Damn. Andrew didn't want them joining him and Miss Parnell. He couldn't chance any of them finding her out, which meant he had to limit her exposure. "Just wandering about, considering our options. We were at Fenwick's. Excellent game there tonight."

Charles's eyes lit. "Indeed? Perhaps that's where we should go." He glanced at the others.

Miss Parnell coughed. "Capital faro table. I made an excellent haul." She did that low, gravelly voice that was disturbingly seductive.

"Then it's settled," Charles said. "Mayhap we'll catch up with you later."

Andrew nodded, relieved that they would not be banding together. "We'll keep an eye out."

They parted ways, and Andrew led her across St. James's to Cleveland Row.

"Thank you," she said. "I didn't want them to join us."

"I didn't either." He peered down at her as they neared the hell. "See, I *do* have your best interests in mind."

She gave him a look that said she was still deciding. He shook his head, marveling at her obstinacy. They climbed the steps of the next hell, and again Andrew was greeted by the massive footman, who was just as capable of tossing one from the premises as inviting one inside. "Evening, your lordship. You have a guest this evening?" The footman's eye glinted as he studied Miss Parnell closely. Too closely.

Andrew resisted the urge to lay a calming hand against the small of her back. "I do. This is Mr. Davis Smith," he said smoothly. "We're here to play upstairs." That was code for the private whist game.

"Ye're always welcome, my lord." The footman glanced over his shoulder, then nodded subtly. Some sort of communication with someone out of sight had just occurred. "Come in, come in." He inclined his head toward Miss Parnell to include her too.

She'd retained a calm demeanor through the exchange, not a hint of discomfort. Again, he was impressed with her.

"Ye know where to go," the footman said.

Andrew did. "Thank you." He looked around the hall, but it was empty. Whomever the footman had exchanged looks with was now gone. Andrew surmised it was the owner of the hell—Mr. Jessup. He ran a mostly fair game but was known for a ruthless streak with those who somehow offended him, usually without them realizing what they'd done. While the whist game wasn't dealt by an employee, a banker managed all wagers and kept a percentage to account for Jessup's expenses.

Andrew led Miss Parnell up the stairs. "Remember to stay in character. This room may contain people you've met before, depending on who's here tonight."

Her eyes glinted with alarm. "Do you think someone will recognize me?"

"Doubtful. Just do your part to ensure they don't. I'll do mine to attract most of the attention."

She chuckled softly. "I'm certain you excel at that."

He laughed in return. "Quite. Perhaps now you'll admit it was a good idea for me to accompany you."

She gave him a suffering glance, but the amused glint in her eyes said she was glad, and that made him glad too. "Yes. Now, may we play?"

He stopped himself from offering her his arm. "Let's."

As he guided her toward the whist parlor, he hoped he wasn't leading them both into the lion's den.

Chapter Three

FOR THE FIRST time in her life, Lucy was content to allow a gentleman to do all the talking for her. Grandmama would be so impressed. No, she'd be stunned. *Then* she'd be impressed.

Poor Grandmama. Lucy felt a trifle bad about sneaking out, but it wasn't as if she had somewhere else to be. Their invitations weren't many, and Grandmama was slowing down. She preferred to stay at home most nights and went to bed early. That was the main reason Lucy was determined to retire with her. A maid of all work would care for Grandmama's cottage, but she wouldn't ensure Grandmama took care of herself, nor would she read to her or share memories that would make Grandmama smile.

Yes, Lucy was doing this for herself, but she was doing it just as much for Grandmama, if not more.

Lucy peered at Dartford across the table. They were halfway through the first hand, and he was a very good player. But then she'd expected nothing else. The Duke of Daring seemed to excel at *most* things.

She glanced at the other two gentlemen, both of whom she'd never met before, thank goodness. Even if she had, it was unlikely they'd recognize her. Still, Lucy kept her head down and contributed just enough to the discussion so as not to seem rude. Dartford kept his word and carried the conversational burden, not that it was great. It seemed the other men preferred to concentrate on their cards for the most part.

Lucy understood. When she'd first learned to play,

she'd had to focus quite heavily on the game. Now it was second nature for her to track the cards and strategize while conversing with her tablemates. That was what happened when your father taught you to play cards as soon as you could count.

The wagering was frustratingly light on this hand. Lucy longed to raise the stakes but was waiting for a signal from Dartford. He spoke of horses and shooting, and Lucy had to bite her tongue to keep from contributing, since those were two of her favorite subjects.

Lord Henderson, a gentleman in the thick of middle age with a ruddy countenance and a persistence for clearing his throat, squinted at Dartford. "Used to set up targets—baskets hanging from trees—on the estate when we were young. I'm an excellent shot, if I may boast."

"Yes, yes," the fourth member of their table, Mr. Wells, said. He was a few years younger than Henderson, or perhaps it was just that he looked more robust. "You shoot at Manton's at least once a week. Though I daresay you aren't as good as you once were." He laid down his card, and they took the trick.

Dartford led the next. "I haven't been shooting at Manton's in an age." He glanced around the table. "I just picked up a pistol from Purdey's last month."

Henderson laid down his card, a pathetic two of clubs. "Bah. It's a Manton or nothing for me." He cleared his throat for what had to be the dozenth time.

"I've always been partial to Wogdon myself," Wells said.

Lucy had shot her father's Manton pistol when she was younger, before he'd lost it in a wager. The weapon she carried now wasn't anywhere near the caliber of the guns they were discussing. She looked at Dartford. "I should like to shoot one of Purdey's pistols."

Dartford arched a brow as he peered at her. "Yes, I seem to recall you like pistols."

Lucy swallowed a chuckle at his comment.

"I'm in need of a new rifle." Wells put down the four of hearts. "I'll have a look at Purdey's."

How Lucy wished she could afford such things. But what would she do with it? It wasn't as if she'd be invited to hunt grouse come August. Perhaps she could set up a target range when they moved to their new cottage. She stifled a smile at Grandmama's horror if she proposed such a thing.

At last Dartford offered a friendly wager, which was accepted around the table. The betting was small at first, almost inconsequential, but by the end of the hand, Lucy was ahead ten pounds. She hoped the wagers would increase—and that she'd retain her luck with the cards—in the next round, but she didn't show it. Father had taught her how to shield her emotions and reactions as well as he'd schooled her in everything else.

Dartford took over as dealer for the next round. Lucy lost a few wagers and began to worry that she'd suffer her first losing evening.

Partway through the hand, Henderson squinted at Dartford. "I've been thinking about those Purdey guns. I should like to see which one fires better. I'll put my money on Manton."

"How much money?" Lucy asked.

Dartford shot her a look of surprise with maybe just a touch of irritation. She ought to have censored herself, but why? She was playing the part of a gentleman, and *they* were allowed to speak their mind.

Henderson shrugged, then looked around the table. "A hundred quid."

Lucy's heart sank. She didn't have that kind of money yet. Anyway, she didn't know what gun maker she'd place her wager on.

Henderson sat forward in his chair, his eyes gleaming. "We must do this."

Wells chuckled. "How do you propose we execute such an endeavor?"

Dartford looked from Henderson to Wells. "We'll use a vise to hold the pistol. That's the only way to objectively compare them. Although I don't know where we'll accomplish that."

Henderson gave them all a superior perusal. "Manton's, of course."

"He'll let you fire the other weapons?" Wells asked.

Henderson laughed but ended by clearing his throat. "'Course he will, because his gun is going to win."

"My money's on the Purdey," Dartford said.

"And I'm for the Wogdon." Wells turned his head to look at Lucy. "What about you, Smitty?"

How she wished she could afford to participate!

Dartford cocked his head to the side. "Yes, Smitty, which one?"

She glared at him for the briefest moment before reining in her reaction. Gritting her teeth, she tried to somehow silently communicate that she didn't have that kind of money. "I'm afraid I wouldn't be able to say," she said, disappointed that she wouldn't get to see the experiment in person.

"Then you'll have to shoot them yourself so that you can form an opinion," Henderson said. "When we're finished here, we'll head over to Manton's." He signaled for a young lad, apparently an employee, to come to the table.

Wells blinked at Henderson, his jaw slack. "What, now? Tonight?"

"Why not?" Henderson gave the boy instructions to find his coach on the street and send his footman to Manton's to make the arrangements. "Now, let us finish. I want to make my hundred quid."

Lucy doubled her focus, intent on winning. Three tricks later, she and Dartford had won, and she was just shy of a hundred pounds richer. An excellent result, but still not enough to enter the shooting wager. She eyed Dartford, wondering if he'd summon a reason to take her home first. She couldn't imagine how he'd do that without abdicating his own participation in the wager.

Henderson stood. "We can ride over to Davies Street in my coach."

"Just so," Dartford said, smiling. He unfolded himself from his chair and stretched his shoulders. "After you, Henderson."

Henderson led the way, followed by Wells. Dartford hung back a few paces and sidled closer to Lucy.

"You're letting me go?" she asked him as they departed the room.

"I'm glad to see you've accepted that I will decide what you should and shouldn't do—for your safety, you understand."

His audacity and arrogance were aggravating, but she couldn't deny that he was useful. Or that in his presence she felt, yes, safer. Protected, even.

But it wouldn't do for him to know that. She stopped for a moment to roll her eyes at him and then exhaled in an exaggerated fashion. "Thank goodness for you."

His dark gaze was direct, almost intimate. "Careful,

that breathy sound was very womanly."

Something about the way he looked at her and the manner in which he said "womanly" made her flesh tingle. She refused to consider that she might find him attractive. "Don't ask if I can participate in the wager. I don't have the funds."

"I could spot you what you need."

A tempting offer, but she'd learned from her father's mistakes. Never ever borrow, particularly if there was any chance you couldn't pay it back. What most people failed to comprehend was that there was *always* a chance you couldn't pay it back. Nothing in life was certain.

"No, thank you," she said, starting toward the stairs.

He walked alongside her. "It's only a few pounds."

She shook her head. "I don't borrow."

"An admirable characteristic. How about if I *give* it to you?"

"A gentleman does not give…*me* money." She'd been about to say a gentleman doesn't give *a lady* money. But ladies didn't frequent gaming hells either. Perhaps she was being foolish. She had money at home—her winnings from her other nights of gambling. In this instance, she *knew* she could pay him back. On the other hand, if she placed the wager and lost…she'd be out a hundred pounds.

"Think about it on the way," he said as they followed Henderson and Wells down the stairs.

Outside, they climbed into Henderson's coach. He and Wells took the front-facing seat, which left the rear-facing one for Lucy and Dartford. The small space required she sit far too close to him. Dartford was a larger than average man, so their thighs nearly touched. Lucy's legs were not as padded as her upper body. She wished they were so that she was not so aware of his presence. Or more accurately, of the fact that she *was* attracted to him.

Blast.

As they traveled to Manton's, they argued as to which gun would fire most accurately. By the time they'd arrived, the wager had increased to a hundred and fifty pounds. Lucy couldn't bring herself to take that much from Dartford.

Manton himself, a man who was much the same age as Wells and Henderson, greeted them, and Henderson had to pay him a fee to open at this hour as well as to allow them to shoot the Purdey and Wogdon, which Henderson's footman had somehow obtained.

Henderson coughed as he turned from Manton and looked at Lucy. "If you'd care to shoot all three weapons, you can then make a decision about your wager."

It wasn't a question. He assumed Lucy was going to place a bet. She sent Dartford a panicked look. He responded with a subtle inclination of his head and a reassuring stare.

That feeling of protection rushed over her again. The independent woman she thought herself to be wanted to hate it. But somewhere, in places she hadn't known existed, she liked it very much.

Lucy let out a breath and tried to focus on the thrill of being able to fire the weapons. She was inside Manton's! And she was going to shoot three of the best pistols ever made.

Manton led them to the shooting gallery. The room was large, easily the size of a grand ballroom, but with a rectangular shape. The ceilings were high, with massive chandeliers that were not currently lit. Instead, lanterns had been placed about the space. It wasn't a terribly bright environment, but Lucy didn't care.

"You'll shoot at the wafer." Manton indicated a disc hanging at the opposite end and handed her the first gun. "We'll start with the Purdey. He used to work for me, you know."

Lucy took the weapon and hefted it in her hand. She glanced at Dartford, who was watching her intently. His gaze was a mix of concern and anticipation. He didn't think she could do this. She was going to really have to hide her emotions now.

She took her place and held the pistol out, marking her aim. She cocked the weapon and fired, hitting the wafer square. Exhilaration rushed through her.

"Excellent," Manton said, taking the gun from her and giving her the second one in its place. "My man will change out the wafer. This next one is the Wogdon."

As they awaited the new wafer, Dartford moved close to her and murmured, "Was that luck?"

She turned her head and whispered, "Skill." A sense of giddiness rushed through her. She never imagined she'd be able to demonstrate her ability to people who would genuinely appreciate it.

"I see." He took a step back.

"Ready?" Manton asked.

Lucy took aim again and fired. She hit the target, but not as accurately as the first time.

"Damn me," Henderson said. "You're not bad."

Pride burned in Lucy's chest. She longed to rip off her disguise and show them that she was a woman. She'd have to settle for imagining their shocked reactions. "Thank you."

Manton took the Wogdon from her and eyed her

fingers. "Most gentlemen remove their gloves when they shoot here."

Lucy curled her hand into a fist and dropped it to her side. She couldn't think of an appropriate response—which was an unnerving and singular sensation—so she said nothing.

"Finally, here's mine." Manton handed her the pistol he'd designed.

It felt familiar, even though it was different from her father's. Or maybe she just wanted it to feel that way. But why? It wasn't as if she missed her father. That wasn't precisely true. She missed the man who'd taught her to play cards and to shoot. It was the only time in her life that she'd been interesting or important to him.

She raised the weapon and took aim. Without hesitation, she pulled the trigger. Again, she hit the wafer in the center.

Manton chuckled. "I wouldn't want to face you at dawn. Why haven't I seen you here before?" He studied her face for a moment, and Lucy began to feel uncomfortable. Coming here had been a folly, no matter how wonderful.

She shrugged and looked away.

"Well, be sure to come in. You need your own Manton."

Lucy turned her head to Dartford. He looked rather pleased.

"What's your wager, then?" Henderson asked.

In her excitement over shooting, she'd almost forgotten how she'd been cornered into placing a wager she couldn't afford. "Ah…"

Dartford stepped toward her, his gaze encouraging. "The Purdey, right?"

"Actually, I would say the Manton." And she wasn't

just choosing that because its manufacturer was standing a few feet away, nor was it due to nostalgia. She'd liked the feel of it best. Which meant nothing about accuracy, she realized.

Manton gave the pistol to one of his men to stage it for the experiment. "If you'll just give us a moment."

Henderson rubbed his hands together. "All right, if the Manton wins, Smitty and I will each take home an extra hundred and fifty quid, and if one of the others wins—which they won't—one of you gents will take home an extra three hundred. Not bad."

Cold sweat chilled the back of Lucy's neck. If she lost… She couldn't think of it.

After another few minutes, during which Lucy's nerves bundled into tight masses all over her body, and her insides churned like boiling water, Manton declared the experiment ready.

Each pistol was fitted into a vise and carefully aimed at a wafer. Manton pulled the trigger on each in succession, and every one hit the wafer. His man went and pulled them down, then brought them to Manton.

Manton laid them on a nearby table in the order in which they'd been shot, which was the same order as Lucy had done. The Purdey was shot near the edge, and the Wogdon came closer to the middle. The Manton, however, had hit dead center. It was the clear winner. Which meant Lucy had won.

Her tension became elation, and this time she couldn't help the smile that crested over her lips. She didn't even realize until Dartford stared at her, his eyes wide. He moved his head from side to side, slowly, almost imperceptibly. Lucy pressed her lips together and grimaced.

"Well done, Smitty," Wells said. He pulled the money

from his coat and handed it to Henderson before turning to Dartford. "I'll let you pay Smith."

Dartford nodded. "Of course."

Henderson cleared his throat. "Shall we return to Jessup's?"

"Thank you, but we've somewhere else to be," Dartford said, much to Lucy's relief.

"Another time, then. Evening." Henderson and Wells left together.

"Come, we'll get a hack." Dartford thanked Manton, who urged Lucy to come back and shoot anytime she wanted.

Lucy was noncommittal. She was just eager to leave. She was weary of playacting, and her throat felt ragged from affecting a masculine voice for so long.

Once they were outside, Dartford let out a whistle. "I see the pistol you carry isn't just for show. You're a hell of a shot, Miss Parnell. How do you explain that?"

"My father."

Dartford hailed a hackney coach and directed the driver to Bolton Street. They climbed inside, once again sitting beside each other.

"Most fathers don't instruct their daughters on how to shoot a gun or how to gamble. I take it he wanted a son?"

"Probably." Lucy had come to realize that Gerald Parnell simply didn't know how to treat a daughter.

He shifted on the seat, angling toward her. "You're an interesting woman. And wealthier than when we started tonight—I'll send the funds over tomorrow. Will that satisfy your needs, or are you going to make me do this again?"

She laughed softly, glad she didn't have to censor herself any longer. "Was it that bad?"

"Not at all. In fact, I rather enjoyed myself. Did you?"

Immensely. "Yes." Not for the first time, she thought she ought to have been born a man. "Thank you for your help. I, ah, I don't have quite enough money to stop."

He folded his arms across his chest and let out a beleaguered sigh. "I don't suppose you're ever going to tell me why you need it."

She rather thought he'd earned the right to know, especially since he'd proven so helpful. Her gaze found his in the dim light provided by the coach's lantern. "My grandmother wishes to retire to the country, and I need to go with her. Only…there's not enough money for that."

"I see. You seem to have at least some money? You had to have started this gambling scheme with something, and I know you've won a bit since then."

Yes, she'd scraped together about twenty pounds to start. But that had been difficult. They didn't have as much as Grandmama had led her to believe the past few years. Grandmama was nearly down to her marriage settlement, the interest from which she needed to live on. And it wasn't enough to support them both without living very frugally. Grandmama had made it clear that Lucy needed to marry. Except Lucy didn't really want to. And anyway, no one had ever shown any interest. She offered her opinion too freely, had a very small dowry—and now none—and to call her beautiful would be an exaggeration.

"We have just enough to finish the Season. But if I can raise the necessary funds, I'll find a cottage near Bath as soon as possible." The sooner she could remove herself from the pointlessness of London

Society and see Grandmama settled, the better.

He sat back against the squab and was quiet as they wound their way through the streets of Mayfair. They were nearing Bolton Street when he turned toward her once more. "Here's the problem. I'm not sure you should do this again, and certainly not more than once or twice more, and absolutely not without my company. I must insist that you agree, or my earlier threat will stand."

"I'm so glad you recognize it as a threat."

He chuckled, his eyes gleaming in the shadowy coach. "Yes, let's be direct with one another, shall we?"

Lucy blinked at him. "I am always direct."

"Unless you're trying to fool people into thinking you're a man." His sarcasm was simultaneously annoying and charming.

"Yes, that. A necessary transgression, I'm sure you agree."

His brow arched. "I hardly think you care whether I agree."

He had her there. She grinned. "Maybe a little. I mean, I *do* care. A little." She'd come to like Dartford during their brief acquaintance, in spite of his moments of arrogance and imperiousness. She looked forward to another adventure or two with him. "You have my word that I won't venture out without your assistance. Shall we set our next appointment?"

His eyes widened briefly. He seemed a bit surprised at the ease with which she'd agreed. "Excellent. Tell me when, and I'll meet you as I did tonight."

"Four nights hence, at half past eleven."

The hackney drew to a halt on Bolton Street, but not in front of her house. They stepped out of the cab, and Dartford paid the coachman.

With her house in sight, weariness seeped into Lucy's frame. She longed to pluck all the padding from her body and scrub her face clean after discarding the fake sideburns.

Dartford walked with her toward the house. "What would your grandmother say if she knew you were doing this?"

Lucy suffered a pang of guilt. "She'd be horrified."

"What does she think you're going to do once she retires?"

They'd reached her house. Lucy stopped and turned toward him. "She expects me to marry."

"And is that a possibility?" he asked. Shadows played across his face, but she could see his eyes clearly. They were dark, intelligent, often filled with humor. His cheekbones gave definition, while his chin, square with a slight cleft, provided character. He bore an appealing countenance. No, that wasn't at all fair. He was exceptionally handsome. And an earl. Precisely the kind of man her grandmother had hoped she would marry but who'd consistently ignored her the past five years. An Untouchable.

She tamped down a scowl, suddenly annoyed anew at her predicament, which was silly since she'd abandoned the idea of marriage. A choice she didn't regret in the slightest.

She gestured to her costume and the sideburns stuck to her face, currently making her itch. "Would I be doing this if it were?"

He shrugged. "Perhaps it *is* possible, but you don't wish to marry, so you choose this instead."

That actually summed up her current attitude quite accurately. She would choose this over marriage. "As it happens, I *don't* wish to marry."

"Indeed?" He cocked his head to the side. "How surprising. We are alike, then, because I don't wish to marry either. Some distant cousin will need to inherit the title."

She wanted to ask why but didn't. That would encourage him to ask her the same, and she had no intention of explaining that to him. Besides, it was best if they didn't become too…close. This was a necessary partnership, but they weren't going to be lifelong friends.

"Are those comfortable?" He reached out with his fingertips and brushed the sideburn glued along her right jawline.

She ignored the frisson of delight that sparked down her neck. "Not particularly. In fact, I'd like a few days to recover from wearing them."

"I should like to see you without them." His dark gaze penetrated through her carefully constructed wall, and his deep voice shot straight into her chest, stirring the inconvenient attraction she felt toward him.

Her breath caught. "I doubt you ever will."

His mouth ticked up in a half smile. "Don't tease me. Please. Not when I've been so helpful. Think of all you won tonight."

All she'd won. It wasn't just the money. Not to her. She'd won respect with her shooting, even if she couldn't tell them she was a woman.

She took a step back, determined to put space between herself and this suddenly dangerous man. "I appreciate your help, but I won't share credit for my winnings. They are mine alone."

He gave a slight bow. "My apologies," he murmured.

"I'll see you in a few days." She turned from him.

"Not if I see you first," he said.

She looked back over her shoulder to see him smiling. “Don’t forget my hundred and fifty pounds.”

“I would never. I’ll be looking for you, Miss Parnell. Good evening.” He touched the brim of his hat and strolled away down the street.

Lucy hurried down the servants’ stairs into the scullery, where her maid was waiting. She doubted she’d see him—she’d gone five years in London without encountering him before. And yet, a small part of her couldn’t help but anticipate the possibility.

Chapter Four

TWO DAYS LATER, Andrew drove his barouche west from London. He carried three other gentlemen: Charles, Beaumont, and Lord Thursby.

"Faster!" Charles called from the rear of the vehicle as soon as they left the traffic of the city.

Andrew grinned, more than happy to oblige. He urged the horses to a greater speed, their hooves pounding the road on the way to Westbourne. The day was cool but dry. The feel of the brisk air against his face was exhilarating. It was moments like these that made his life palatable. Worthwhile, even.

The memory of the first time he'd ridden so fast that he'd nearly lost control assaulted him. Sometimes that happened when he drove—he'd relax and the old thoughts and dark emotions swelled inside him until he could feel the loss of his family anew. Especially the most agonizing—the last one to die, his beloved brother. After weeks of harrowing illness during which each one had been stricken and taken from him, Andrew hadn't had any tears left to shed. So he'd climbed on his horse and ridden as fast as he could. He'd ridden as if he could overtake death and bring Bertie back. But he couldn't.

Realizing his hold on the reins was far too tight, Andrew forced himself to release the tension burrowing through him. He shoved the bitter memories to the recesses of his soul, to where they festered and ate at him, but where he could ignore them for the most part.

He drove the team faster, aware that a corner was coming. He didn't slow. He heard an intake of breath behind him. Beaumont probably. He didn't like to go quite as fast as the rest of them. Thursby was a member of the Four Horse Club along with Andrew, while Charles was hoping to gain membership. That was, in fact, the purpose of their endeavor today. Charles was going to practice so that he might finally be invited to join.

Andrew took the corner without slowing. The barouche tilted, but the wheels never left the ground, and the horses were confident, eager even, under Andrew's hand.

"Hell's teeth, man!" Beaumont exclaimed. "Are you trying to kill us all?"

Thursby, a convivial gent nearly ten years older than Andrew's twenty-nine years, laughed and looked back over his shoulder. "You're in excellent hands with Dart."

Andrew slowed the horses as they reached Westbourne. "It's time for Charles to take his turn anyway."

"Heaven help me," Beaumont said. "He's nowhere near as skilled as you."

"There's no call to be an arse," Charles said. "I've become quite good."

Andrew wasn't certain he'd term Charles's abilities as "quite good," but they were more than adequate. The question was whether he'd be good enough for the Four Horse Club, and it would be up to him and Thursby to recommend him. So far, they hadn't felt comfortable doing so. It was a select and prestigious group, and its members had to demonstrate superior skill.

Andrew pulled into the park and drew the team to a halt.

"I thought you might invite your new friend, Smitty," Beaumont observed.

Andrew turned his head. "And where would s—he have sat?" Damn, he'd almost referred to her as a she.

"I heard he's quite the sharpshooter," Charles said to Andrew. "We should meet at Manton's one day. I'll wager you can hit more targets than him."

A thought occurred to Andrew. If Miss Parnell came along with him to a few events such as a phaeton race or shooting practice, she could wager without the danger of the hells. There was still a risk that her identity would be exposed, but she was awfully good at her disguise. It was something to consider. He'd ask her about it at their next appointment or perhaps earlier if he managed to see her.

He hoped it was the latter. The desire to see her dressed as a woman had become a fascination. Last night, he'd dreamt of her without the sideburns. He envisioned her with dark blonde hair, rich and thick like honey. She possessed a trim waist with a supple curve to her hips. In the dream, he'd started to remove her clothing, but he'd awakened before he could see what was underneath.

"Are you ready to switch?" Charles asked, jolting Andrew from his reverie.

"Yes." He leapt out of the barouche to check the horses while Charles moved to the driver's seat. Thursby climbed to the backseat, which Charles had vacated. After surveying his team, Andrew took Thursby's place beside Charles. "I think I shall attend Lady Colne's ball tonight. Anyone else going?"

Charles turned his head and stared at him. "You're

going to a ball? Why?"

Beaumont sat forward, his fair brows drawn into a knot. "Yes, why?"

Thursby, the only married one among them, chuckled. "Perhaps Dart has decided it's time to do his duty. We all get there eventually." He'd wed just three years ago, so he spoke from experience.

Andrew shuddered. "Marriage is not my plan, gents, rest assured. It's just been a while, and you know me, I like to do a little bit of everything." In truth, he hoped to encounter Miss Parnell. His curiosity was quite simply getting the best of him.

"This is true," Charles said, nodding. "How goes your plan for ballooning?"

Flying was Andrew's newest scheme. That distant memory assailed him again. Bertie's feeble voice telling Andrew not to worry, that he would soon get to fly—with the angels. Bertie had been obsessed with flying, saying he longed to be a bird and soar high above the trees. Andrew meant to do it for him.

"I've corresponded with Sadler, and we're finalizing plans for his ascension next week." James Sadler was the leading aeronaut in England, a brilliant fellow who was as much an inventor as a balloonist. He had an exhibition scheduled from Burlington House and had agreed to take Andrew with him for a fee, which Andrew had willingly paid. He looked up at the sky, clotted with gray-white clouds, and imagined the sensation of being up there, of looking down at everything in miniature detail.

"Damn me," Beaumont said, whistling. "You couldn't pay me to do that, and I certainly wouldn't pay for the chance!"

"I don't know. It might be fun." Charles grinned at

his passengers and rubbed his hands together. “Everyone ready?”

“Remember to focus on the corners,” Andrew said. “And watch your grip. My team is sensitive. They won’t like it if you’re too heavy-handed.”

Charles nodded. “I appreciate you allowing me to practice with them.”

They started out slowly, with Charles steadily increasing their speed. His skill had improved, and Andrew began to think they could perhaps finally recommend him. The breeze whipped over them, bringing that sense of freedom and abandon that Andrew loved. The first turn approached.

“Lean into the curve,” Andrew said. “Keep your grip firm.”

Charles drove faster, and Andrew’s assessment faltered. “Careful,” he warned.

But Charles didn’t slow, and when they reached the turn, the barouche tilted.

Andrew grabbed the side of the vehicle and prayed it wouldn’t overturn. With his other hand, he reached out and grabbed at the reins. “Charles!”

Charles dipped to the side but didn’t relinquish the reins. Andrew lurched forward and snatched them from his friend, whose grip was hard and fast.

“Charles, the horses!” Andrew called.

Charles let go at last, then tumbled from the side of the barouche.

“Bloody hell!” Beaumont cried.

Andrew steered the horses to slow and finally stop. “I need to check the team,” he said, climbing down. “You see about Charles.”

Thursby jumped down. “He looks to be standing up.” He and Beaumont hurried to Charles, while

Andrew spoke softly to his horses. They were a magnificent team and seemed none the worse for Charles's carelessness.

The trio returned to the barouche before Andrew could make his way to them.

Charles's coat was torn, and there was a hole in his breeches. His head hung at a sheepish angle, and his face was bright red, probably as much from embarrassment as exertion. "My apologies, Dart. I thought I had it."

"You did well until the turn."

"I'm afraid I became cocky." He winced. "Are the horses all right?"

Andrew buried his annoyance since there was no lasting harm done. "They're fine. I'm sorry to say you're going to need a little more practice. You need to work on your turning technique before you add in the speed."

Charles nodded. "I will. Thank you."

Andrew glanced down at Charles's rumpled form. "You all right?"

"I am. Knee's a bit beaten up, I think." He gestured to the hole above his boot, where blood trickled over the fabric of his breeches.

Andrew gave one of the horses a final pat. "Let's get back to town, then. I'll drive," he said wryly, provoking laughter from Thursby and Beaumont and even a smile from Charles.

Once they were on their way, Thursby turned his head toward Andrew. "I'll be at Lady Colne's this evening. It will be a pleasure to see you there. Perhaps you'll join me at hazard."

Mention of gaming brought Miss Parnell to mind once more. But then it seemed she was never terribly far away. This was a new sensation, this interest in a woman, but then he enjoyed her company as much as any of his acquaintances'. She was a welcome change to his routine, another adventure he could claim.

Going back to Thursby's invitation, if Miss Parnell wasn't there, gambling would be his only interest. "I may just do that."

If she were there, however, would he dance with her or merely satisfy his desperate curiosity?

Thursby looked at him askance. "If you change your mind about venturing onto the Marriage Mart, there's quite a good crop this year. Holborn's daughter is lovely but seems a bit fast."

This aroused laughter from everyone.

Beaumont leaned forward from the back. "Said a reformed rake for whom 'fast' was merely his behavior before sundown."

"Yes, well, reformation happens to all of us at some point, if we're lucky," Thursby said tersely. "As I was saying, there are young ladies that may be worth your time to know. Miss Emmaline Forth-Hodges is bound to make an excellent match, or so my wife says."

"Sutton's interested in her," Charles said.

Beaumont snorted. "Bah, that won't go anywhere. Sutton doesn't really want to marry."

"Or perhaps he's just exceptionally selective."

Andrew smiled at their banter. He knew Sutton vaguely. He had a bit of a reputation for disappointing young women. He showed interest, but when it seemed a formal courtship was imminent, he backed away. One might expect that young ladies would stop showing him favor, but he was still a wealthy earl with multiple estates. Women would be drawn to him until he ceased to draw breath.

Which was why Andrew generally avoided things like balls, for he was also a wealthy earl—although he had just one estate. "You can stop suggesting marriageable women, Thursby. As I said, I've no plans to take a wife."

Just as he had no plans to reform. Not that he was a rake as Thursby had been, but he liked his carefree lifestyle and had no desire to alter it. Especially for a wife or a family. The mere thought of those things summoned those torturous memories he preferred to keep buried. Families meant love. Love meant pain. And he'd endured enough pain for his entire lifetime, however long it lasted.

LUCY WALKED INTO Lady Satterfield's drawing room that afternoon at her grandmother's side. Grandmama's hip was bothering her today, so she'd decided to use her cane, which she did from time to time.

"I'll find you a chair, Grandmama," Lucy said, glancing around the room. She'd been to Satterfield House on several occasions, but this was only her second visit this Season. The first had been Lady Satterfield's annual ball, which was the first grand event each Season. That was when Lucy's dearest friend, Aquilla Knox, had become Lady Satterfield's ward.

"Over there will be just fine." Grandmama indicated a pale blue settee that would afford a view of the door to see who came and went as well as the tall windows that faced the street.

Lady Satterfield sailed toward them. She was tall, her hair still dark though she was in her fifties. She smiled warmly. "Lady Parnell, it's a pleasure to see you. And

Miss Parnell, you look lovely. I'm delighted you could both join us today."

"Thank you, my lady. I appreciate all the kindness you've shown Aquilla." Lucy wanted to ask where she was but didn't wish to appear rude.

"Oh, I adore Aquilla. It's been a joy having her here with us this Season."

Lucy knew Aquilla felt the same way—they corresponded nearly every day. Aquilla had only come to London to visit Lucy for a short time. Her parents weren't giving her any more Seasons, since her last four had been utter failures.

Fortunately, however, Lucy, Aquilla, and their friend Ivy had met Lady Satterfield's stepdaughter-in-law, the Duchess of Kendal, at the ball, and she'd taken an instant liking to them. Upon hearing that Aquilla had to return to the country with her parents, Lady Kendal had invited her to spend the Season with her. Five years ago, Lady Satterfield had sponsored her in just such a fashion, and she'd wanted to perform the same kindness for someone else. As it happened, however, Lady Satterfield had ended up being Aquilla's sponsor, an arrangement that suited everyone marvelously.

"I just need to see Grandmama to the settee," Lucy said to the countess.

"Of course." Lady Satterfield stepped aside so that Lucy and her grandmother could move farther into the room.

Lucy took her grandmother's cane once she was seated and rested it against the edge of the settee. When she looked up, Aquilla was coming toward her, a bright smile lighting her face. But then Aquilla was usually smiling. Lucy believed it was her God-given mission to bring light and grace to those who needed it most.

"Lucy!" Aquilla took her hand and squeezed it, then dropped down next to Lucy's grandmother. "Grandmama, you look lovely in that shade of blue." She pressed a kiss to the older woman's cheek. She'd spent enough time with Lucy over the past five years to count herself as a member of their tiny family.

Grandmama patted Aquilla's knee. "You're such a good girl, my dear. How are you enjoying being Lady Satterfield's ward?"

"It's ever so wonderful." She beamed at them. "I've never been to so many balls, and Lady Satterfield loves to shop. I must admit I've developed quite a fondness for it."

Lucy was glad. Aquilla deserved to be happy.

Grandmama's gaze focused near the doorway. One of her friends had just arrived. "Agatha is here. You two take yourselves off and talk of fripperies and dance partners." She waved them away.

Aquilla laughed softly. "Yes, Grandmama." She stood and linked her arm with Lucy's, and they walked toward the windows.

Lucy eyed her friend's yellow frock. "Is that another new gown?"

Aquilla smoothed her hand over the top of her skirt. "Yes, do you like it? Lady Satterfield has been far too generous. My mother would suffer an apoplectic fit." Because she'd never wanted to invest too much in Aquilla, particularly after her first Season had been such a disappointment. Aquilla was very pretty, with dark, curly hair and vivid blue eyes, but she liked to talk—so much so that by the middle of that first Season, she'd become a wallflower. Right alongside Lucy, who had developed a similar reputation. Not for the quantity of her speech, but for the brashness of it. Lucy had learned to curb her tongue—somewhat—in the intervening years, but the damage had been done. As a result, both she and Aquilla were firmly on the shelf.

Which was fine with Lucy. Aquilla, however, wanted a husband.

"I'm sure it will be a valuable tool in your husband hunt," Lucy said. "How are things progressing?"

They corresponded nearly every day, but Aquilla hadn't said much on that front.

She gazed out the window and sighed. "Dismal, I'm afraid."

"You told me last week that you'd had invitations to dance."

"Yes, but they never lead to anything else. I think they're just favors to Lady Satterfield or Lady Kendal. That and they want to ask me if I know the Forbidden Duke and Duchess." She rolled her eyes. "Can you believe that nonsense?"

Lucy chuckled. "Yes. We were in awe of Nora when we first met her, if you'll recall." Nora was Lady Kendal, who was also known as the Forbidden Duchess. The nickname came from her husband who disdained most of Society in favor of his family and his dukedom. He'd cultivated a reputation for being detached and unapproachable—forbidden, as it were. Or, as Nora called him, he was an Untouchable. Like the Earl of Dartford.

Aquilla giggled. "I suppose we were rather intimidated. I'd forgotten since I've become so comfortable." Her gaze flicked down over Lucy's costume. "You should come shopping with us. It's been ever so long since you've had a new gown."

And it would likely be an eternity still. "I'm afraid I

cannot."

Aquilla frowned. "Why not? We used to like to shop for ribbons and things."

That was true. They'd squandered many an afternoon that first year they'd met. Lucy smiled faintly at the memory. "I'm afraid there's no money for me to do that. I'll barely make it to the end of the Season, and then Grandmama is moving to Bath."

Aquilla's eyes widened. "What happened? You've never mentioned this before."

"It's a new development. There just simply isn't any money. You know how deep in debt my father was when he died."

His entailed holdings, along with his baronetcy, had reverted to the crown, and they'd had to sell off everything they could. The bulk of the proceeds had settled his vowels, leaving just enough to live on these past seven years.

Aquilla nodded sympathetically, her gaze stricken. Empathy was another of Aquilla's strengths. "Bath isn't terribly far. We can visit each other."

"Assuming I go to Bath with Grandmama. Right now there isn't enough money to support us both. Grandmama is insisting I find a husband."

Blue eyes wide, Aquilla gaped at her. "But you don't want a husband."

"No, I don't."

Aquilla pressed her lips together. "Perhaps you should revise your opinion. There has to be a gentleman out there that you can tolerate. Not all men are like your father or your grandfather."

Selfish, dissolute men who'd led their lives without a whit of responsibility or a care for their wives or children. They'd both left their families in debt and, in

Lucy's case, with no prospects for her future, save what she could manage for herself. No, she wouldn't put her faith in any man.

For some reason, she thought of Dartford. Not because he was marriage material, but because she supposed she *had* put her faith in him. And so far, he hadn't let her down. She reminded herself that their acquaintance was young. There was plenty of time for him to disappoint her in spectacular fashion.

"Or like Caruthers," Aquilla said softly.

They hadn't spoken of him in a very long time. A young buck, he'd paid Lucy attention during her first Season. He'd led her to believe he wanted to court her, and Lucy—naïve fool that she'd been at twenty—had thought she'd broken her mother's and grandmother's curse when it came to men. They'd shared dreams and chaste kisses, had talked of their future. And then he'd disappeared. A month later, she'd heard he'd eloped to Gretna Green with an heiress.

He'd broken the curse, all right. He'd ensured Lucy wouldn't take a husband at all.

"Let's not mention him," Lucy said. "In hindsight, I should've packed Grandmama up back then and moved to Bath." They could've saved a great deal of money if she'd avoided the past several Seasons. "Anyway, I'm not the one we should be focusing on. You're the one who wants a husband, and with Lady Satterfield's help, I daresay you'll find one."

"I don't know, but both she and Nora are so optimistic. I don't want to disappoint them."

Lucy shook her head. "You mustn't think of it like that. This is about you and your happiness, not theirs." But how like Aquilla to think of them first. "I'm confident your new alliances will bear fruit. You just have to be patient." Lucy knew how terrible that sounded. Aquilla had already been waiting five years. And she never complained.

Determination lit Aquilla's eyes. "You're right. Nora says I'll marry an Untouchable like she did. I'd be happy with a vicar or even a lawyer."

An Untouchable. Dartford's handsome visage floated through her mind again. It was a shame he wasn't interested in marriage. Lucy might have encouraged him to pursue Aquilla and vice versa. Inexplicably, a jolt of distaste sparked through her.

Aquilla moved closer and spoke softly. "Tell me what you're doing about your money situation."

Lucy couldn't bring herself to speak the truth, not even to her dearest friend. But at the same time, she wanted to tell her about Dartford and about shooting at Manton's. That was a memory that would make her smile for a long time, probably forever.

"Will you trust me when I say that I have a plan and it's coming along nicely?" She'd have the money she needed soon. Just a few more nights out with Dartford.

Aquilla narrowed her eyes. "That sounds rather cryptic. Why the secrecy? You know you can tell me anything."

Yes, she did. For all that Aquilla liked to talk, she didn't break confidences. Even so, Lucy didn't want to tell her about it until she was finished. Maybe she was just being superstitious since she'd been quite lucky so far. "I know, and I shall. Soon. It's…complicated."

Aquilla exhaled. "I'll pretend I'm not insulted."

Lucy winced. "That is certainly not my intent. I'll share everything with you soon, I promise."

A figure came toward them. It was Nora, the Duchess of Kendal. She smiled and greeted them both warmly.

"How have you been, Lucy?" she asked. "I haven't seen you since my mother-in-law's ball." She laughed. "Which isn't surprising, since I rarely go out. I'm fortunate to see Aquilla when we come for dinner once a week, and of course, she's been to Kendal House."

"We haven't been out often either," Lucy said. "My grandmother isn't quite as spry this Season."

Nora nodded. "I understand. I daresay the same thing is happening to Lady Dunn. We haven't seen her as much this Season, and she's not here today. I shall have to pay a call."

"I'll come with you," Aquilla said. "I'd love to see her and Ivy."

Ivy Breckenridge was Lady Dunn's companion and the final member of their spinster-wallflower trio. That reminded Lucy of something. "I've been thinking that we need our own name, like The Untouchables."

Aquilla's eyes lit. "We do! Do you have something in mind?"

"I do, but it might be too pretentious—The League of Invincibles. Because nothing keeps us down."

Nora grinned. "That's not pretentious at all. It's splendid."

"And accurate," Aquilla agreed. "I'll come up with a special handshake."

"May I be a member even though I'm married?" Nora asked.

"Marriage has nothing to do with membership," Lucy said. "Of course you can be a member."

"Excellent. And anyway, you won't be unmarried for long. Aquilla's Season is going swimmingly, and I have high hopes for Lady Colne's ball tonight." Nora looked at Lucy. "Your grandmother indicated that you wanted to go and has arranged for Lady Satterfield and Aquilla to pick you up."

Lucy wanted to groan. She did *not* want to go. Furthermore, they hadn't been invited. Yet it seemed that Grandmama had neatly maneuvered an opportunity for Lucy to attend. She might be slowing down physically, but her acumen was as sharp as ever.

Aquilla angled toward her. "It will be just like Seasons of old." Her blue eyes sparkled with anticipation, and Lucy couldn't help but be swept up in her enthusiasm. Just because she didn't want a husband didn't mean she couldn't help her friend find one. Besides, she missed adorning the wall with Aquilla.

"Yes, it will." All of Lucy's ball gowns were from last Season and the one before, but that wouldn't matter, not when she would spend the evening in the shadows.

The conversation turned to Nora's two children, and soon Lucy's grandmother was ready to leave. When they were settled in their small carriage, Lucy didn't prevaricate. "I see you organized my evening for me."

Grandmama patted her hand. "Indeed I did. You can't be expected to find a husband if you aren't out. I spoke to Lady Satterfield about this at length. She will take you along with her and Miss Knox, since I am not able to keep up today."

It was even worse than just tonight. She'd organized Lucy's entire Season. How was she to maintain her plan with Dartford if she was out with Lady Satterfield and Aquilla? "Thank you. But don't be disappointed when I am still unwed at the end of the Season."

Grandmama pursed her lips. "My dear, I hope not. Your time is running out. It's now or never, I'm afraid. You know what's at stake."

Just their entire livelihood. They could live, but it

would be a pale imitation of the life they currently enjoyed. It was going to be an adjustment, but one that Lucy was more than prepared to make.

"I do," Lucy said quietly. She wanted to tell her grandmother what she'd told Aquilla, that she was working on a solution. But she wouldn't even say that much. Once she had the money in hand and could set the move to Bath in motion, she'd tell both of them that they needn't worry.

Her next appointment with Dartford couldn't come soon enough. In the meantime, she'd suffer through tonight and do whatever she could to help her friend's cause. Aquilla wanted a happily ever after, and she would have it.

Lucy would settle for comfortable ever after.

Chapter Five

ANDREW ARRIVED AT Lady Colne's ball fairly early, but not *too* early. He was instantly besieged by those of his acquaintances who attended these sorts of events. And then he was assaulted by matchmaking mamas parading their daughters in front of him as if he were at Tattersall's surveying horseflesh. It was more than a little discomfiting.

He was pleasant but noncommittal, and his attention was divided between those seeking his company and the woman he was looking for but wasn't sure he could find. Since he had no idea what she really looked like.

He supposed he did have at least an idea—the shape of her face, her height, the tilt of her head. Her eyes. Those lush, expressive eyes that reminded him of the forest at Darent Hall, his country seat. If he could just hear her speak, he'd know her for certain.

Because he'd dreamed she had dark blonde hair, that was what he found himself searching for. He could be wrong, however, so he told himself to study every face and form for a hint of his friend Smitty.

A tall, regal woman approached him. "Lord Dartford, how charming to see you here." The woman was vaguely familiar, but he wasn't completely sure how he knew her. She seemed to understand his consternation, bless her, for she said, "I'm Lady Satterfield. I was a friend of your mother's when we were in our first Season. I came to Darent Hall a few times, but you were only a boy."

And just like that, Andrew's heart began to pound.

Cold sweat dappled his neck. He didn't want to feel this. Not here. Not now.

He tried to summon a pleasant response but only managed, "Yes, I remember you." He didn't really, and now he understood why. He generally shoved everything to do with his family as far away from his mind as possible.

She cocked her head to the side. "It's quite all right if you don't." She took his arm. "Come, walk with me a moment."

The irony of being rescued from the herd of matchmaking mamas by another matchmaking mama wasn't lost on him. *Was* she a matchmaking mama? "Where are we going?" he asked.

"I thought you needed rescuing. You don't come to many balls anymore. Perhaps you underestimated the vulturelike atmosphere."

He laughed, surprised that his emotions could veer so swiftly, but exceptionally glad. The tension she'd provoked by mentioning his mother eased. Her touch was surprisingly comforting. "Thank you. I *had* forgotten."

She led him to the edge of the ballroom. "I must confess I'd hoped to introduce you to my ward, but I can see you need a moment to regain your equilibrium."

He marveled that she'd noticed his discomfort. "I'm fine, thank you." He was now. "I'd be delighted to meet your ward." It was the least he could do to repay Lady Satterfield's kindness, even if she was the one who'd caused his momentary distress.

"All right. She's over here with her friend."

They skirted the wall until they came upon a pair of young women. Both were dark-haired, one with corkscrew curls grazing her temples, the other with a more severe style.

The one with the curls was facing him. Her bright blue eyes connected with Lady Satterfield first, acknowledging her, then moved to Andrew. She smiled warmly.

The second one was angled away from him, but now she turned. The familiar moss and earth tone of her luminous eyes shot straight into his chest. His breath hitched.

It was *her*.

She wasn't blonde. But she was stunning. Not classically beautiful, but far more attractive than the pale misses who'd clustered around him when he'd arrived.

Lady Satterfield let go of his arm. "May I present Lord Dartford?" She gestured toward Miss Parnell's companion. "This is my ward, Miss Aquilla Knox, and her friend, Miss Lucinda Parnell."

Miss Knox curtseyed. "Pleased to meet you, my lord."

He bowed. "The pleasure is mine." His gaze moved to Miss Parnell. "Miss Parnell."

"Lord Dartford." Her voice was as dusky and seductive as he recalled. In fact, it was even more alluring now that he had her feminine features to go with it.

"May I have the next dance?" he asked. Belatedly he realized he should've asked Miss Knox to dance, but he feared Miss Parnell had stolen his wits.

She narrowed her eyes slightly and didn't immediately respond. Instead, she glanced at her friend.

Miss Knox gave her an easy smile, and Andrew knew she must do so often. Not like Miss Parnell, who kept her emotions very close. At least when she was dressed as a man. Would she behave differently now that she was without her disguise? What was she really like? Andrew longed to find out.

She was utterly lovely, with a strong but feminine jawline and supple lips that made him wonder how she could ever pass for a man. The sideburns, which he didn't miss in the slightest, completely changed her face, he realized. She'd been smart to don them.

He was glad, however, that she wasn't wearing them now. And that she'd disposed of her padding and her men's costume. She was lithe and lean, with subtle curves and long legs. He imagined her riding a horse with ease. If she could shoot like a man, he suspected she probably rode like one too.

"The next set is starting soon," he prompted. She still hadn't responded to his invitation.

She continued to hesitate, and her friend delivered an elbow to her side. Andrew stifled a grin as Miss Parnell tossed a glare at Miss Knox.

"Go!"

Andrew couldn't hear the word but read Miss Knox's lips, and the glower she delivered Miss Parnell gave the utterance its exclamation point, at least in Andrew's mind. Miss Knox gave her a little push for good measure.

Miss Parnell frowned but moved forward. Andrew offered his arm, which she took—in a clearly reluctant fashion if the slowness of her movements were any indication.

Andrew bowed to Lady Satterfield and Miss Knox. "Ladies."

He led Miss Parnell toward the dance floor. "Why didn't you want to dance with me?"

"Don't take it personally. I don't like to dance with anyone."

He glanced down at her. "Not a very good dancer?"

She sucked in a breath and then laughed. He liked that sound. Almost as much as he liked watching her animated face. "I'm an *excellent* dancer."

He arched a brow at her. "I'll be the judge of that."

She rolled her eyes. "I suppose you're superior on the dance floor. You don't seem to have any deficiencies."

He grinned, enormously pleased with her observation. "I'm so glad you noticed."

The set finished, and the music started for the next dance. A waltz. Andrew couldn't believe his good luck.

Miss Parnell's nostrils flared. It was a slight reaction, but Andrew caught it.

"What's the matter?" he asked.

"I haven't waltzed very much. I wasn't paying attention to the sets, otherwise I would've told you I couldn't dance this one."

He lightly clasped her waist and took her hand. "I thought you said you were an excellent dancer."

She scowled at him as she curled her fingers around his and placed her hand on his shoulder. "You are most ungracious."

He laughed again, enjoying her immensely. "Come now, surely if you can shoot a gun with deadly accuracy, you can't let a waltz defeat you?"

She squared her shoulders, which drew his attention to her chest. Though she wasn't well-endowed, she was nicely formed for her frame, and the bodice of her raspberry silk ball gown fit her to perfection.

"No, I shan't. I'm invincible, don't you know?" She gave him a saucy look, and he was completely enchanted.

They moved with the music, and he was glad he remembered how to waltz. "I have a confession to make. My waltzing experience is rather limited as well."

"Charlatan."

He laughed again. "That's ironic coming from you."

She lifted a shoulder. "One might say I'm uniquely qualified to recognize deception."

He chuckled, enjoying himself far more than he had in a long time. And with a woman. On a dance floor. At a ball. Who would've thought that would be possible? He looked down at the woman in his arms and liked what he saw. She wasn't what he expected, and yet she was everything he'd hoped.

Hoped?

Jarred by his thoughts, he focused on sweeping her around the dance floor instead of exploring why he found himself reacting to her in this fashion.

She took a wrong step, and he had to grip her more tightly to steer her back on course. This brought them closer together, and he caught a nose full of her scent—something floral and spicy at the same time. Intoxicating.

"What are you even doing here?" she asked. "The Duke of Daring doesn't extend his adventurous spirit to insipid Society events."

"You are well versed in my behavior." He wasn't sure if that was good or bad. Neither, he decided. She wasn't husband hunting. He had nothing to fear from her.

"There isn't much to do when you're stuck along the wall. Aquilla and I used to dream up disaster situations. We assigned roles based on what we knew of people, so it was helpful for us to have a sense of what people are like."

"Disaster situations? I'm not sure I follow your meaning."

She cocked her head to the side. "As an example, the chandelier might fall to the floor, crushing people and starting a fire. Who would die, who would flee, and who would stay to rescue people?"

He stared at her, not certain whether he should laugh or be alarmed. "Dear Lord, you two are frightening."

"Three, actually. Our other friend typically joined us. And to be honest, she usually thought up the disaster. I'm afraid she's as disdainful of Society as the Forbidden Duke."

"The who?" He vaguely recalled that nickname, but wasn't sure he knew to whom it belonged. "I don't follow gossip and reputations like you do."

"No, because you aren't as bored as we were. You were off shooting and gambling and racing." She sounded wistful.

He felt sorry for her. For all women, actually. He'd never really thought of what it must be like to struggle with the constraints Society placed upon them. "You've reminded me of what I wanted to speak with you about tonight. Yes, I was hoping to encounter you. *That* is why I came to this insipid ball."

She blinked up at him, looking momentarily surprised and something else. Pleased maybe? "What is it?"

The music drew to a close, and the dance ended. Andrew escorted her from the dance floor. "Shall we promenade for a bit?"

"Yes."

"We'll just take a turn around the terrace." He walked with her through the ballroom to the door leading outside. "Is your grandmother here? I should like to meet her."

They moved onto the terrace, which was lit with bright lanterns. Other people were present, either strolling or deep in conversation. "Why, so you can tell her about my escapades?"

"Escapades. An excellent description. No, we have an agreement. So long as you let me accompany you, I will keep your secret. I just wanted to meet her."

"Oh. She isn't here." She looked up at him and smiled. "But that's nice."

His chest constricted the tiniest amount, and he coughed. "Yes, well, about…about my idea. I was thinking that instead of going to gaming hells, you should accompany me to some gentlemanly events where wagering occurs."

Her brow furrowed. "Like at Manton's?"

"Just so. In fact, we could go to Manton's again. Charles has already tried to wager that I could outshoot you—he heard of your prowess with a pistol."

She laughed, and it was filled with devilish glee. "I should like that."

He couldn't help but laugh with her. "I'm sure you would. You could also attend one of the phaeton races."

"Will you be racing?"

"Probably not. If I'm racing, I can't remain at your side, and it seems prudent for me to do that."

"I won't disagree, but I admit to being disappointed. I'd like to watch you race."

They'd reached the far end of the terrace, where there were fewer people. In fact, there was no one within fifteen feet of them, and if he steered her to the shadowy corner, they could perhaps pass unnoticed. Hell, why was he even thinking that?

He stopped and turned with her, intent on taking her back. But he was frozen. By her floral-and-spice scent. By the lovely contours of her face as the lanterns' light spilled over her. By the open, guileless intensity of her gaze.

She looked back toward the ballroom. "Anyway, I understand why I can't. But I like your plan. Especially if I get to shoot again."

"Then that's what we'll do. Let me sort out the particulars. You'll need to work out how to leave your house as a gentleman in daylight."

She tossed him a concerned glance. "Oh dear, that *is* a problem. I'll come up with something."

He guided her back to the door to the ballroom. "Then we both have assignments. We shall share our plans when I see you night after next. Unless you'd prefer to cancel that appointment."

"No. That will give us each time to plan, as you said." They neared the ballroom. "Thank you."

"Shall I deliver you somewhere?" he asked, anxious to be gone. Now that he'd accomplished his goal, he wanted to leave. Never mind dancing with Miss Knox.

She withdrew her arm from his. "That isn't necessary. Thank you for the dance."

"Thank you. You've quite satisfied my dancing requirements for the next year at least."

She smiled again, and he was glad he'd come. It had been worth seeing her like this, even if he was a damn fool for thinking so.

"You've done the same for me. Two years, probably." She shrugged. "Maybe even for a lifetime."

She had to be joking, but something about the statement rang true. He wanted to say that wouldn't happen, but then he recalled that she didn't wish to marry either. And she hadn't been eager to dance with him. Quite the contrary. It seemed they were birds of a feather, and didn't that make her even more dangerous than she'd been in that dark corner on the terrace? He'd looked at her out there and for a brief moment had wanted to sweep her into his arms and see if she tasted as good as she smelled and as delicious as she looked.

He bowed. "Good evening, then."

She curtseyed. "Good evening."

He strode from the ballroom as if the flames of hell licked at his feet. If he wasn't careful, things could progress to a place he didn't want them to. He took a deep breath. They wouldn't.

He and Miss Parnell had a temporary association. She would earn the funds she needed, and then she would be gone from his life.

He would go back to his solitary, carefree existence where he wasn't threatened by loss or pain.

Or love.

LUCY DIDN'T MAKE it ten steps back toward Aquilla before a gentleman asked her to dance the next set. Shocked, she said yes. As soon as they finished, another gentleman—a baronet—requested the next. She wanted to decline, but after years of seeking dance partners and nearly always coming up short, she didn't really know how.

Finally, when the music ended, Lucy dashed back to Aquilla before another gentleman could corner her. Aquilla was still there and had been joined by their friend Ivy Breckenridge.

Lucy glanced around and saw that another gentleman was coming toward them. She tugged at both Aquilla's and Ivy's hands. "Quickly, we must find the retiring room."

Aquilla grinned broadly. "Yes, let's. I want to hear everything! This is your most successful night *ever*—and just when you need it most."

Lucy wanted to scowl, but she'd wait until they were out of the ballroom. "This is not at all what I need."

They exited the ballroom and made their way to the retiring room.

"I don't understand," Ivy said, "Aquilla told me you must find a husband immediately because you're out of money."

Lucy tossed an exasperated glare at Aquilla. "That's all you told her? You didn't bother mentioning that I have no interest in finding a husband?"

Aquilla shrugged, not the least bit bothered by Lucy's irritation. "I assume you'll come around."

Lucy groaned and then stopped short. "I don't want to go to the retiring room, where people could overhear us."

Ivy took the lead. "This way." She guided them to a small sitting room, closing the door behind them as they went inside. "Lady Dunn and I mistakenly found ourselves in here after we arrived. The retiring room is farther down the corridor, so we learned."

Lucy looked around the chamber, which was lit with two lanterns. The hearth was dark and cold.

Aquilla must've noticed the same things, for she said, "The lanterns seem to invite company; however, the lack of a fire to provide warmth seems to do the opposite."

"It's set for an assignation," Ivy said, her distaste

evident in the curl of her lip.

"Is it?" Aquilla asked as she strolled into the room and touched the back of one of the pair of ivory settees. "How do you know?"

"I just do." Ivy turned to Lucy. "I was surprised when Aquilla told me you were seeking a husband. I thought we were of a similar mind on that topic."

Ivy had as much interest in wedlock as Lucy did, which was to say none. In fact, Ivy was even less interested, if that were possible. Whereas Lucy had once hoped for success on the Marriage Mart, Ivy had never even tried. She'd been a lady's companion for as long as Lucy and Aquilla had known her—and was quite content with her lot.

"My grandmother wants me to find a husband. She wishes to retire to Bath, and does not have enough money to support me." Lucy allowed the scowl she'd earlier repressed to come forth. "If I'd had any idea we were wasting money with these fruitless Seasons, I would've packed us off to Bath years ago."

Aquilla turned and looked at Lucy, her blue eyes bright and sympathetic. "Come now, it hasn't been that bad, has it? We've had fun, I hope."

Lucy regretted her earlier annoyance. She went and took her friend's hand, giving it a quick squeeze before letting go. "We've had plenty of fun. I am grateful to you both for making it tolerable." She smiled at Ivy, who'd gone to stand near the cold fireplace.

Ivy nodded in agreement. "Indeed. Well, if you don't mean to marry, what *is* your plan? I'm certain you could take up as a lady's companion with little effort."

Lucy had considered that, but the truth was that she didn't like the idea of having to answer to someone else. She enjoyed the independence that life with her grandmother offered, particularly their time away from London. After her father's death, when they'd had to move away from Stonewood, they'd spent the Season in London and the rest of the year near Bath. It was where she and Grandmama were most comfortable and why Grandmama wished to move there permanently.

For Lucy, she spent as much time outside as possible—walking, swimming, shooting, riding, if she could borrow a horse. She wouldn't be able to do any of those things if she were a lady's companion.

She tipped her head to the side, weighing whether she ought to tell them both what she was doing. "I don't think I'd make a very good companion."

Aquilla glided toward her, the silk of her beautiful new aqua-colored ball gown swirling around her ankles as she moved. "Lucy does indeed have some other plan." She glanced toward Ivy, her mouth pursed. "Not that she's saying what it is."

Ivy arched a red-gold brow at Lucy and crossed her arms. "Is that so? You're keeping secrets?"

Lucy resisted the urge to roll her eyes. Ivy was the most secretive among them. No, secretive wasn't the right word. She was…guarded. She spoke very little of her family, and when she did, it was brief and with disdain. Lucy and Aquilla had always wanted to know more—such as how Ivy had become as polished and educated as if she'd been prepared for Society—but Ivy didn't encourage those kinds of discussions. She always said she preferred to focus on the present and the future, that the past was precisely where it belonged. Lucy and Aquilla surmised that she'd buried some deep hurt, but didn't know what it was.

"Yes," Aquilla answered for her. She too had crossed her arms, making Lucy feel as though she were being chastised.

She pinned Aquilla with a mutinous stare. "Is it a secret if I say I plan to tell you?"

Aquilla, never one to willfully cause discomfort, threw her hands up. "No. And I'm sorry for badgering you." She smiled encouragingly at Lucy, then darted a look at Ivy. "She'll tell us in time."

"Well, my curiosity is piqued," Ivy said. "But I can be patient."

Again, Lucy considered just telling them, but they'd say it was dangerous, and she'd have to explain that she had a protector in Dartford. She realized he was the piece she didn't wish to disclose. Aquilla's eyes would widen, and she'd titter about how wonderful that was and probably suggest that he could be her husband. While Ivy's eyes would darken, and she'd frown. Then she'd caution Lucy, perhaps even saying that Dartford was anything but protection. To her, all men sought to seduce women into bed.

Neither one of her friends would understand Lucy's current situation. So she didn't tell them.

"I have a plan to make money so that I can retire with Grandmama. Things are going very well. I will tell you all about it soon." When she had the necessary funds in hand, and they wouldn't be able to try to talk her out of anything—because she'd be finished.

For some bizarre, unpleasant reason the thought of being finished with Dartford sparked a flash of annoyance. She liked him; that was all. And with him, she was able to do things she couldn't, such as shoot at Manton's. Their conversation from earlier came back to her, and she felt a rush of anticipation. To think that she could do that again—shoot at Manton's—or any number of other things, filled her with excitement.

"Are we ready to return?" Aquilla asked. "Actually, I'm not at all certain why we left."

Ivy looked at Lucy. "It seemed as though Lucy wanted to tell us something, but I would guess that is not the case."

"No, I did want to talk to you, but mostly I wanted to leave before someone else could ask me to dance."

Aquilla moved closer. "You didn't like dancing? Lord Metcalf is an excellent dancer."

The baronet who'd claimed the second set. Or third, if she counted her dance with Dartford. She'd liked *that*, if she was honest. Dartford's touch had been warm and sure, masculine. What an odd thing to think. But with him, she'd felt feminine in a way she never had. Was it because he'd only ever seen her as a man, and tonight she'd been more aware of herself as a woman? Or was it the way he'd studied her, as if he couldn't quite believe she was a woman? Or that he was shocked to find she was an *attractive* woman?

"Lucy?" Aquilla's voice drew her back from her musings.

"Yes, he's an excellent dancer, but that isn't the point." Was she speaking of Dartford or Metcalf, she asked herself. *Metcalf.* She couldn't think of Dartford right now. "I don't want a husband, and all of this…attention is a nuisance."

Ivy laughed, causing both Lucy and Aquilla to turn their heads. "Four years ago, you would've been ecstatic."

"Well, it's not four years ago. I am older and wiser, and I don't have the patience for this now. Really, where were these nincompoops when I wanted them?"

Ivy laughed again, harder this time, and Lucy joined her, giggling. Belatedly, Lucy realized that Aquilla wasn't laughing. She was watching them both with a slightly perturbed frown.

Lucy sobered and turned toward her friend. "Sorry. I know you'd love to have this attention, and if I could divert it toward you, I'd do so in a trice."

Ivy joined them and touched Aquilla's arm. "I've never understood your desire to wed, but I support your happiness wholeheartedly."

Aquilla exhaled. "It's all right. None of that is your fault. I'm being ridiculously maudlin. We each have our own path, and none is better than the other."

"Still, I'm being thoughtless," Lucy said, wincing.

"No, you're not. If you were, you'd still be laughing." Aquilla smiled at both of them. "Truly, you are the two dearest friends anyone could want. Who needs a husband?"

Ivy grinned. "Indeed." She turned her gaze to Lucy. "Do you plan to hide for the rest of the evening?"

Lucy sighed. "I suppose not." She looked at Aquilla. "How late will Lady Satterfield wish to stay?"

"Not much past midnight, I should think."

Lucy was relieved to hear it.

Ivy turned toward the door. "I need to check on Lady Dunn. I settled her in the gaming room. She'll likely want refreshment soon."

"We'll all go," Lucy said. They departed the room together.

Ivy left them to attend her employer, while Lucy and Aquilla went back to the ballroom—slowly.

"Marriage wouldn't be so bad, you know," Aquilla said softly. "My parents are quite content."

Content, yes, but Lucy didn't think they could be described as happy. They certainly didn't engender a sense of love or family, which made Aquilla's eternal optimism and charm a curious thing. If Lucy was going to bother with marriage, she wanted those things—family and love. She also demanded trust. She needed to know she could depend on a husband. That was paramount. She refused to end up like her grandmother, scraping for a comfortable retirement.

She supposed some gentleman *could* come up to scratch, at least providing dependability and a family. But after years of being ignored, she just didn't think that was likely. "Tonight is peculiar, a one-time oddity," she said. "I doubt this will encourage anything at all. Tomorrow, Society will go right back to not even seeing me."

Aquilla looked at her askance. "I don't know if I believe that. The Duke of Daring asked you to dance. That's extraordinary, don't you agree?"

He'd only done so because he knew her, not because he was interested in a courtship. "No."

Aquilla looked at her as if she'd gone mad. "He never dances!" She placed her finger against her chin in a contemplative pose. "In fact, he rarely attends balls. I wonder what he was doing here." Her gaze turned expectant as if Lucy might know.

And of course she *did* know. He'd been looking for her. She ignored the rush of heat flashing through her. "I have no idea."

"He didn't say when you were dancing? What *did* you talk about?"

"Waltzing."

Aquilla eyed her with skepticism. "How mundane. You're a better conversationalist than that."

"I might have told him about how we conjure ideas of potential disasters."

Aquilla's gaze filled with horror, but was quickly

replaced with humor as she dissolved into giggles. "You *didn't*."

Lucy smiled, recalling his reaction. "He wasn't terribly amused. I daresay I needn't worry about him pursuing me in the future."

Aquilla shook her head. "Pity. He's my favorite of your dance partners this evening. What of the others? Any idea why they wanted to partner you?"

Her question didn't offend Lucy in the slightest. It was, after all, very strange, and they both knew it. "I would guess it was borne of male competition. They want what they think they need to battle for."

"How primitive."

A thought blasted into Lucy's brain. If Dartford dancing with her could spark interest in Lucy, then surely it would do the same for Aquilla. She decided right then that she'd persuade him to do just that. "Perhaps Dartford will dance with you and then *you* can bask in all the attention."

"Well, that would be lovely. Unlikely, but lovely." She exhaled. "It's also probably pointless. You said yourself that nothing would come from your success tonight."

"For me," Lucy clarified. "You, on the other hand, will be a far more engaging dance partner than I am, and you'll charm them all into calling on you and vying for your hand. It will be a true competition."

Aquilla laughed. "I do appreciate your confidence—you're a darling. Let us not forget that I don't charm gentlemen so much as drive them away."

With her chattiness. Yes, Lucy knew that, just as she knew that the right man, someone who would love Aquilla for all that she was, would come along. "Well, let's just see what happens, shall we?" She linked her arm through Aquilla's and swept her back into the ballroom.

Later, as she tried to sleep, Lucy's brain was full of ideas and plans. She could scarcely wait until her next appointment with Dartford. Beyond earning more money for her goal, she was excited to learn what he had planned for other activities. And she'd convince him to lend his support to Aquilla. Perhaps he could even do more than dancing. Other gentlemen revered him. Surely if he spoke highly of a lady, their interest would be stirred.

As she fell asleep at last, she thought of racing in Hyde Park and shooting at Manton's, not in her men's costume, but dressed as herself. She imagined Dartford cheering her on and sweeping her into his arms, and she felt something more than protected. Something that would've filled her with alarm if she'd remembered the dream in the morning.

Fortunately, she didn't.

Chapter Six

HAVING ARRIVED EARLY for their appointment, Andrew waited for Miss Parnell at the corner while keeping an eye on her house. He'd been thinking of her far too much—of how alluring she was in a ball gown, how she felt in his arms, how tempting she'd looked outside on the terrace.

It was a good thing she'd be dressed as a man tonight. He didn't think he could see her in full feminine regalia again without doing something he'd likely regret.

Or not regret. Life was cruel that way.

At last he saw her come up from the servants' entry. She hurried toward him, her movements looking more like a woman's than last time.

When she reached him, he said, "Your gait is too feminine."

She looked down at her boots. "Really? I've been practicing."

Hell, maybe it was him. Maybe he couldn't see her for a man at all now that he'd seen her other side. "I'm sure it's fine. Just be mindful."

He turned with her toward the main thoroughfare. "We're not going far. Just to a hell on Piccadilly."

"Faro?" she asked.

"Or hazard if you like."

"It's silly, but hazard seems so much riskier. I know that makes no sense whatsoever because both are games of chance, but I've just always been partial to cards."

He glanced over at her as they walked. "Why is that?"

"Probably because my father always seemed to lose at hazard. One night, he lost five thousand pounds, plus our coach."

"It's no wonder you're in need of funds now." He cringed, not meaning to be ungracious. "My apologies."

She flashed him an artless smile. "It isn't your fault. We manage the best we can with what we're dealt, don't we? Yes, I realize that's a reference to cards." She chuckled.

Andrew had spent the better part of his life managing in precisely that fashion. He took extra care to try to stack the deck, to use another card reference he'd just heard recently, if at all possible. That meant keeping people from getting too close and filling his life with distractions.

Like Miss Parnell.

Only, she was a distraction he probably didn't need. But it wouldn't be forever, he reasoned. Their association would be over soon enough.

"What did you come up with regarding other events?" she asked, jarring him from his thoughts.

He'd given it plenty of consideration. "I think we'll start with the phaeton racing. The next one is Tuesday." Three days from now. "You'll be able to wager on several heats. Just be warned that you won't win every one."

"But you'll guide me, won't you? I have no idea who's a better driver."

"Of course."

"What do you drive when you race?" she asked.

"A high-perch phaeton. I'm working with someone to design a new one. There are a few modifications I'd like to make to increase my speed."

"Is that wise? It's dangerous enough, isn't it?" She waved her hand. "Never mind. I forgot with whom I was speaking. You're the Duke of Daring. Of course you want a faster vehicle."

He laughed. "Don't move your hand like that. It screams woman."

He began to worry that everything she did would signify her sex, but again assured himself that this was his problem based on his knowledge. Knowledge that others would not have.

"Damn," she said. "I'll do better when we get there. I think I've become too comfortable with you."

Damn indeed. He paused. "Perhaps this isn't wise in the long term."

She stopped a few steps in front of him and turned. "What do you mean?"

"Only that it's a risk every time you go out as you are."

She frowned. "I haven't had any problems aside from you." Her eyes lit. "*You're* the only one who's seen through my disguise. I think this is your difficulty."

Just as he'd thought. "I'm sure you're right." He started forward again, and they continued along the street.

"Perhaps I ought to have been born a man," she said. "I should think that would've suited me better."

What a shame that would've been. "I'm glad you weren't."

"Why?" She tossed him a quick glance. "Forget I asked. I'm not sure I wish to know."

Good because he didn't want to tell her. Another thought occurred to him. What if her wish to be a man had something to do with why she didn't want to marry? Maybe there was a more…*basic* explanation for her attitude. "Is there a reason you'd prefer to be a man? You've said you have no wish to marry. Perhaps you're not, ah, like other women."

She slowed and tipped her face toward him. "What do you mean?"

"Only that if you're more comfortable as a man, that might explain why you don't wish to marry. Perhaps you don't, ah, prefer the company of men." He regretted saying it almost immediately. Yes, he was flaunting every convention by escorting her around London near midnight without a chaperone, but that didn't mean there weren't *boundaries*.

She stopped abruptly and said nothing for a moment. When she turned, she eyed him warily. "I'm not entirely sure what you mean, but I assure you that I have no preference for either men or women." Her eyes widened, and he was certain she suddenly understood. "Oh. Well. I don't wish to marry because I'd prefer to rely on myself. As for the other…" She looked away and started walking again. "I've actually kissed a man. It was nice."

Andrew stared after her, momentarily unable to speak. When he found his voice—and his feet—he caught up to her. "Whom have you kissed?"

She slid him a sly look. "No one you know."

"You might be surprised." *He* was also surprised. By the fervor with which he wanted to learn this man's identity and smash his face in. Which was wholly ludicrous.

"No, really. He was a sheep farmer's son. This was years and years ago. Before my debut."

Andrew's shoulders relaxed. He laughed.

"Why are you laughing?"

Because he'd been an idiot. And because he'd stepped into a steaming pile of sheep manure with this conversation. "The idea of you with a sheep farmer. My apologies. I don't mean to offend."

"He was a well-mannered boy. Joshua." She wrinkled her nose. "But he did smell like stale hay."

Andrew laughed harder. "Stop, please."

She blinked at him. "Perhaps you should tell me of your lady loves."

Andrew instantly sobered, his laughter turning into a cough. "Yes, well, no. I don't think so." He wasn't a rake by any means, but neither was he a monk.

"Is that why you don't wish to marry? Perhaps you're not like most men."

He couldn't tell if she was joking or not. He stopped and turned toward her. She halted a step in front of him and pivoted.

He pinned her with an exacting stare. "I assure you, Miss Parnell, I am exactly like other men. I like to gamble and race, and I like women." He edged toward her. "*Emphatically.*"

She stared up at him, her hazel eyes enticing and mysterious at the same time. Her tongue peeked from her mouth and licked her lip, an action he'd never seen her do before and wasn't sure he wanted to see again. Certainly not when she was costumed as a gentleman.

"Don't do that." He didn't explain, nor did she ask. "We're here." He'd never been more relieved to arrive at a destination. "Ready?"

She inhaled deeply and smoothed her fingertips over her fake facial hair. "I am." She'd lowered her voice and flattened her lips, looking more like Smitty than she had all evening, thank God.

"That's disturbing," he said softly. "How quickly and

easily you do that." He shook his head, then turned to take the stairs up to the door.

They were greeted by a footman and then made their way to the main gaming room, where faro and hazard tables were set up.

Charles waved from a faro table in the corner. "Dartford! Come here."

Andrew leaned close to Miss Parnell. "I sought to avoid them the other night, but if you're going to make a go of this, we must join them."

"Let's go." She started without him, but Andrew easily caught up.

They waited until the round was over, and then Charles stepped away from the table. "I need a respite," he said. "The others are at hazard." He inclined his head toward Beaumont and a few others from their group. He gestured to a doorway leading from the room. "Have a drink with me."

Andrew glanced at Miss Parnell. He didn't know if she could drink. But given everything he knew about her, he expected so. She didn't return his gaze. Instead, she followed Charles into the parlor where a footman offered them whiskey, gin, or port.

She took the port, which surprised him.

"Not a whiskey drinker?" he asked.

She eyed the glass he'd taken from the tray. It contained gin. "Neither are you, I see."

Charles chuckled. "Not Dart. He typically goes for blue ruin. He lives like a man who doesn't have a tomorrow, isn't that right, Dart?"

Miss Parnell eyed him quizzically but was quick to mask her perusal.

Charles sipped his drink. "Smitty, I hear you're quite the marksman."

"So it would seem," she said, pitching her voice as low as Andrew knew it could go.

"I should like to see you take aim at the wafer some time," Charles said. "We'll have to arrange a shooting day."

"Indeed."

Andrew liked that she was noncommittal. They needed to take this slowly. "I've invited Smitty to join us for racing on Tuesday morning."

"Capital idea," Charles said. He looked at Miss Parnell, scrutinizing her a little more than Andrew would like. "Do you race?"

"I do not, but I should like to try."

Charles rocked back on his heels. "You're a driver, then. What's your vehicle?"

She glanced at Andrew, and he lightly shrugged. She'd need to maneuver these sorts of conversations.

She cleared her throat in a thoroughly masculine fashion. Andrew nearly applauded. "A phaeton."

"High perch?" Charles asked.

"No." Her tone was that of disappointment. Damn, she certainly seemed to crave excitement as much as he did. How extraordinary. And yet troubling at the same time. He didn't want to like her more than he already did.

Beaumont and the others joined them. "If it isn't the mysterious Smitty," Beaumont said. "We haven't seen you in a while. Everyone wants to see you shoot."

Miss Parnell wore a high, stiff cravat to shield the slender, alluring column of her neck, but it didn't cover the blush that spread up her face. She turned her head slightly and brought her hand up to smooth her sideburn, likely in an effort to mask her reaction. She liked the praise. Who wouldn't?

"He's coming to the races on Tuesday," Charles said. "Mayhap we can set up a target so he can demonstrate his skill. I'll still wager Dart can outshoot him."

Beaumont narrowed his eyes then grinned. "I'll take that wager! Fifty pounds."

"Fifty pounds," Charles agreed.

Charles looked toward Andrew and inclined his head toward the corner. "Dart, might I have a word?"

Andrew didn't want to leave Miss Parnell, even if it was just to move across the room. He preferred to hear what was said to her and what she said in response. But he couldn't think of a reason to decline Charles without drawing attention to their situation. So he went along with him but kept his body positioned so he could see Miss Parnell with the others.

Charles threw back the rest of his whiskey and rotated the glass several turns in his hands. "I'm a bit short tonight, Dart. Will you loan me a hundred pounds?"

Andrew flicked a glance at his friend but kept his focus on Miss Parnell. "How much have you lost?"

Charles tugged at his collar. "Ah, five hundred."

Andrew looked at him fully. "Hell. It's early yet. What happened?"

"Just got caught up. But don't worry, I'm done with faro."

"You should be done with everything. Why not take the role of spectator for the rest of the evening?"

Charles's dark brows knitted as his mouth formed a pout. "That's never fun."

He thought of the losses Miss Parnell's father had suffered and the impact it had on others. Charles didn't have a family, but he likely would someday. "It's better than losing in excess of five hundred pounds." Andrew slapped Charles on the shoulder. "You'll thank me."

"I could just go home and fetch more blunt. Aye, that's what I'll do."

Andrew saw that Beaumont was talking to Miss Parnell. He wanted to go back and hear their discussion. "Careful, Charles. Don't get in over your head."

"I won't."

Now Beaumont led Miss Parnell back to the gaming room. Time to go. Andrew turned to Charles. "Do what you must, but I don't wish to contribute to your downfall. Sorry, chap."

He hurried to join the others in the gaming room.

LUCY SIPPED HER port as she watched Dartford speaking with Charles, who looked a bit nervous. "What's that about?" she asked the nearest gentleman, who happened to be Beaumont.

The viscount looked over at the pair in the corner and shrugged. "Charles is probably asking for funds. Sometimes he gets caught up and loses his allotment for the evening.

"Allotment?" she asked.

"His father keeps him on a tight rein. It's a good thing, else he'd likely be in debtor's prison already."

Lucy hid her scowl behind her glass. She didn't like Charles, she decided, despite his geniality.

Beaumont turned to face her. "Did Dart also invite you to the balloon exhibition this Saturday?"

Lucy gave Beaumont her undivided attention. "What balloon exhibition?"

"Sadler's ascending from Burlington House, and

Dart is riding with him."

He meant to fly? Lucy had never seen a balloon ascent. She measured her tone, lest she sound overly interested. "How extraordinary."

"We're not going to the ascension. We'll be waiting for him at Darent Hall, where they'll descend." His blue eyes lit with excitement. "But don't tell him—it's a surprise. Charles is already wagering on where the balloon will land. We plan to arrive early and choose landing sites. Whoever comes closest will win the pot."

How Lucy longed to join them. But how would she get herself to Dartford's seat in Kent? It was a good twenty-five miles away. Plus, Dartford wouldn't be happy to see that she'd come, not without his company. She inwardly frowned. It wasn't up to Dartford to dictate her actions. She'd go if she wanted to. Except she still didn't have a means of travel. She realized, rather belatedly, that it was past time to involve her friends in her scheme. They would provide support and suggestions—one of them would have an idea to help her participate in this balloon excursion so that she could wager on the outcome. If she could win the pot, it might be enough to reach her goal.

"Sounds like fun," she said.

"You'll join us, then?"

"I'll try." She'd do everything possible.

He arched his brows at her. "Just remember it's a secret."

She nodded and wondered how Dartford would react to the surprise. Hopefully, she'd find out.

Beaumont threw back the rest of his whiskey. "I'm going to the faro table."

Lucy was itching to increase her purse. "I'll join you." She tossed a glance at Dartford, but he appeared to be deep in conversation with Charles, who was still fidgeting agitatedly with his glass.

The faro table was about to start a new round, so their timing was impeccable. Soon, Lucy was caught up in the game. She didn't notice when Dartford came into the gaming room, but sensed his presence when he moved behind her, just a moment before she saw him from the corner of her eye.

He sidled up to the table, taking a position to her right, while Beaumont was on her left. "You shouldn't do that," he murmured.

She glanced his way. "What, leave your sight? That's absurd."

"It isn't. We had an agreement."

"I was only in the next room, and I wasn't alone." She'd kept her voice low, but now she pitched it even softer. "Do I need to be concerned about Beaumont?"

"No." The answer came swiftly. "Never mind. You're doing well," he said. "After this, we can return to Jessup's to play whist if you'd like."

"Actually, there's a hell I wanted to visit further down Jermyn Street. They allow deeper play."

He looked at her intently, and she feared he would refuse. In the end, he nodded. "You're a judicious gambler, but then I should expect nothing less." Was there admiration in his gaze? She wasn't certain. Nevertheless, she appreciated his words. She had no wish to become like her father, not that she believed she would.

After two more rounds, they left. Beaumont and the others went another direction, and Charles went home.

As they walked to Jermyn Street, Lucy inquired about Charles. "Beaumont said he was asking you for money. Is that true?"

Dartford exhaled. "Yes. Unlike you, he is *not* a judicious gambler."

"I see. And did you give him money?"

"No."

She suspected he hadn't, but hearing that she wasn't wrong about him made her belly flutter. It was an odd, new sensation, but not at all unpleasant.

As they approached the hell, Dartford's tone turned serious. "I see where we're going. This is not like the other hells we've been to. In this instance, I will expect you not to leave my sight, and the moment I indicate we should leave, we *will* leave. Those are my terms, and they are not negotiable. Do you agree?"

She trusted him. As much as she'd probably ever trust any man. "Yes. But I need to win. At least a hundred pounds."

"I understand. We'll leave after that, and I'll hail a hack to take you home."

She wasn't certain of his intent. "Alone?"

His brow furrowed. "Of course not. I wouldn't do that."

No, he wouldn't. She was stuck with him whether she liked it or not.

She liked it.

They entered the hell, and right away she noticed the difference. Not everyone was as well dressed as they were. Or as clean. There was an odor of sweat and liquor. It was louder, more raucous.

Dartford guided her toward the nearest faro table, using his body to both cut through the throng and as a shield to protect her. They both played the next hand. This game moved faster than the others in her experience. It would be easy to lose track, especially if you were drinking whiskey or gin, as so many of the men around her were doing.

As the final card was turned, the man next to her grew upset at his loss. He leaned over the table, sneering at the dealer. "I'll come back tomorrow with my friends, and we'll see if you cheat me again."

A brawny footman was on him in an instant. But the angry man wasn't small and put up a fight. He jostled into Lucy, sending her sprawling. In the process, her hat slipped from her head.

Before she could reach for it, Dartford had slammed it back onto her scalp. He hauled her to her feet, his hands coming under her arms and clasping her sides. His fingertips crushed into her breasts, but she had enough padding that it didn't hurt. What it did do was jolt her into a very specific, very provocative awareness.

"Let's go." He kept one hand on her side and turned her toward the door.

She stepped away from him—it wouldn't do for anyone to see him touching her. Plus, his touch was doing that fluttery thing to her belly again.

As soon as they were outside, Lucy tried to turn back, but he urged her down the steps. "I have winnings to collect."

"Not enough to make going back in worth it. Things were about to erupt in there." He kept his hand on her side. "I told you we'd leave when I said so. The situation was precarious enough as it was."

Lucy tried to plant her feet on the bottom step. She desperately wanted to go back inside. "I need to collect my money." Not only did she not win the hundred pounds she'd hoped, she'd laid out everything she'd won earlier in the evening and a bit more. She glowered up at him and tried to move away. "I'm at a loss as it stands."

He looked down at her, frowning. "I said it wasn't negotiable. I'm sorry you lost money, but you knew this was a risky endeavor from the start." He pulled her away from the hell. "Actually, you didn't, otherwise you never would've done it, especially without help."

Yes, she'd known it was a risky endeavor, and if she were honest with herself, she'd admit that if she'd gone into that hell alone tonight, she would've turned right back around and left.

She exhaled loudly, trying to expel the frustration of losing money. "Yes, yes, you're a bloody hero." She twisted her body away from him, and he finally let her go.

He slowed his pace. "Are you all right?"

"I'm fine."

"Good. However, you were very nearly exposed when you lost your hat. It's quite evident you are not a gentleman when you lose that accessory."

She'd considered adopting a wig. Perhaps she'd been foolish not to. "I'll invest in a wig."

His brows drew together, darkening his countenance. "I'm beginning to think you should cease this activity entirely."

She bristled inwardly. "No. We'll just stick to hells you know are acceptable."

"I'll think about it."

She stopped and threw him a mutinous glare. "This is not your decision. I don't *need* you to continue."

"You do if you want your grandmother to remain ignorant of your activities."

"You're a beast."

He hailed a passing hackney coach. "I am merely adhering to the terms of our agreement."

He spoke as if they had some signed contract. Like a

marriage.

She adopted her most imperious tone. "Perhaps this agreement has run its course."

The coach stopped, and he gave directions to return them to Bolton Street. He held the door while she stepped inside. Again, they had to sit beside each other on the only seat.

He sat next to her, stretching his legs out in front of him as much as the confined space would allow. The lantern hanging outside the window offered meager illumination, but she could see the stern set of his features—his mouth drawn, his brows dipped low.

She straightened on the seat, worried that their association might be at a premature end.

"I'm sorry," he said, surprising her. "When I saw you hit the floor, I was…concerned."

She had the sense he was tempering his words. But that would mean he was something more than…concerned. "I said I'm fine."

He turned his head toward her. "I understand that. Now." He removed his hat and tossed it on the floor. He raked his hand through his hair, tousling the dark locks. "All right. We needn't terminate our arrangement. We'll limit ourselves to hells that are more…sedate."

Lucy giggled, drawing his sharp attention.

"What?" he asked.

"It's rather amusing to utter the words 'hell' and 'sedate' in the same sentence, don't you think?"

He visibly relaxed, his shoulders dipping. Then he grinned. "Yes." He collapsed back against the seat. "Good God, that was alarming. You sure you're all right?" He looked over at her and waved his hand. "Of course you are. You're made of better stuff than most of the men I know."

Lucy immediately thought of at least one gentleman of his acquaintance. "Such as Charles?"

"Probably. I can tell your opinion of him diminished when you learned of his penchant for gambling. Don't judge him too harshly."

She considered removing her hat as he'd done. What would be the harm? They were done for the evening, and she could put it back on before departing the hack. "You're kind to defend him, but I don't know that I can help myself. My father's habit all but ruined me and my grandmother."

Dartford nodded. "I do understand, but Charles isn't a bad sort. Besides, he's young yet. He may come around before he has a family."

Lucy pulled her hat from her head and set it in her lap. "I pray that he does, but it's none of my concern."

Dartford straightened, his attention fixed on her. He reached out and touched a lock of her hair that must have come loose. "Perhaps you do need a wig," he murmured. "I'm happy to procure it for you and have it delivered."

It would make things simpler if he could do that. But right now she was thinking that nothing about this was simple. Sitting here with him touching her hair was…complicated. "That would be exceptionally helpful. Thank you."

He didn't release her hair. If anything, he moved a bit closer. "Sometimes I forget there's a beautiful woman hiding beneath this disguise."

Heat rushed up her neck and flooded her cheeks. "You flatter me. I am not beautiful." No one had ever called her that. "My chin is too pronounced, and my eyes are squinty."

His mouth curved up. "Your eyes are lovely. They remind me of a forest—all dark and mysterious—just waiting to be discovered. And your chin"—his gaze dipped to her mouth—"is just the right size to support that incredible mouth of yours."

Oh dear, the fluttery feeling returned tenfold. "You shouldn't say such things." She whispered the words, but they sounded deafening in the dim cocoon of the coach.

"I shouldn't do many things. Probably." His head lowered and before she could think about his intent, his lips covered hers in a delicate, delicious kiss.

The sheep farmer's son's kiss had been nothing like this. Her heart raced, her stomach cartwheeled over itself, and her flesh tingled.

He released her hair and cradled the side of her neck as his mouth played over hers, coaxing, teasing, arousing. He pulled back slightly. "Like that," he murmured. "I definitely shouldn't do that."

She let go of her hat and pulled at his lapel. "No." She kissed him this time, surrendering to the forbidden urge inside her. One or two kisses didn't matter. One or two kisses were *nice*. Didn't she deserve one or two kisses?

His hand curled around her neck, and he tilted his head, slanting his lips over hers. She sighed against his mouth, and he took advantage, sliding his tongue along her lower lip. She vaguely remembered tongues being part of that long-ago kiss and suddenly wanted to revisit that sensation.

She gripped his coat tighter as she opened her mouth, inviting him inside. A deep groan sounded from somewhere in his chest, firing her excitement. She slid her hands up and clasped his neck as his other hand came around her waist. His hand splayed over the top of her hip, and he pulled her toward him, turning her on the seat. Her hat slipped to the floor.

His tongue swept into her mouth in deep, lush strokes. A singular and unexpected thrill swirled through her—it was *desire*. She held tight as he kissed her, and she supposed she kissed him back. She copied his movements, sliding her tongue against his, moving her lips, and clutching him as if she would float away and drown if he let her go.

The coach came to a sudden and shocking stop. They broke apart, both of them breathing heavily. Dartford blinked at her and swore under his breath.

"I apologize," she said, covering her mouth in horror. How fast he must think her—

"Do *not* apologize," he said sharply, but not in anger. "I was just surprised… I forgot that you look like a man right now." He snatched his hat from the floor and crammed it on his head. "I'll be damned if you feel like one, though," he muttered.

The heat that had fled when the coach had stopped rushed back over her. He'd said she was beautiful. He'd kissed her as if she *was* beautiful.

He reached down and plucked up her hat, then thrust it toward her. "Here. I need to pay the driver." He bounded out of the cab as if it had burst into flames.

Again she felt a pang of distress. He'd said she shouldn't apologize, and he'd seemed to like kissing her… But he seemed to regret it just the same.

Lucy made sure her hair was tucked up into her hat. She straightened her coat and pulled her already-high collar up beneath her jawline. Her knuckles brushed the faux beard, which she could feel even through her gloves. Yes, she looked like a man. How odd that must have been for him.

His face appeared in the doorway. "Are you coming?"

She half expected him to offer her his hand, but of course he couldn't. She came up off the seat. "Yes."

He stood to the side as she stepped down. The coach pulled away almost immediately.

"I'm afraid I'm the one who must apologize," Dartford said. He looked everywhere but at her. "I don't know what came over me. You may be assured that won't happen again."

Yes, he regretted it. She was certain. And while she knew he shouldn't have done it, she was glad that he had. Not that she planned to tell him that. "Thank you. We'll go on as if that *didn't* happen." She picked at an invisible speck on her coat—anything to divert her attention from his horrid awkwardness. "Do you think you can procure a wig tomorrow so that I may have it before the phaeton races?"

He nodded. "Yes, of course. I'll make it a priority."

He looked at her then, his gaze dark and intense, and she wondered if she'd ever be able to regard him the same way. She hoped so. She didn't want to develop a tendre for any man, let alone this one. She simply needed to keep her focus. Maybe she ought to think of him as a brother. She nearly laughed out loud at that thought. Then she wanted to cringe. No, definitely not a brother.

"I'll just stand here until you're inside." He turned his head, once again moving his focus to anything but her.

"Of course. Thank you again for your assistance this evening." She pivoted to go into the house, but stopped when he spoke.

"We race in Hyde Park at nine o'clock. How do you

plan to leave without your grandmother seeing you?"

This was where Lucy needed to involve her friends. She'd tell her grandmother that she was visiting Aquilla. "She never rises that early. I'll be able to meet you in the park." She'd sneak out of the house in her costume with her maid's assistance.

He looked at her again, and it seemed the seductive haze of their kiss had dissipated. He was all business and concern. "How?" He arched a brow at her. "I should like to know how you will accomplish the feat of leaving your house in broad daylight without anyone noticing you're dressed as a man."

Lucy wasn't entirely sure. Which was why she needed her friends. She edged toward the house, eager for this evening to be over. "I'll manage. Thank you."

He frowned. "You'll let me know if I can assist in any way?"

"I shall, but I daresay you've done enough." She hadn't meant it to sound as if he'd done *too* much but wondered if he'd taken it that way.

He looked away and stiffened. "I see. I'll send you the wig tomorrow."

She resisted the urge to make sure he knew how much she appreciated his help and his concern. She'd never known a man like him before. Couple that startling realization with his intoxicating kisses, and she feared she was in far more trouble than she'd been at the gaming hell.

"Good night." She turned and practically dashed inside, eager to toss away her gentleman's costume and, for the first time, relish the fact that she was a woman.

Until she recalled that, for the first time, she'd come home with less money than she'd left with. She needed to regain what she'd lost and more. As much as she hated losing money, she was glad to have something to focus on besides kissing Dartford.

Tuesday's phaeton races couldn't come fast enough.

Chapter Seven

ANDREW WAITED UNTIL Miss Parnell was safely inside her house before starting up the street. He walked with purpose and speed, his mind churning over the foolishness he'd perpetrated in the hack. He'd never meant to kiss her. If he could take it back, he would.

Would he?

Perhaps not, he realized somewhat grimly. Still, it couldn't happen again. Not that he expected it to. She'd seemed utterly horrified afterward and had practically run inside to escape his company. He didn't blame her. He'd behaved in a reprehensible fashion. He was supposed to be her protector—like an older brother. He shuddered at the thought, both because of the implications of being related to her by blood while also being attracted to her and because he couldn't imagine having family again.

Family.

He threw that thought right out of his brain before he had to resort to the gin bottle.

Quickening his pace, he turned his mind to other, more pleasant things such as the balloon ride next week. By the time he reached his house, he felt much more relaxed and could almost forget about what had happened in the coach.

Almost.

His valet greeted him in his bedchamber. "Good evening, sir. You're in early tonight."

"A bit, yes." Thanks to the fracas at the hell. He supposed he could've got up with Beaumont and the others, but after the incident in the coach, he preferred his own company.

Tindall took Andrew's coat and followed him into the dressing room that adjoined his bedchamber. Not for the first time, Andrew considered elaborating on their conversation, but it was important to him to keep relationships with his retainers aloof and disconnected. They were employees who came and went, not an extension of his family as they'd once been. Again, his mind threatened to hurtle down that dark path, but he refused to allow it.

"Tindall, you've been with me over two years now."

"Yes, my lord."

"And you're aware that I don't keep valets longer than two years?" Andrew had told him that when he'd hired him. He made a point of hiring young men who sought a valet position but had little or no experience. Andrew gave them the experience they needed as well as an excellent reference. It was a mutually beneficial arrangement.

"I am, my lord. I did wonder why you'd kept me on this long."

Andrew wondered why too. He'd told himself it was too close to the Season to turn him loose, but it would've been a good time for Tindall to make a transition. Now he felt like a clod.

Andrew pulled off his cravat and handed it to the young man. Well, a few years younger than Andrew's twenty-nine years, anyway. "It's probably time for you to move on. Of course I'll provide an outstanding reference."

Tindall bent his head as he folded the cravat in half. "I do appreciate that, my lord." When he looked up, his dark eyes were bold, and his chin jutted. "I wonder if you might allow me to stay on a month or so. My mother is ill, and I'm afraid all my spare time is being spent caring for her and overseeing her care. I pay a woman to attend her while I am at work."

Andrew's fingers froze in unbuttoning his waistcoat. A wave of ice slammed into him, and a cold sweat broke out on the back of his neck. "Your mother is ill? Why didn't you say something?"

Tindall blinked. The courage was gone from his gaze, replaced with confusion and uncertainty. "I didn't wish to trouble your lordship."

"It's no trouble. I…I want to know these things." No, he didn't really. Just the thought of this man's mother dying… "Is she terribly ill?" Andrew wanted to bite the question back. He didn't really want to know.

"It's serious, yes." Tindall spoke slowly, cautiously.

Andrew should let the subject drop, but he found he couldn't. "Never mind what I said before. Stay on as long as you need to. And I insist on sending a physician to see her. I'll take care of it first thing tomorrow."

Tindall bowed his head again, smoothing his hand over the silk of the cravat. "I am overcome by your generosity, my lord."

Generosity, ha. It was a simple thing. A necessary thing. A basic human right. Ailing people needed the care of a capable physician. People like his parents and his sisters. And his brother.

The cold sweat spread, and his skin felt as if it were coated in frost. His discomfort must have shown—he'd likely gone pale if this was like similar occasions in his past—for Tindall's eyes widened. "My lord, are you all right?"

Damn it. This hadn't happened to Andrew in some time. Years maybe? When he'd been younger, the bouts had been more frequent, daily and weekly at first, then lessening over time. He'd thought them long gone.

He'd hoped.

But he'd thought of his family more this evening, had let them creep back into the places he kept dark and quiet—ignored. Now he was overwhelmed with emotion. He wanted none of it.

"I'm fine," he said tightly. "Nothing a bit of gin won't cure. Fetch me a bottle?"

"Indeed, my lord." Tindall set the cravat on a chest and left with alacrity.

Andrew removed his waistcoat and tugged off his boots and stockings amid a barrage of memories he didn't want to see. His mother coughing until she couldn't breathe. His sisters praying together as their fevers raged. His father trying to find a physician and only hastening his death as he spent hours out in the snow. His brother's cold, still body.

Yet Andrew had been spared. For so long, he'd just wanted to die with them. And sometimes he still wished he had. Barefoot, he went into his chamber and stared at the low fire burning in the grate.

When Tindall returned, Andrew took the glass and bottle from him. "Thank you, I don't require anything further." He turned from his valet lest he see the way his hands shook.

Tindall didn't immediately leave. Andrew fought the urge to snap at him to go already but was glad he didn't when Tindall said, "Thank you again, my lord. I appreciate your kindness more than I can ever say."

Andrew couldn't speak, so he only nodded. At last he heard Tindall walking across the room and the click of the door as he left.

Still shaking, Andrew sank into the chair situated by

the fireplace and set the glass on the table beside it. He opened the bottle and poured the gin, careful not to splash any of the liquid outside of the tumbler. He set the bottle down with a clack and picked up the glass. He didn't sip but took a long gulp and closed his eyes as it burned down his throat.

The images still played and the familiar emotions—guilt, loss, anger, sadness—consumed him. He finished off what he'd poured and filled another. That went down faster than the first. Another.

Finally, his shaking began to lessen and the sense of panic dissipated. He was here. Whole. Alive. But so empty inside.

He stood up and paced. He wanted it that way. He *needed* it that way. He never wanted to feel that helplessness and devastation ever again.

He strode back to the bottle and poured another glass. As he finished that one too, numbness stole over him. When he collapsed into bed a short while later, relief sagged through his frame. He fell into a deep, dreamless sleep, the kind he'd cultivated for nearly two decades. The kind that kept the demons at bay.

TWO DAYS LATER, Lucy greeted her friends, whom she'd invited for tea. Ivy arrived just before Aquilla and said she had the entire afternoon free. Her employer, Lady Dunn, was very generous with the amount of free time she gave Ivy, which allowed Ivy ample opportunity to conduct her charitable activities.

Aquilla arrived in a flurry of pale yellow muslin, unruly dark curls, and cheerful chatter. She never failed to brighten a room or Lucy's mood. She found it nearly impossible to be sullen around her, not that Lucy was feeling sullen. No, she was feeling quite determined.

As soon as Aquilla came into the drawing room, she noticed the flowers on the table near the window. She glided over to them and sniffed before darting a playfully accusing stare at Lucy. "You didn't tell us you received flowers! Who are they from?"

Lucy rolled her eyes as she sat down. "How do you know they're mine? Maybe they're for my grandmother."

Aquilla pulled off her gloves. "That's absurd. Of course they're for you. What I don't know is which of your dance partners sent them. Was it Dartford?" She glanced at Ivy and smiled. "I do hope it's Dartford."

"It wasn't." Lucy bristled, which was surprising since she didn't care who they were from. "They're from Lord Edgecombe."

Aquilla perched on the settee and set her gloves on the arm. "How splendid. Did he pay a call?"

"No, he just sent the flowers with a note that he hoped to see me soon for another dance." Lucy, of course, hoped no such thing.

"Edgecombe is a charming fellow, if a bit reserved," Aquilla said. "I daresay I frighten him, but then I either scare the sense out of a gentleman or bore him to tears." Her tone was free of dismay, her features light and open. Still, Lucy hated for her friend to think of herself that way.

"That isn't entirely true," Ivy, who'd sat down beside her, said quietly. "You just haven't met the right one yet."

Aquilla smiled brightly. "Just so."

They caught up on Society nonsense while they drank tea and ate cakes. Lucy dismissed the elderly butler and went to close the door after he left.

Aquilla leaned forward on the settee. "Are we to be secretive today?"

Lucy sat back down on the chair angled toward the settee that held Aquilla and Ivy. "I have a matter of importance, and yes, secrecy, I need to discuss with you." She didn't want any of the small staff to overhear, with the exception of her maid, who was, of course, a key player in Lucy's deception. She was upstairs keeping Lucy's grandmother busy in her sitting room answering correspondence from a friend in Bath.

Aquilla's bright blue eyes sparkled. "How intriguing."

Lucy smoothed her palm over her skirt and straightened her spine. "You both asked what I was doing about our financial woes, and I'm now prepared to share all of it with you." She took a deep breath, uncertain of how they would react. She knew they would support her, but that didn't mean they wouldn't be shocked or scandalized. "I've been dressing up as a man and visiting gaming hells in order to increase our coffers."

Aquilla's jaw dropped. Ivy's eyes widened. Lucy worried the fabric of her dress between her thumb and forefinger.

Aquilla finally spoke. She shook her head, the curls framing her face bobbing with her movement. "I can't imagine it. A man?"

"Yes."

"No one has seen through your disguise?" Ivy asked.

Lucy allowed a small smile. "I'm quite convincing actually. I wear padding beneath the costume to hide what few curves I have." She was not as tall and womanly as Ivy or as attractively formed as Aquilla. "However, there is one person who paid close enough attention to puzzle it out."

Aquilla gasped. "What happened? This sounds terribly dangerous."

"It isn't." Or it wasn't until two nights ago. But that had been a riskier hell, and she wouldn't make that mistake again. "Besides, I have a…guide who looks after me. The person who suspected I was a woman."

Ivy frowned. "You seem to be dancing around this person's identity. It has to be a gentleman, but who?"

Aquilla, who was closer to Lucy than Ivy, scooted to the edge of the settee. "Yes, who?"

She'd known she had to tell them. "Dartford."

"Oh, this is better than flowers," Aquilla said in a low, appreciative tone that was the aural equivalent of rubbing one's hands together. Or so it sounded to Lucy.

Ivy pressed her lips together. "I should have known. That is why he danced with you at the ball."

Lucy could take that assumption as an insult—as though Lucy couldn't expect a man like Dartford to want to dance with her—but she didn't. She and Ivy were as pragmatic and honest as the Season was monotonous. "Yes."

Aquilla sat back now, her gaze turning speculative. "How extraordinary. And you say he knew you were a woman right away?"

"Not *right* away." Though it *had* been fairly quick.

Aquilla gave her a sly look, her mouth curving up. "He took an interest in you."

Ivy smiled at her with pride. "Well, I think this is just wonderful. Have you been doing well?"

"Yes, until my most recent outing. We visited a more raucous hell and had to leave before I could collect my winnings." That still stung.

Aquilla's brow creased, and her demeanor changed. "Even with Dartford along, I'm not convinced this isn't dangerous."

Neither was Lucy, but not for the reasons they did. She'd thought far too much of Dartford's kisses and, worse, considered kissing him again. "As it happens, we will be doing less of that. Dartford came up with the brilliant idea of me attending some gentlemanly pursuits with him and wagering on them as his set does. It's a far easier and safer way to generate the money I need."

"You say Dartford came up with this?" Ivy asked. She sounded skeptical, as if she couldn't quite believe he'd been helpful. But then Ivy's opinion of men was fairly low.

"Yes, after we had an impromptu shooting exhibition at Manton's one night."

Aquilla lurched forward again, laughing. "You did what?"

Even Ivy grew animated, her green eyes shining. "Yes, do tell."

Lucy related the entire story, relishing their rapt attention and joyful engagement.

"I wish I could've seen it," Ivy said. "I think I need to start dressing up as a man."

Lucy laughed. "The trousers are quite liberating."

Aquilla swung her head toward Ivy, grinning. "Can you imagine what Lady Dunn would say?"

Ivy laughed. "She couldn't know!" She looked at Lucy. "Just as your grandmother doesn't know?"

Lucy nodded. "Yes, which is why secrecy is important."

Ivy picked up a cake from her plate. "But how will you explain the fact that you have enough to retire with her?"

"I've given this plenty of thought, and I plan to tell her that I made an investment last year and that it paid well. She won't ask for specifics."

Ivy swallowed her bite. "That could work."

Time to broach the reason she'd invited them today. "I find I am in need of assistance with another aspect. It's easy for me to sneak out after Grandmama has retired for the night. However, tomorrow I am going to attend phaeton races in the park at nine o'clock. Grandmama will still be abed, but I don't want to be seen leaving the house as a man. Furthermore, I need to have a reason for not being here should she realize my absence."

"That last part is simple," Aquilla said. "You're spending the day with me. Shopping, visiting the museum, whatever you decide."

Lucy had hoped she would offer just that. "Thank you."

Ivy cocked her head to the side. "How elaborate is your disguise?"

"There's the padding underneath the clothes, and my maid helps me stick sideburns along my upper jaw, here." She indicated where the hair was affixed. Her skin was still a bit tender from wearing it two nights ago, and for that reason alone, she looked forward to not having to do it anymore.

"Ingenious," Ivy breathed. "Could you dress inside a coach?"

Lucy pondered this idea. "It would be difficult. And what would the coachman say if I entered as a woman and left as a man?"

"If you had others with you, he may not notice, but that would require you to take an entourage."

"I volunteer!" Aquilla offered cheerily.

Lucy contemplated donning the necessary padding and trying to pull on the breeches in the confines of a coach and decided it would be more trouble than she wanted to bear, if possible. This gave her another idea—she'd be donning a new costume for a daytime excursion and perhaps Judith could stitch the padding into the coat. She'd discuss it with her. "I think it would be far easier if I went somewhere and dressed, then left from there."

"Actually, I believe you're overthinking this," Ivy said. "You aren't going to be doing this regularly. You simply need to leave the house when there is no one on the street—have your maid look out for you."

Aquilla nodded. "I agree. Just walk to the corner where I'll have Lady Satterfield's coach waiting for you. Your maid can let the rest of the staff know that you are out—with me."

Lucy was hesitant. She looked from Aquilla to Ivy and back to Aquilla again. "You think it will work?"

"It should," Aquilla said.

Ivy shrugged. "The key is to keep an eye out before you leave, and not to do this overly much. How long do you plan to keep up this charade?"

"A couple more weeks should do it. Maybe less. On Saturday, I need to find my way to Kent, where I could potentially win enough money to put an end to this."

Aquilla's eyes grew wide. "Kent? What's going on there?"

"Dartford is ascending in a balloon from Burlington House and plans to descend at his house in Kent. His friends are going to surprise him there—you must keep this part secret."

Ivy interrupted her with a wry look. "Every bit of

this must be kept secret."

Lucy grinned. "Well, yes. Anyway, they're going to surprise him and there will be extensive wagering on where he lands. Whoever comes closest to the actual location will win the pot."

"That sounds like such fun." Aquilla mock-pouted. "Are you sure you can't just persuade them to invite women?"

Lucy laughed. "Even if I could, you wouldn't be among them. That would be rather unseemly, wouldn't it?"

Ivy picked a crumb from her skirt. "That settles things. I *am* dressing up as a man."

They all laughed for a moment. Smiling, Lucy drew them back to the issue at hand. "Any suggestions on how I shall travel to and from Kent?" She looked mostly at Aquilla, who had more access to vehicles than Ivy.

Aquilla tapped her finger against her cheek. "It's one thing to borrow Lady Satterfield's coach at nine o'clock in the morning. How shall I explain the need for a coach for most of the day?" She dropped her hand to her lap. "Do you know who has more vehicles than she knows what to do with?"

Lucy shook her head. "Who?"

"Nora."

Lady Kendal? Lucy wasn't sure she wanted to involve a duchess in her scheme. "I'm not sure it would be wise to ask her." She glanced at Ivy to gauge her reaction.

Aquilla looked between Lucy and Ivy. "Nora will be delighted to help. She's rather championed us, if you haven't noticed."

Lucy *had* noticed. She and her grandmother had received more invitations over the last few days, and she was fairly certain Lady Kendal and Lady Satterfield were responsible. "You're certain she won't be scandalized by what I'm doing?"

Aquilla arched a brow at her. "Don't forget she survived her very own scandal."

"Which is why she likely wouldn't appreciate my activities."

"On the contrary, she will understand what you're trying to do and why you're doing it—even if I don't." Aquilla fixed her attention on the tea tray.

"What do you mean?" Lucy asked.

Aquilla gave a light shrug as she glanced toward Edgecombe's flowers. "I still think marriage is a viable option."

Ivy gently touched Aquilla's arm. "Leave it."

Aquilla nodded and gave Lucy an apologetic look. "I only want you to be happy."

"And I shall be," Lucy said. But for some strange and disconcerting reason, she thought of Dartford and not a quiet cottage with her grandmother. The more she thought about it, the more she needed this ruse to end soon.

"I want to understand this ballooning scheme," Ivy said, her tone somewhat dark. "You said Dartford's friends are going to surprise him. This means he isn't aware of what you're doing? You'll be venturing to Kent alone, without his protection?"

Lucy had considered this, but she wouldn't be alone. She'd be with Dartford's friends, whom she almost thought of as her friends. She didn't feel intimidated by any of them. "I won't ride to Kent with them, and I daresay Dartford will arrive shortly after we do." At least that was what she hoped happened.

Ivy looked at her intently. "He won't be angry? In my

experience, men hate it when women act independently."

Would he be angry? He'd repeatedly threatened to expose her scheme to Grandmama. She worried for a moment but decided his ire was worth the risk of what she could earn. "He'll accept it. We're both eager to be finished." Especially after what had happened the other night. She only hoped things wouldn't be terribly awkward when she saw him tomorrow morning.

"Dartford is an odd fellow, isn't he?" Aquilla asked. "He's attractive, possessed of an excellent title and more than adequate wealth, even if his holdings aren't vast. He's of a perfectly marriageable age, and yet he shows no inclination."

"Because he doesn't wish to marry." Lucy belatedly wondered if she ought to have kept that to herself.

Aquilla's attention perked. "He said that? That is the general consensus about him, but I'm not sure if he's ever come out and made that clear. He's quite adept at avoiding gossip and lingering on the periphery of Society while still being a favorite."

Ivy gave her a pointed look. "An Untouchable, you mean."

Aquilla laughed. "Yes. His desire to remain unmarried makes him even more of an Untouchable."

Lucy had to agree, and it was perhaps the primary reason she trusted him. They were of a like mind, and she found that most pleasing.

"It's too bad, though," Aquilla said. "He'd be excellent husband material—if you wanted that." She looked at Lucy, who stared at her for a moment.

"You're incorrigible."

"I know!" Aquilla waved her hand as if she were swatting at a fly. "I'm sorry. It's just that he's quite marvelous, really. He's doing you a rather spectacular favor, one that most men wouldn't."

"She's right," Ivy said. "I find it suspicious. You're certain he doesn't want anything from you? Do we have any cause at all to be concerned? He hasn't tried to…compromise you, has he?" Her lip curled as she asked the last.

Lucy immediately thought of him kissing her. And then of her kissing him. He might have initiated it, but it had been a thoroughly mutual act. "No. He's simply doing me a favor—exactly as Aquilla said. I know it's difficult to believe." He'd said that helping her was just another adventure. It was for her too, and so far, she was having the best time of her life.

Lucy looked at Aquilla. "Lady Satterfield's coach will be waiting for me a bit before nine tomorrow?"

Aquilla nodded. "I can't promise I won't be inside…"

"You mustn't," Lucy said more sternly than she probably needed to, especially when she realized Aquilla had only been joking. "I didn't mean to snap at you. I just can't risk anyone learning that I'm a woman."

"And what would my being in your coach have to do with it?" Aquilla asked.

"Indeed," Ivy agreed. "But Aquilla, dear, your reputation would be in shreds once people realized you were the mistress of London's newest gentleman gambler." This provoked laughter from Lucy and Aquilla. Ivy looked at Lucy. "What do you go by?"

"Davis Smith, though Dartford has taken to calling me Smitty."

Aquilla and Ivy exchanged looks and smiled, nodding. "I rather like that," Aquilla said. "Don't be surprised if we call you that—in private, of course."

Lucy could see that her friends were enjoying this. They'd been supportive and helpful and altogether wonderful. She regretted not telling them sooner.

Aquilla drew her gloves on. "I'll let you know as soon as I've organized your transportation for Saturday. And we'll use the same explanation for your absence. We'll say you're attending an all-day picnic with us. Oh, that sounds lovely. Perhaps I'll convince Lady Satterfield to journey to Kent…"

This elicited a bark of laughter from Ivy and a giggle from Lucy, who now *knew* her friend was jesting.

"Thank you." Lucy reached over and patted her friend's knee and gave Ivy an appreciative nod. "I have the best friends ever."

"We do, don't we?" Aquilla stood, and Ivy joined her. They said their good-byes, and Lucy felt good about sharing everything with her friends.

Well, not *everything.*

Why hadn't she told them about the kissing? Because Aquilla would've tried to play matchmaker, and Lucy didn't want that. Plus, Lucy was trying very hard to forget it had ever happened. Discussing it with her friends would ensure it lived forever.

Only, she was certain it would anyway, despite her best efforts to the contrary.

Chapter Eight

ANDREW PACED BESIDE his phaeton in Hyde Park the following morning. It was just past nine and Miss Parnell had not yet arrived. She'd sent him a note yesterday afternoon indicating that she'd arranged transportation to meet him here, but didn't disclose what it would be. He hoped she hadn't run into trouble.

The first race was due to begin soon. If she didn't arrive presently, she wouldn't be able to place a wager.

At last he heard the sound of a coach. He craned his neck as the vehicle drew to a halt and wasn't disappointed when Miss Parnell alighted. She wore a different costume, one that was more suitable for this time of day. She came toward him quickly.

"I was beginning to worry," he murmured.

"Smitty!" Beaumont called out as he saw her. "So glad you could join us. We were just about to start. He gestured toward a middle-aged man who was writing in a book. "That's Nevins. He records all the wagers."

"Come, I'll introduce you," Andrew said smoothly. He wanted to guide her on how much to wager and on whom. He kept his voice low as they walked. "Bet on Harcourt. Thirty pounds."

"Is that enough?"

"For this first race, yes. You don't want to draw overt attention to yourself."

She nodded.

He studied her, trying to discern whether she was wearing the wig he'd sent. He'd procured one that was the same color hair as hers. Unable to see for himself, he had to ask. "Are you wearing the wig?"

"Yes, thank you. It fits quite well."

He was glad. He'd been able to approximate the size of her head after cupping it the other night. Bloody hell, why was he thinking of that right now? He glanced at her, wondering if she'd thought of their…*interlude* at all.

He'd actually spent far more time contemplating it than he ought, which should have been not at all, largely due to his efforts to banish the other episode from that night from his mind. So far, reliving Miss Parnell's delicious kisses had proved an excellent diversion from the ghosts of his past.

She stopped and looked around. "Where is Harcourt?"

"He and the other racer, Lord Edgecombe, have already gone to the start. This is where they'll finish."

She looked at him, her hazel eyes widening. "Edgecombe?"

"Yes, do you know him?"

"I do," she said softly.

A sliver of jealousy needled into Andrew's chest. "How well?"

She shrugged. "Not terribly. We danced at Lady Colne's ball. Thanks to your attention, I was besieged with more dance partners than I knew what to do with. It was most taxing."

He laughed as the jealousy he'd felt slipped away. "I won't burden you again."

"What you *should* do, actually, is dance with my friend Miss Aquilla Knox. She could use the attention. She wants to marry, and she'll make an excellent wife."

"I have no plans to attend another ball anytime soon,

but if I do, I shall make a point of it."

She looked at him with open appreciation. "Thank you."

"Last call for wagers!" Nevins's shout pulled Andrew from the intoxicating depths of Miss Parnell's eyes.

"Come." Andrew introduced her to Nevins and a few other gentlemen. She'd become quite good at adopting more masculine mannerisms—she held her shoulders a bit higher and walked with a longer stride. It had to be exhausting.

They went to stand just off the track as they waited for the race to start.

Beaumont leaned toward Miss Parnell. "Once, a gentleman lost control of his horses, and we had to scatter like rats in daylight." He laughed. "Damn near knocked us all down."

She shot Andrew a concerned glance. He subtly shook his head in response. They'd be fine. He'd keep a close eye on things. He always did, but he was especially alert today with her here.

The race began. They could see Edgecombe and Harcourt across the park. Edgecombe started off much better than he usually did, and for a brief moment, Andrew worried that he'd given her bad advice. But Harcourt quickly overtook him, and in the end, it wasn't much of a contest.

Harcourt crossed the finish line amidst cheers, and Edgecombe received a similar welcome a few moments later. They steered their vehicles off to the side. The next racers were already queued at the starting line.

Edgecombe climbed down from his perch and shook his head. "I thought I had it for a moment there." He was always a good-natured sport. He gestured toward Andrew's phaeton. "You're not racing today?" All the racers typically left their vehicles near the starting area.

"Not today."

"That's too bad. Always easy money when you race." He chuckled, and his gaze fell on Miss Parnell. "I don't believe we've met."

Andrew moved closer to her. "Allow me to present Davis Smith. Smitty, this is Edgecombe."

She offered her hand, and Andrew could see the strength with which she gripped the other man. "Pleasure to make your acquaintance."

"Indeed." Edgecombe's eyes squinted slightly, and Andrew didn't like his scrutiny.

Andrew nudged Miss Parnell. "Time to make our next wager." He nodded at Edgecombe as they passed by him. "I didn't care for the way he was studying you," he whispered.

"I don't think he recognized me."

"Still, I think it's wise if you steered clear of him."

"Probably."

Her agreement made him relax. He advised her on the next wager and hoped he was right. This would be a much closer race. The cheering grew to a rousing crescendo as the phaetons careened, side by side, around the final corner. Unfortunately, his pick crossed the finish just behind the other racer.

Andrew grimaced at Miss Parnell, who was frowning. "I'm not always right," he said quietly so only she could hear. They stood at the edge of the group.

She gave him a sardonic look. "How refreshing to hear a gentleman say so."

Andrew coughed. Charles had walked toward them as she spoke, and she hadn't been using her disguised voice. Plus, her comment wasn't one that Smitty would've uttered. Charles, however, didn't appear as though he'd heard.

He greeted them with a jovial smile. "Dartford and Smitty. Together again, I see. Smitty seems to be our newest member." He looked at Miss Parnell. "Of our group."

Andrew laughed. "We have members? I wasn't aware."

Charles waved his hand. "You know what I mean. Say, why aren't you racing today? I can't remember the last time you didn't."

"Just taking a respite."

Charles chuckled. "Going to give others a chance, eh? Or maybe no one wants to race you since they always lose."

"I'd race him." A tall, lanky fellow strode toward them. He was young—near Miss Parnell's age—but with a robust confidence and a bold swagger. Yet at the same time, Andrew wouldn't call him arrogant.

Andrew wasn't a braggart, and if he said he could do something, he did it. And usually with aplomb. "I'll take you up on that sometime, Greene."

Greene nodded and turned his attention to Miss Parnell. "Robert Greene."

She shook his hand, demonstrating the same strength and assurance she had earlier. "Davis Smith."

"We call him Smitty," Charles interjected. He looked at Andrew with beseeching eyes. "Come on, Dart. Race Greene."

Greene arched a brow in question, then gave a shrug. "I'm up for it."

Miss Parnell cleared her throat. "You aren't scheduled to race someone else today?"

"I am not. But I always bring my vehicle, just in case." He indicated his elegant phaeton and grinned.

Andrew eyed the vehicle with envy. It was new and reminded him of the model he was having made. The carriage on both was a bit smaller than typical and the wheels taller. He was excited to see it finished. "When my new phaeton is ready, we'll race."

"I'll look forward to it," Greene said. He turned to Miss Parnell. "Do you race?"

"I don't." She eyed Greene's phaeton. "But I should like to."

"Perhaps you should race me, then. You could borrow Dart's vehicle."

Andrew didn't like where this conversation was going. "I don't think he's ready for that, are you, Smitty?"

She made a grimace—a very manly one—and shook her head. "Unfortunately not, but I think you should have a go." She looked pointedly at Andrew.

Hell. She wasn't supposed to say that. He'd been clear about his intention to stay with her today.

Charles elbowed him in the arm. "I think it's unanimous. Go on."

To refuse now would create a scene, and he didn't want that. He began to question his idea to bring Miss Parnell along. Still, he had to admit it was better than a gaming hell. He could, at least, trust these gentlemen not to erupt into fisticuffs. At least not at this time of the morning. Late at night, after they'd all been drinking? That was another situation altogether.

"All right, then." He looked at Greene. "Will you alert Nevins?"

"Certainly." Greene rubbed his hands together as he ambled off.

Miss Parnell looked at him expectantly. "I need to place my next wager."

She started toward Nevins, and he rushed to catch up. He glanced around to make sure they were out of anyone's earshot. Still, he kept his voice low. "Why did you do that?"

"Do what?"

"Don't be obtuse. You're too smart for me to believe that. Plus, you sound guilty."

She chuckled. "Do I? I wanted to see you race, and who knows when I'll have another opportunity." She spoke in her deeper "man" voice, which was probably for the best. More and more, however, Andrew longed to see and talk to her without her disguise.

Now it was his turn to laugh. "I see. Well, I don't want to disappoint you."

"I wish I could ride with you." There was an edge of wistfulness to her tone that he'd heard before. "But I'd slow you down."

He eyed Greene and turned his head to look at the man's phaeton again. "Yes, but I think I could still win. However, if you rode with me, you wouldn't be able to wager."

She stopped before they got to Nevins. "I could actually go with you? It wouldn't be odd?"

Andrew came to a halt beside her. "Not terribly. Sometimes faster drivers do it to offer an advantage to someone less experienced."

"Like Greene?"

"Greene's one of the better drivers, especially for his age." Andrew grinned. "He'd probably take offense if I said I was taking a passenger. However, I like this idea. I won't have to leave you unattended."

She frowned. "But I can't wager. Even so, I don't know when I'll have a chance to do this again…" She looked up at him, her eyes sparkling, her lips parted.

"Let's. Please."

He was powerless to resist the feminine lure of her gaze and the breathless seduction of her plea. "Then let's place your wagers on the next races before we head over to the start."

He instructed her on the races leading up to his, which would be last. After Nevins recorded their bets, Andrew turned to Greene, who lingered nearby.

"Greene, I'm going to take a passenger to make things interesting."

Greene's brow climbed. "Who?"

"Smitty, here."

Greene raked his gaze over Miss Parnell, and Andrew felt a ridiculous urge to plant his fist in the other man's face. "I'll take someone too then." He glanced over at the men gathered near the finish. "Beaumont."

Beaumont was several inches taller than Miss Parnell, and several stones heavier with his athletic build. "Are you certain you choose him?"

Greene smiled. "Like you said, to make things interesting."

Andrew nodded. "As you say."

He and Miss Parnell walked to his phaeton. "Can you climb in by yourself? I can't help you without drawing notice."

"I've been scaling trees my entire life. This is easy." And so it was as she vaulted up into the vehicle.

He joined her on the seat and picked up the reins. "Do you know how to drive?"

"I do."

He handed her the ribbons. "Then you drive over."

She turned her head, blinking, her mouth open in shock. "You'll allow me?"

He leaned back in the seat. "Why not?"

"I'm… Thank you." She clutched the reins for a moment before guiding the pair of horses forward. She proved a sure and steady hand as she drove them to the starting area.

As they drew near, the next race started. His team didn't flinch as the gun sounded, and neither did Miss Parnell.

They watched the race, and she cheered as her driver won. She turned her head toward him, laughing. "I'm doing well today. Thank you. I needed to make up for the other night when I lost money."

"Well, that is our intent, isn't it?"

"Yes." She touched his sleeve, and he pretended the movement didn't send a jolt of desire straight through his belly. "But you've given me so much more. These are experiences I never would've been able to have without you. I'll remember—and treasure—them forever."

He stared at her, thinking they were far too close, but realizing he couldn't move away without falling from the vehicle. Was she speaking of everything they'd done together or just this—the racing, the shooting, the gambling?

She turned her head, but he saw the blush creeping up her neck.

Hell. They'd done a good job this morning of ignoring that the other night had ever happened. And yet now there was a…*thing* between them. What he didn't know was if she regretted that event or if, like him, she secretly hoped it might happen again.

Which it bloody well could *not.*

They sat in mostly awkward silence as they waited their turn. The next two races ran. She lost the first wager and won the second. Finally, it was time for him and Greene to pull up to the starting line.

Nevins's younger brother started each race by firing a shot into the air. He asked them if they were ready. Andrew nodded, then looked over at Greene, who nodded too.

Andrew tipped his head over toward Miss Parnell but kept his gaze on his team. "Lean with me on the turns, and hold on."

She gripped the side of the phaeton just before the gun fired.

Andrew drove his team forward, and they leapt from the line to an early lead. The course wasn't terribly long and featured two turns, the second of which was quite sharp. It had tripped up many a less-experienced driver.

At the first turn, he miscalculated slightly, and they lost a bit of their lead. On the straightaway, Greene nearly caught up to them.

"Faster!" Miss Parnell yelled.

He realized he wasn't driving quite as fast as he would if she weren't with him. From the corner of his eye, he saw Greene pull up alongside him.

Gritting his teeth, he decided he didn't want to lose. Not that he ever did, but especially not today. He wanted to win—for her. As she'd said, she would likely never have the chance to do this again, and he wanted it to be a memory that made her smile. "Hold on."

He increased their speed as they approached the second turn. "Lean into me!"

Her body came up against him, and he took the corner perhaps faster than he ever had. The wheels of the phaeton creaked, and he thought that the far side had lifted off the ground—an inch or two at least. His muscles clenched, and he sent up a silent prayer as they came around.

With the turn behind them, she sat straight again and cheered. "Magnificent!" Her laughter filled the air, and he couldn't help but grin.

They'd pulled ahead of Greene through the turn, and now Andrew widened their lead. When they crossed the finish line, it was a clear win.

Beside him, Miss Parnell gulped air. "That was absolutely exhilarating. Thank you." Her eyes were glossy with excitement, her lips curved into an enchanting smile.

"You don't look remotely like a gentleman right now." No, she looked like a beautiful woman he wanted to kiss. "Pull yourself together, because we are about to be mobbed."

Sure enough, gentlemen rushed toward the phaeton shouting and laughing. "Damn me," Charles said, grinning. "That was the finest corner I've ever seen." He looked at Miss Parnell. "It's a testament to his driving that you didn't fall out."

"And Smitty's balance," Andrew said, laughing. "Charles, you would have fallen out regardless of who was driving."

Charles's smile didn't fade. "True."

Andrew climbed out of the vehicle and watched as Miss Parnell did the same. She was quickly surrounded, and Andrew grew nervous as men slapped her back and jostled her. He didn't like their proximity and started toward her to provide a buffer.

Greene approached him before he could reach her. "Congratulations. That was an incredible turn."

Andrew didn't take his eyes from Miss Parnell. She was smiling, but in that reserved way with her lips pressed together. "Thank you. You put up an excellent race."

"I tried." Greene's brow furrowed. "Did you hear anything odd? I swear I heard a woman laughing."

Andrew stopped cold, ice coating his neck. He pulled his gaze from Miss Parnell for a moment and looked at Greene as if he'd sprouted another nose. "No."

"Ah well. Next time, I'll choose someone closer in size to your passenger—though I was hard-pressed to find someone of Smitty's short stature."

Because for a gentleman, Miss Parnell was small. At least in height, and even though she padded herself, she didn't appear very large. Another conversation he didn't care to have today and more scrutiny he'd rather she didn't receive. He glanced at Greene before taking his leave. "Please excuse me."

He cut through the crowd and finally reached her side. He whispered next to her ear, "You need to go."

She nodded. "My coach is waiting." She started to turn, but that bloody Greene had caught up to them and stopped her, his hand catching her elbow. Andrew miraculously stopped himself from slapping his hand away. Touching her like that was precisely what had led Andrew to realize she wasn't what she seemed.

Miss Parnell extricated herself quickly and efficiently, however. Andrew hoped she'd been fast enough to prevent Greene from discerning anything.

"Smitty, I hear your shooting is something to be seen," Greene said. "Perhaps you'd care to demonstrate?"

Hellfire. She needed to leave, but he didn't think she would, not with the temptation of shooting dangling before her.

She coughed. "I shall sometime."

She started to turn, but Greene said, "Why not now?"

"Because I didn't bring my weapon." Her tone was dark and clipped—both manly and haughty.

Andrew stifled a smile, unsurprised that she could hold her own. "We'll arrange a shooting exhibition soon."

"Next Tuesday after the racing," Greene said. He pinned Miss Parnell with a direct stare. "I shall look forward to it."

She made a sound that was a sort of grunt of agreement. Yes, she was becoming quite an accomplished *man*.

She collected her winning from Nevins and searched Andrew out with her eyes. Once their gazes connected, she inclined her head toward where her coach stood.

Andrew nodded slightly and left the crowd, joining her on the way to her coach. "Who loaned you their vehicle?"

"Lady Satterfield."

Andrew nearly tripped. "She knows of your charade?"

"Heavens, no. My friend Aquilla is her ward. She arranged it."

"How enterprising."

"When are we going out again?" she asked as they neared the coach.

"I don't know. The other night has given me pause." He realized as soon as he said it that she could interpret that one of two ways.

She looked at him sharply. "You don't mean to end our agreement prematurely, do you? I still require more funds."

He was relieved—but maybe also a trifle annoyed—when she didn't mention him kissing her. He didn't like thinking that she was so unaffected while he had been just the opposite. "No, I said I would help you reach your goal, and I shall. Tonight?"

"Half past eleven at the corner."

He stopped a few feet from the coach. "Perhaps we should go tomorrow night to give your poor face a respite." When she blinked at him, he clarified. "So you don't have to wear the facial hair again."

She looked away. "I appreciate your concern, but I shall be fine." She turned and walked away without another word, leaving him to wonder if he'd annoyed her.

But that was preposterous. She was merely keeping their relationship to what they'd agreed upon—him helping her to make the money she needed to retire to the country with her grandmother.

He suddenly realized London was going to be rather dim without her in it.

Chapter Nine

AS LUCY LEFT her house that night, she wondered if she shouldn't have heeded Dartford's suggestion. Despite applying generous amounts of cream to the area, her skin still felt a bit raw.

No, it was good they were going tonight. Grandmama had informed her that they would attend a dinner party tomorrow evening. Lucy hoped the redness on her face would fade by then.

Dartford leaned against a streetlamp, his features cast in seductive shadow. She didn't need to see him to picture the lines of his face—the strong angle of his nose, the cleft in his chin. He presented an attractive figure, a handsome gentleman lounging carelessly, just waiting for Something Exciting.

And yet he was only waiting for her. She was *not* exciting.

She'd worried that this morning would be uncomfortable given how their last meeting had ended, so she'd made a calculated effort to avoid the subject. He'd clearly done the same, which was for the best. Still, here they were together again, at night, in the same situation that saw them kissing several nights ago.

Not precisely the same. If he suggested they take a hack, she would firmly refuse…

He pushed away from the lamppost. "I thought we'd return to the hell where I met you."

She nodded, uncaring where they went so long as she could make money. If she could do well tonight and again on Saturday with the balloon excursion, she could stop this. However, after the exhilaration of this morning's race, she wasn't sure she wanted to. Especially since next week there would be a shooting exposition, and she was expected to participate. It was too good to pass up.

They turned down Piccadilly and made their way to the hell.

"You had a good time this morning?" he asked.

"Quite. I look forward to next week." Whether she had enough money or not, she decided in that moment she wanted to go. At least once more.

"Since you know of the plans to shoot, you'll need to bring your pistol."

She slowed, realizing what he was implying. "You know I don't have a proper one."

"I do. You can borrow one of mine." He glanced at her. "How did you leave your house without notice this morning?"

"My maid and I watched for the street to be clear, and I left as stealthily as possible. Aquilla and Ivy told me not to overthink it, and I daresay they were right. Lady Satterfield's coach was waiting for me on the corner."

He sent her an approving glance. "You needn't bother with Lady Satterfield's coach next week. I'll pick you up in the same place."

They'd be alone together again in a coach. She wasn't sure that was wise, but she was even less sure she should mention that fact. So she didn't.

Instead, she sneaked quick looks at him and recalled the feel of his mouth on hers and the way her body responded…

"Miss Parnell?"

Had he said something? "Yes, what?"

"I asked what pistol you wanted me to bring—the Purdey or the Manton?"

She shrugged. "Whichever you prefer. Although, I am partial to the Manton."

"The Manton it is, then." They neared the hell, and he reminded her of his "rules." "Stay in my sight please, and when I say it's time to leave, we leave."

"I know."

"You understand why I demand these things, don't you? You see how our last excursion could've ended in disaster?"

She stopped and turned toward him. "It did."

He nearly tripped. "I beg your pardon?"

She gave him an indignant stare. "I went home without my winnings, if you'll recall."

He coughed and smoothed his hand over the front of his coat. "Ah. I thought you meant…never mind."

She hushed her voice low even though there was no one on their side of the street. "You thought I meant the kissing." The last word came out like a hiss.

He averted his gaze from hers. "I, ah, yes."

"I did not. I'm quite content to behave as though it didn't happen. I thought that's what we were doing."

"Yes. Just so." He turned away from her without looking her in the eye. "Let's get to the hell."

When they arrived at the hell, they went directly to a faro table where Lucy lost nearly every turn of the card. It was her most crushing defeat yet. She grew irritable, and Andrew urged her to take a respite. They went to the salon, where she took a glass of port and Andrew gin.

"I don't know how you can drink that," she said.

"Have you tried it?" he asked.

"No."

He grinned. "Well, then. What kind of guide am I if I don't ensure you sample it?" He handed her the glass despite her lack of agreement.

She gave him her port to hold, which he took from her fingertips. "What if I don't want to try it?"

"I won't believe you. You'll try anything once, I think."

She felt an imprudent pride at the admiration in his tone. She had to quash the urge to arch her brow in a saucy fashion. She couldn't flirt with him when she was dressed as a man. She couldn't flirt with him ever! She sipped the gin and coughed at its tang. "Damn."

Better prepared, she tried it again. She didn't cough this time, but she still didn't particularly care for the taste. She handed him the glass and took her port, which she promptly used to banish the lingering taste of juniper from her mouth.

"Well, you tried it," he said, toasting her with his glass.

She looked up at him, cocking her head to the side. "Satisfied?" She realized—a bit too late—that she was flirting with him anyway. She straightened and took another drink of port.

He seemed to recognize her foolishness when he didn't answer. Or maybe he was distracted because at that moment, several members of his set entered the salon—Beaumont, Charles, and Greene among them.

"Dart and Smitty," Charles said. "I was certain we'd find you tonight." He looked at Dart. "I've noticed you don't meet us at the club on the nights we run into you with Smitty. Where do you two start your evenings?"

Charles's gaze lingered on Lucy. She lifted her glass to shield her face. She didn't like it when anyone looked at her too closely, and unfortunately that was bound to happen the more time she spent with these gentlemen. Perhaps she should count herself lucky and skip next week's races.

"It varies," Dartford answered casually. He looked at Lucy, perhaps reading her discomfort. "Shall we return to the table?"

Yes, she had losses to recoup. "Let's." She tossed back the rest of her port and set her empty glass on the tray of a passing footman.

Greene stepped forward. "I'll go with you."

Lucy glanced over at Dartford, who gave an infinitesimal shrug.

At the table, Greene took up a place beside her. "How did you meet Dartford?"

"Here, actually. We, ah, have a few things in common." She looked at Dartford, who stood on her other side, and hoped he would provide assistance.

"Such as shooting and driving," Dartford said. "Smitty likes exciting things."

She tried not to think that he was flirting with her, because of course he wasn't. Still, she could imagine that he was. She internally shook herself—this entire flirting nonsense had no place in her plans and deserved none of her attention.

Greene's mouth curved up. He was attractive, with dark blue eyes and a wide smile that invited you to talk with him and trade stories. "Then you are peas in a pod," he said.

They turned their attention to the table to place their bets. As with the previous round, Lucy lost far more than she won. By the end, she was fuming and more than a little distressed. She couldn't afford to keep losing like this. She was already quite behind. This was precisely the sort of wagering that led one down a path to ruin.

But Lucy wouldn't do that. Her situation was completely different—she didn't wager for amusement. She looked around at the gentlemen at the table, realizing that they all did, as far as she knew. She suspected some of them might need the extra funds for one reason or another, but couldn't imagine them being as desperate as she was.

How she hated that word. Damn her father.

Her lip curled as she turned to Dartford. "I'm ready to move on."

He nodded, his expression surprisingly grim. He, of course, knew she was losing, and she noticed he hadn't been doing as well as usual. Even so, he was still ahead of her.

Dartford collected his meager winnings, and they left. Greene came along, and Lucy noticed the entire group was leaving with them.

"Where are we off to next?" Greene asked pleasantly.

For some reason, Lucy wished they would go their own way. She was just feeling grumpy over her losses and was eager to turn her night around.

"Let's go to Turner's," Charles suggested as they descended the front steps.

Beaumont scrunched up his nose. "I was thinking Polton's."

Charles's face reddened. "I can't, ah, go to Polton's." He glanced away as his voice trailed off.

Dartford slapped Charles's shoulder. "No problem. Turner's it is." He nodded toward Beaumont, who nodded in response.

Lucy had no idea where Turner's was located so she waited for Dartford to guide her. They hung back and walked at the back of the pack.

"It's not far," Dartford said softly. "Don't worry, your luck will turn around."

"And if it doesn't?" She didn't have to work very hard to make her voice sound hard and gruff.

He clapped her shoulder in much the same way as he'd done with Charles, but she imagined it must have felt different. His hand lingered just a second too long, his fingers caressing her as he let go.

A shiver danced up her spine, and her inclination for them to be alone returned with greater force. She almost asked him if they could go to Polton's anyway.

When they arrived at Turner's, Charles didn't go inside with the others. He waited for Dartford and asked him for a quick word. The way he looked at Lucy gave the clear impression that she was not invited to listen. Dartford frowned but couldn't object without drawing unwanted attention, so she went inside without him. She knew he'd follow as quickly as possible given how much he didn't like leaving her alone.

Not that she *was* alone. Greene approached her as soon as the footman admitted her into the hall.

"Smitty, shall we hit the hazard table?"

She shook her head. "I don't play hazard, but don't let me stop you."

"Not at all. I'm keen to follow your lead." He smiled warmly, and nothing about his demeanor should've bothered Lucy. Still, something about the way he looked at her made her slightly uneasy. Oh, she was being ridiculous. She was just feeling testy after losing so much money.

"Faro, then," she said, deepening her voice. She ambled to the table, walking as laboriously as possible to disguise her femininity. She worked very hard to keep up the façade, but she had to admit it was beginning to wear on her. Her back, particularly the space between her shoulders, always ached the day after she played Smitty. All her muscles felt tired as she worked to stand and walk in very specific ways. Between that and the facial hair situation, she wouldn't miss her Smitty disguise. She would miss being Smitty, however.

As she placed her bets on the faro table, Andrew joined her. She longed to ask him what Charles wanted—was it money again? She saw that Charles had come inside too and had gone to the hazard table, so he must not be out of funds.

Lucy was relieved when she won the first two turns, but then she lost every single one after. She turned from the table in disgust, her hands shaking.

Dartford hadn't wagered. He came over to her, noted her agitated state, and simply said, "Let's go."

She was more than ready. Without a word, she strode toward the door.

Greene's voice followed her. "Are you leaving?"

She spun on her heel, anger and disappointment seething through her. "I know when to stop. I wish you better luck."

Greene looked as if he might say something more, but Dartford gripped his bicep as he walked by. "Good night."

Dartford was right behind her as they exited the hell. She quickly descended to the street and turned toward St. James's. She didn't have to think about lengthening her stride, because she was in a hurry to put this night behind her.

"Wait," Dartford called, but he easily caught up with her. "Slow down."

She threw him a dark glare. "You can keep up."

He snagged her elbow and drew her to stop. "I'm not the villain here."

She crossed her arms over her chest, uncaring if she looked like a man or a woman or a monkey. "I suppose you're going to tell me there is no villain."

"Actually, I think you were targeted to lose. Charles noticed that the dealer was cheating at the first hell. That's what he wanted to tell me outside. Charles often suspects cheating to explain his losses, but in this case, I think he was right."

She dropped her arms and simply gaped at him. "Why was I targeted?"

"Because you've won so much recently. Hells don't like smart players. I admit I don't always try very hard to win. But then I see gambling as an amusement, not a money-making opportunity."

She snorted and spun on her heel, continuing along the pavement. "How fortunate for you."

He easily strode alongside her. "Why are you angry with me?"

"I don't know. I'm not. I'm just…angry."

"I understand."

"I don't know how you can. You don't have an uncertain future. You never have to worry where you'll be in five years." She'd slowed her pace and realized she'd been speaking far too loudly. Yelling almost.

"No, I don't," he said quietly, but still loud enough for her to hear. "And I'm sorry that you do."

She knew he meant it. He was kind and thoughtful—she saw it in the way he treated his friends as well as in the way he helped her. Yes, she was angry, but not at him. If she was angry with anyone, it was her father.

"I hate what he did to us," she said so low that she

wasn't sure he could've heard her.

They turned onto St. James's. "I know. But he can't hurt you anymore."

Emotion welled in her chest and flooded her eyes. "Can't he? I'm in this mess, aren't I?"

He grabbed her elbow again and pulled her into a narrow close between two buildings. It was dark and damp since it had rained all day. In fact, she was surprised it wasn't raining now—it smelled as if it would.

She couldn't make out his face but felt his proximity. They didn't touch, but all she had to do was sway forward and their bodies would connect. She fought to stay away.

"Can I… Do you want me to hold you?"

Oh God. They were dressed as gentlemen on St. James's. Yes, they were in a dark alley, but if anyone saw them…

Temptation overwhelmed her. She twitched, and her hand bumped against his. His fingers slid along hers. She exhaled softly, the sound echoing around them in the small space.

"Thank you, but no." Her mouth declined his invitation, but the rest of her screamed for him to touch her, to take her into his arms, to kiss her.

She stalked from the close before she did something foolish.

He followed her, and they walked in near silence until they'd crossed back over Piccadilly.

"So what happens now?" she asked. "Is there any hell who won't try to cheat me?"

"It's hard to say. They may feel vindicated by tonight's fleecing." He winced. "Sorry. It might be best if you didn't go out for a while."

"Yes, I am coming to the same conclusion." They neared her corner. More than ever, she needed to win the pot at the balloon descent. And now she *had* to go to the races next Tuesday.

"I should have seen this coming and organized a plan for you to lose more than you did. I'm afraid I was too focused on helping you achieve your goal as quickly as possible."

They stopped near the lamppost that he'd been lounging against earlier. "It's all right," she said. "I don't blame you. You've done far more good than harm. Besides, I daresay I could use a respite from this bloody costume."

He chuckled softly. "Excellent. It will all work out, then."

She hoped so. "I'll see you in a week."

His brows drew together. "It will be strange to go so long without seeing you. I enjoy our time together." He spoke plainly, but she longed to know if there was more to it than simply enjoying her company. Did he want her the way she wanted him?

He'd offered to hold her, but as she'd noted, he was kind and considerate. It didn't mean he was attracted to her in the same way that she was attracted to him. Yes, he'd kissed her, but since then, he'd given no indication that he wanted to repeat the activity. For her own sanity, she had to assume they were friends and nothing more. Besides, she didn't want anything more—he didn't fit into her plans, even if he was quite the best man she'd ever met.

"Yes, it will be strange." Except she'd see him in four days, but he didn't know that. She looked forward to surprising him. With a bit of reluctance, she pivoted. "Good night."

"Good night, Miss Parnell," he said softly.

She imagined she heard a wistfulness in his tone that couldn't possibly exist. She didn't bother to admonish herself. She'd take joy wherever she could find it.

Chapter Ten

ANDREW LOOKED OUT over London as they ascended higher. As Sadler had warned him, the air was much colder up here, and growing more frigid by the moment. He'd donned a greatcoat and his thickest gloves at Sadler's recommendation.

The takeoff had been nothing short of breathtaking. The crowd at Burlington House had been massive—so large, in fact, that he hadn't seen any of his closest friends.

Close friends? He couldn't think of them that way. He'd taken the opportunity of Miss Parnell's hiatus to take his own break from visiting the usual hells. Instead, he'd gone off on his own and spent the last few evenings taking in boxing matches at the Bucket of Blood. He'd watched a particularly entertaining bout last night with a viscount named Sevrin who knew far more about pugilism than anyone Andrew had ever met. He'd decided to add it to his list of things to try.

For now, he was content to soar high above the earth. His heart swelled as he thought of Bertie and how much his brother would've loved this. He half expected to suffer an attack and was worried what might happen in their current position amidst the lowest clouds, but so far he'd felt surprisingly peaceful.

"How are your ears?" Sadler asked.

He'd warned Andrew that the change in altitude would likely cause pain and encouraged him to swallow and work his jaw to ease the ache. "Fine, thank you. How fast are we going?"

"Not terribly. The wind is pretty calm, but I think it's going to pick up as we move east. Our speed should increase a bit."

A sharp pain jabbed through Andrew's ear and shot down the side of his neck. He brought his hand up and held the side of his head.

"Your ear?" Sadler asked. "Just do what I told you."

Andrew nodded and moved his jaw.

The pain lessened but didn't disappear entirely. Bertie wouldn't have liked the earache, but he would've endured it for this. Without warning, the familiar helplessness washed over him, and the world blurred beneath him.

He couldn't think about Bertie anymore. Miss Parnell immediately came into his head instead. He saw her as he wanted to—as a woman, with her dark hair swept into that feminine style at the ball, her body draped in raspberry silk, the creamy column of her neck graced with pearls.

Had she been wearing pearls that night? He didn't think so. She likely didn't have any jewelry, or if she had, she'd sold it. He hated how she'd sounded the other night. Angry and frustrated, then defeated. But only for a moment. She'd rebounded because that was the kind of woman she was. She was forthright and witty and absolutely fearless.

She'd love this, and he suddenly wished he'd brought her along—as Smitty, of course. He'd tell her all about it. He'd explain the floating sensation, the icy temperature, the gut-twisting view, even the earache. She'd thrill to his every description.

What was he doing? He shouldn't be thinking of her like this. He'd been so relieved when she hadn't accepted his overture in the close the other night. At least one of them had retained their wits. More and more, he found himself helplessly drawn to her, and that was bad.

He needed distance.

And he'd have it. He was already devising a way to ensure she had all the money she needed. He'd goad Greene into another race—it wouldn't be difficult—only this time, she wouldn't go with him so that she could wager. He'd tell her to bet on Greene, and Andrew would lose. Yes, it was cheating, but it was for an excellent cause. If he thought she'd just accept money from him, he'd have given it to her days ago.

As predicted, the wind picked up, and the balloon moved faster. The buildings of London grew more sparse, giving way to greener spaces and tall church spires.

Andrew turned to Sadler. "When can I parachute?" They'd corresponded about this possibility.

Sadler chuckled. "You like this."

"Very much." But it was more than that. It was for Bertie. This was the first step, but parachuting was as close to flying as he could get, and he'd do it for his brother.

"I'm doing another ascent in two weeks. You could jump then."

"Perfect." He saw Darent Hall. It wasn't exceptionally large as far as country houses went, but it was beautiful. Designed by Henry Flitcroft seventy years ago, it was situated on a hundred acres of spectacular parkland. Andrew didn't spend as much time here as he ought because there were too many memories.

The wind increased, jostling them as Sadler guided them to descend. "Hold on, Dartford, this is going to be a bumpy landing. Never fear, I've had dozens of them and walked away from each. Maybe with a little help." He winked at Andrew.

Andrew wasn't afraid, but then he never was. He didn't fear death, not when it would reunite him with the people he loved most. He began to shiver and chose to blame the cold air.

The pain in his ears intensified. He winced as they dropped closer to earth.

It started to rain lightly. He squinted at the lawn beneath them and saw specks. They were people, he realized. Who was down there waiting for him? The staff? They knew he was descending today. Perhaps they'd come outside to watch.

The ground neared, and he could make out the identity of the group. It was Charles and Beaumont and the others. He saw a smaller figure, and his stomach dropped. She wouldn't have come here.

Just as they were about to touch the ground, the wind picked them up again. A moment later, they dropped, hitting the earth with a thud and bouncing back up. Andrew's ears throbbed, and a headache formed just over his brows.

"Hold on!" Sadler called over the wind as the balloon came back down hard.

They bounced again, Andrew's body jostling with the force of the movement. Thrown off balance, he let go of the side of the gondola. They dropped once more, and again jolted back up. This time, however, Andrew catapulted from the gondola and hit the ground. The last thing he saw was the bright blue and yellow of the balloon rising above him.

EVERYTHING HAD HAPPENED exactly as planned. Lucy had traveled to Darent Hall in a barouche belonging to Nora. She'd arrived and placed her bet after careful consideration. There was a wide lawn where the balloon was expected to land, but Lucy had chosen a spot closer to the edge. It was a wager of utter chance, so all she could do was pray that she would win.

She'd actually considered not coming at all since she'd lost the other night. However, she found she didn't want to miss this, even if she didn't make a wager.

There were about a dozen gentlemen besides Lucy, including Charles, Beaumont, and Greene. They milled about the lawn drinking from flasks, and Greene said they should've set up a shooting exhibition to pass the time. He was still eager to see Lucy shoot, but she didn't have Dartford's Manton pistol yet. Tuesday would be here soon enough. She would shoot, and she would win back all the money she'd lost and more.

At last the blue-and-yellow balloon came into view just as a fine mist began to fall. Everyone cheered. Lucy grinned briefly before reining in her expression. She shouted in her deep, masculine voice, joining the others.

They watched it descend, and already a few of the men moaned about the placement of their wagers. They weren't allowed to move their markers after the balloon came into view.

As it neared the ground, they rushed toward the balloon. It hit the ground hard, and Lucy's breath caught as it bounced back up. She stopped short, and the others did too. She watched in horrified fascination as the balloon came down and went back up again—once, twice, and then the unthinkable happened: Dartford fell out of the gondola and dropped to the ground. The fall wasn't great, but it looked hard.

Everyone rushed toward him, but Lucy arrived first. He lay facedown. She knelt down next to him, her knees pressing into the damp earth. She placed her hand on his back and leaned down. "Dartford," she whispered huskily.

He didn't open his eyes, and Lucy's chest tightened. He couldn't be… No.

Beaumont knelt beside her. "Let's roll him over."

She nodded, and they worked together to move him to his back. There was grass and dirt stuck to his face, and a cut above his eye bled. She wished she had a handkerchief to dab at the blood. The hell with it, she just used her fingers, uncaring about ruining her gloves.

Beaumont moved to his other side. "Dart? Come on, man, wake up."

Charles dropped down next to Beaumont. He picked up Dartford's hand and squeezed it. "Open your eyes, Dart."

Lucy could feel the concern in the air. It matched hers as fear gripped her from the inside out. She didn't want to lose him.

His lids finally fluttered open. His dark eyes were unfocused for a moment, and then they found Lucy. He blinked.

"You're all right," she murmured, careful to keep her tone deep and masculine in spite of the distress roiling inside her.

Charles shook his head and smiled. "You gave us quite a scare."

Dartford turned his head. His gaze darted here and

there, taking stock. "What the hell are you all doing here?"

"Waiting for you," Beaumont said, as if Dartford had gone daft in the fall. "We held a contest as to where you'd land. Anyone know who came closest?" He looked around.

"Looks like it might've been Oxley," someone said.

Lucy felt a moment's disappointment, but next to the near disaster that had almost befallen Dartford, she didn't care about losing the wager.

He struggled to sit up, and Beaumont helped him. Lucy also helped, but she wasn't as strong as Beaumont. "You all need to leave," he said darkly. His eyes found Lucy's, and they speared her with their intensity. "Except you."

Lucy didn't understand why he was ordering everyone away, but she was glad he didn't include her. She wanted to make sure he was all right.

"We thought we'd stay and celebrate," Charles said. When Beaumont elbowed him in the side, he added, "But maybe not now."

"Not now, not ever. I didn't invite you." He looked at Lucy. "Help me up."

A few members of his staff arrived then—a younger man and a man and woman of middle age. "Let me help you, my lord," the younger man said.

Lucy was glad for his assistance. She didn't want the other men to see that she wasn't as strong as they'd expect her to be. Still, she lent her help in pulling Dartford to his feet.

He turned his head to look at the older man, perhaps his butler? "Alder, please see that all of these gentlemen are on their way immediately."

"As you say, my lord." He turned his attention to the

group and looked at them expectantly. Then he turned to Lucy. "We'll take care of his lordship."

"Except her. *Him*." He shook his head. "I took quite a fall."

Ice flooded Lucy's veins as she glanced around to see what they'd thought of his slip. Greene watched her with an odd look in his eyes that made her extremely uncomfortable.

"Why does he get to stay?" Charles asked. He sounded a bit petulant, but Lucy wasn't sure she blamed him. Dartford wasn't being particularly hospitable. But as he said, he'd taken quite a fall.

Dartford sent Charles a dark stare. "Because he's a physician."

A what? Lucy blinked, wondering how in the world she was going to pretend to do *that* going forward. What had he just done?

He winced, putting his hand to his head. Blood tracked from the cut over his eyes down his temple and along his cheek.

"We need to get him inside," Lucy said in her most authoritative tone. She turned to the other men. "Go on. He'll be fine." She had no idea if that were true of course, but he did seem all right.

The woman came forward with Dartford's hat and placed it on his head. "To keep the rain off ye." She spoke with a gentle Irish lilt.

The younger man and Lucy steadied Dartford between them as they walked toward the house. It was an arduous procession, and she wondered if they should've brought a cart or something to carry him.

"How's Sadler?" Dartford asked.

Lucy had met all the gentlemen in attendance and didn't recognize the name. "Who?"

"The balloonist."

"I'm not certain, my lord," the younger retainer answered. "Samuel went to check on him."

Dartford nodded, wincing with the movement. "Let me know what he finds out. I've the devil of a headache."

"Is that why you ordered everyone away?" Lucy asked.

"No. I don't like people coming to Darent Hall." His clipped tone said he didn't want to discuss it further, but Lucy was still curious. She put her questions away for later.

The rain increased as they made their way to the house, and by the time they arrived, Lucy's coat was quite wet. The older woman, who Lucy had learned was the housekeeper, Mrs. Alder, had walked ahead of them, and now barked orders to a couple of footmen, who ran to do her bidding, starting with a bath for his lordship.

She turned, her soft smile at odds with the command she'd just displayed. "Go on up. I'm going to the kitchen to fetch a tonic for his headache." She looked at Lucy. "What else do ye require for your treatment?"

Lucy blinked, her tongue freezing in her mouth. "Ah, hot water, clean cloths. The tonic, of course." She didn't sound remotely like a physician. What had Dartford done by spewing that nonsense?

They made their way upstairs, and thankfully, Tindall, Dartford's valet, she'd also learned, supported most of his weight. His bedchamber was at the back of one of the wings of the U-shaped house. It was large, with tall windows looking out over the expansive park and forest behind the house.

A massive four-poster stood against one wall. Tindall

led Dartford to it, and Lucy stepped aside. She was suddenly completely and tensely aware that she was inside Dartford's bedroom.

"I'll go help with the bath." Tindall looked at Lucy. "Can you get him undressed?"

Lucy's eyes widened, and she coughed. She looked to Dartford to intervene, but he was pulling at his cravat and didn't seem as though he'd heard what Tindall had said.

Dartford perched on the edge of the bed and dropped his cravat to the side. It slithered to the floor. "I don't want a damned bath," he muttered. He'd at least heard *that* much. "Though hot water does sound delicious. It was bloody freezing up there." He turned his head toward Tindall, who was just disappearing into an adjoining chamber. "Tindall, a moment."

The valet turned and came back. "My lord?"

"No one is to come into this chamber save you and Mrs. Alder." He gestured toward Lucy. "This...*person* is not what you think. You're going to keep her secret. Is that clear?"

Tindall didn't even flinch at his use of "her." "Yes, my lord." He left without another word or any reaction whatsoever.

"I'm not undressing you," Lucy said, abandoning her masculine voice and any other pretense of her disguise.

The blood had dried on his face, making him look somewhat fierce. "Not even my boots and coat?"

Lucy pulled her gloves off and tossed them onto a chair near the fireplace along with her hat. She longed to take off the wig and the facial hair, but she still had to get back to London, and she didn't want Nora's coachman to see her as a woman. Especially since she'd still be dressed in men's clothing. She also shrugged out of her wet coat and hung it over the back of the chair.

She went to Dartford and took his hat. She considered setting it on the bed, but it was wet, so she dropped it on the floor. Next, she helped him out of his damp coat. She took it to the chair by the fireplace and laid it over the arms. "Someone needs to stoke this fire. I can do it if you like."

"After the boots, please."

She returned to him and knelt. "This is a side of you I haven't seen. Very demanding. And somewhat austere. Why don't you want your friends here? They were so eager to surprise you, and then they were horribly concerned when you landed so poorly." She tugged his boots off in quick succession and set them to the side. His stockinged feet seemed impossibly intimate. She couldn't dare to remove the hosiery and bare his toes. And yet she did. Without him even asking.

She first peeled one away, revealing a muscular calf covered with dark hair. She blushed, the heat in her face welcome after being outside in the chilly damp for more than an hour. She moved to the next leg, going even faster this time and paying less attention to the flesh she revealed with her ministrations.

She jumped up. "Better?"

"My head is killing me."

Mrs. Alder came in then, carrying a tray with a small bottle, a larger bottle that seemed as if it must hold liquor, and a glass.

"I hope you brought gin." Again his tone was on edge, and she wondered at this Dartford she'd never met.

"Of course, my lord." Mrs. Alder poured from the smaller bottle and handed him the glass. "Tonic first, however."

"You're in charge, as always." He lifted the glass and toasted her before drinking the brew. He wrinkled his nose and handed it back to her. "That's even nastier than I remember."

She gave him an imperious look, but her lips curved into a smile. "It hasn't changed a bit." She poured the gin next and gave it to him. She set the bottle on the table next to the bed. "I'll leave this here."

"You're a gem among women," he said before taking a healthy drink.

She turned to Lucy. "What can I get for you?"

Lucy was absolutely tongue-tied. The housekeeper looked at her with kindness and not an ounce of judgment. Did she know she was a woman?

"Mrs. Alder, this is Miss Parnell. She is not a physician, nor, as I'm sure you can see, is she a gentleman. Only you and Tindall will know the truth. I, of course, expect you will tell your husband, but I know he will be typically discreet."

"Of course, my lord." She nodded and looked to Lucy again. "Shall I prepare a room for you?"

"Oh, I won't be staying. I'll just make sure Dartford is all right, and then I'll take my leave."

"As you wish." The housekeeper left, closing the door behind her.

Tindall came back from the other room. "Your bath is ready, my lord."

Lucy took a step back. "I'll build up your fire, and then I should probably go."

"Stay until I'm finished." He stood up from the bed with Tindall's help. "Please."

She shouldn't. But she was powerless beneath the weight of his dark, earnest stare. She nodded and watched Tindall guide him from the room.

Turning, she went to the fireplace and stoked the fire. Once it was crackling and warm, she backed away and stood there until she felt the chill in her bones vanish completely. She walked to the windows and looked out over the lawn below. There was a garden, and a small maze, but it looked a bit overgrown.

It was late afternoon. She ought to leave soon.

Oh, what was she doing here at all? What a fool she'd been to come! She'd lost the wager, and she'd somehow become a physician. How would she maintain that façade in front of those men? And Dartford had slipped up—calling "him" a "her." Had Greene caught it? It seemed he might have, given the attention he'd directed at her afterward. They'd *all* likely caught it, but had they blamed it on Dartford's fall? She hoped so.

She worried that it was time to end this charade once and for all. And she hadn't yet earned anywhere near the funds she needed.

She heard movement and started to pivot.

"You might want to keep your back turned," Dartford said.

Lucy snapped her head back around as another blush stole up her neck. Was he…naked?

A minute later, he called out again. "You can turn now."

She waited a moment and then did so slowly. He was in bed, the coverlet pulled up to his chest, and he wore a shirt, though it was open at the neck.

Averting her gaze, she fished for an appropriate topic of conversation. "Did you learn how Sadler fared?"

"No." Andrew's voice was deep and gravelly, and he cleared his throat. "Tindall, do you know?"

The valet turned on his way to the door. "Ah, yes, I forgot to mention it, my lord. He is sound, and when he learned you would be all right, he left for London."

"Thank you, Tindall. That's all." The low rumble of Andrew's voice resonated in her bones and fired her blood.

She held her ground, afraid to move, as Tindall left them alone. "This is wholly improper," she said.

Andrew's face was clean, but the cut above his eye was red. "Everything about our association is improper."

She couldn't disagree with him. With slow, tentative steps, she made her way to the side of the bed. He looked well for the most part, aside from the cut on his forehead. She reached out to smooth the flesh above the wound but stopped herself. "Do you need stitches?"

"I don't know." He cracked a small smile. "You're the physician."

She scowled at him. "Thanks to you. Why did you say that? I can't be a physician. I don't know the first thing."

He looked up at the bed hanging. "I don't know. I blame the fall. I wasn't thinking clearly. I just wanted a reason that you should stay."

Her insides churned with anticipation. "Why?"

His eyes found hers. "I don't know. I just wanted you here." He sounded mystified, and while that should have confused her, it filled her with heat and elation.

"What are we going to do about this physician problem? Maybe you can tell them you were confounded by the fall."

"Like I did when I called you a she?" He shook his head. "No, I'm afraid the ruse is finished. Davis Smith is going to retire to Edinburgh or somewhere equally distant."

Frustration and anger overtook the other emotions raging inside her. "But *I'm* not finished. I lost more money today on this stupid balloon wager. I'll come up with a new disguise. I'll get a gray wig and be an older man."

He sat up quickly, too quickly because he winced and brought his hand to his head. When he looked at her, his brows were pitched low, his eyes bright with something she couldn't quite name. "Damn it, Lucy, can't you just be a woman for once?"

Chapter Eleven

ANDREW STARED UP at her. Her lips were parted, her breath coming fast. She was angry, but she was also something else. His head hurt. Hell, his entire body hurt, but he was *also* something else. He wanted her. Desperately. And right now he didn't give a damn about the consequences.

He snaked his right arm around her waist and cupped the back of her head with his left hand, pulling her down. He claimed her mouth, his lips moving against hers in fierce possession. He wanted her more than he'd ever wanted anything.

His fingers twisted into the base of her wig. Oh, this would not do. None of it. Not the hairpiece, not the sideburns, not the costume. He wanted *Lucy*.

He pulled his mouth from hers but didn't release her. "I want to see you. Without *Smitty* interfering." He brought his hand around and dragged his thumb along one of the hated sideburns. "How do these come off?"

Her lashes fluttered. "They pull away. You just have to be gentle."

He scooted to the side and tugged her to sit beside him. He sat up and found the end of the faux piece. He pulled at the edge, lifting it up carefully. He moved slowly but noted that she winced. "Does it hurt?"

"A bit. You could go a little faster."

He tore it away, trying to be as delicate as possible. She closed her eyes briefly when he was done. When she opened them again, her gaze was determined. She reached up and pulled the other one away with a quick movement then dropped it on the bedside table. She sucked in a breath, and he could see that her eyes watered. "I think my maid used too much glue today. We wanted to make sure they stayed in place since it was going to be such a long day." She blinked and rubbed at the reddened flesh.

"Let me." He replaced her fingers with his, smoothing her skin while he stared into her beguiling eyes. "You're absolutely fearless, do you know that?"

Her gaze didn't waver, nor did she flinch—confirming what he'd said. "I want what I want."

He cupped the side of her face, his thumb moving over her flesh, soothing her. "And what's that?"

"Freedom. Independence. Security."

"I want excitement. Adventure. But most of all, I want you." He drew her head down and kissed her again. Where he'd taken her by surprise a moment ago, she was ready this time. Her mouth met his with equal fervor, her lips opening and her tongue darting forth to tangle with his.

This was exciting and adventurous—everything he wanted and more. He lay back, palming the back of her head. Clutching at her waist, he pulled her down on top of his chest. He splayed his hand over her lower back, pressing her into him. The coverlet was between them, providing an infuriating barrier. But beneath it, he wore only a shirt. He'd likely scandalize her. Or not. Lucy wasn't the type to frighten easily.

Lucy.

How had he ever thought of her as Smitty? Hell, he'd forgotten to dispatch the wig. He reached up and pulled it from her head.

She broke the kiss. "Ow!"

He winced. "What? I didn't mean to hurt you."

"The wig was pinned to my hair." She sat back and massaged the back of her head.

He released her. "My apologies." He offered her the wig, but she shook her head.

She pulled a pin from her hair and dropped it on the table beside the bed. A second one joined it. Then another. With careful, exacting precision, she removed each pin and deposited them on the table. Lock after lock, the dark mass fell until it reached past her shoulders in a rich, sable curtain.

Andrew dropped the wig, heedless of where it landed. "You're so beautiful. And don't tell me that you're not. You *are*."

Her eyes were wide, luminous, in the dim, seductive light of the chamber. "I never thought so…until I met you."

He brought his hands to her face, stroking her cheeks, reveling in their silky smoothness. He drew his thumbs over her cheekbones and pushing his hands back into her hair. It was thick and soft, and he tangled his fingers among the waves.

He wanted more.

Moving down her body, he clasped her sides and lifted her over him, laying her in the middle of his bed. He came up on his side and loomed over her. Her cravat was undone, and he could see just a trace of her neck. He tugged the silk away and threw it aside. The neck of her shirt fell open, exposing more of her creamy flesh.

She stared up at him, her eyes full of wonder and desire. "My boots are probably dirty."

He pulled his gaze from hers and looked down at her feet. "Then let's dispose of them." He made quick work of it, peeling her boots away and throwing them to the floor. He did the same with her stockings, eager to see her feet. They were pale and lovely. He ran his fingertip along the outside edge, from toe to heel.

She flinched, giggling. "That tickles."

He looked back up at her face, his mouth forming a lazy smile as his headache began to fade from the tonic. "Does it?"

She was still wearing far too much, reminding him of Smitty. And damn it, he didn't want Smitty in his bed.

He wanted Lucy.

He leaned on his elbow beside her and put his fingers on the uppermost button of her waistcoat. "May I?"

She nodded. Her chest rose and fell with deep, ever-quickening breaths.

He realized there was no padding here. "Where is the bulk of your costume?"

"We grew smarter with the day costume. My maid sewed it into the coat. Once I take it off, there's just me."

He moved to the next button, enjoying this leisurely removal of her costume but also eager to see her, as she said, as just her. "Ingenious," he breathed. "But then I'd expect nothing less from you." He moved more quickly, making his way through the waistcoat and then pushing the sides open to expose the shirt beneath.

She gasped, then brought her hand up to the back of his head. She pulled him down. "Kiss me, Dartford."

"Andrew. You should really call me Andrew." No one had called him that since he'd been small, and even then it had only been his brother and his sisters. His parents had called him by his courtesy title. Why Bertie and the girls had called him Andrew remained a mystery he'd never know the answer to.

Darkness threatened to engulf him, just as it had after the balloon incident. Until he'd found her face. He'd been horrified to see that she was among the gentlemen on the lawn, but after awakening, he'd been relieved and...happy. He did the same thing now that he'd done then to keep his sanity intact—he focused on her. He fed on her touch and lost himself in her kiss.

He pressed down on top of her, relishing her body beneath his. He speared into her mouth, his tongue dancing with hers and his body throbbing with need. She arched up into him, pressing her chest against his. He realized there was something missing. He brought his hand up her side and cupped her breast. Only there was no breast.

Well, he knew she had them. He'd seen them at Lady Colne's ball. Rather, he'd seen their shape. He wanted to *actually* see them. Or at least feel them.

He moved his hand back to her waist and tugged the shirt from her breeches. He found the hem and slipped beneath it, skimming his hand up along her bare flesh. She gasped into his mouth. She was warm and soft, and he was going silently but fervently mad with desire.

The shirt lifted with his movements, bunching between them. At last, he reached her chest and encountered linen. She'd bound her breasts. He ran his hand over the fabric, searching for how to remove the offending piece. There was a knot in the middle, but his attempts to loosen it failed utterly.

He ended the kiss, tugging at her bottom lip with his teeth. Her eyes opened. The black of her dilated pupils nearly engulfed the iris, and her mouth was kiss red.

"What torture is this?" he asked as he tried futilely to undo the knot.

"It seemed necessary." She brought her hands up and took over from him, quickly loosening the fabric. "I can't…" She looked away from him.

She wanted him to stop. He didn't blame her. Hell, he was a beast anyway. Disappointment curled through him. "It's all right. I'm afraid I quite lost my head."

She tried to rise. He sat back, giving her the space she needed. She came up off the bed and whisked the shirt over her head, shocking him. "I didn't want you to stop. I just can't take this off without help. Well, I suppose I can, but it's easier with assistance. My maid wraps it rather tightly."

He stared at her, his mouth moistening with need. She was a gift. He had no idea what he'd done to deserve her, but he wouldn't question the grace with which she'd been given to him.

He grasped one of the edges of the strip of fabric and began to unwind it around her. He went slowly, once again enjoying the slow, meticulous removal of her clothing. It was almost unbearably erotic. As much as he hated her masculine costume, he thrilled to the revelation of her form. It made her even more feminine, more beautiful, more irresistible.

When he got to the final wrap, her breasts taunted him. At last their shape was exposed to him. He snatched the fabric away then, desperate to have her free and open to his hungry gaze.

"You can see why it's no stretch for me to dress as a man. I'm afraid my curves are almost nonexistent."

He heard her words but couldn't have disagreed more. Her breasts were small but lush and round, with perfect pink nipples just begging for his kiss. He pushed her back against the pillows and spread her hair out over the white linen. He traced his hands down her neck, along her collarbones, and circled her breasts before cupping them gently. "You are curved in precisely the way you are meant to be, and you are stunning. I don't know why you have these inaccurate views of yourself, but allow me to disabuse you of them right now."

He moved down her rib cage, noting her slender but supple build. She was athletic, graceful, utterly perfect in his eyes. But there was more to see. He found the fall of her breeches and unbuttoned them with quick flicks of his fingertips. The sound of her breathing ceased, and he realized she was holding her breath while he worked.

He grasped the waistband of the breeches and tugged them down, glad to see there were no smallclothes barring his view. The thick, dark thatch of her curls greeted him as he stripped the garment away. Her breath came back in fast pants.

"*Lucy*." He dragged his fingertips along the arc of her hip and the curve of her thigh. "If you have any flaws, I don't see them. All I see is a beautiful woman I want with every part of my being." He untangled himself from the bedclothes and came over her, bracing his hands on either side of her head. He still wore his shirt, but that was all that lay between them now. "If you don't believe me, let me show you."

She thrust her hands into his hair. "Yes. Please." And she kissed him again, her tongue tracing over his lips before plunging into his mouth and claiming what she wanted.

He kissed her deeply, pressing his body against hers. She twisted and arched beneath him, stirring his arousal. The hem of his shirt just covered his cock, and he had no plan to reveal it to her. This moment wasn't for him but for her. He meant to give her an experience she'd never forget. This woman who'd been deprived of so much deserved nothing less.

He stroked the side of her neck, feeling her pulse strong and sure against his fingertips. He dragged his mouth along her jaw, kissing and licking, tasting her. She pulled at his hair, moaning. He smiled against her, reveling in her uninhibited response.

Caressing her collarbone, he moved lower until he found her breast. He cupped her again before coming to the nipple. With thumb and forefinger, he pulled and lightly squeezed. Her moans grew louder and her chest came up, seeking more of his touch. He brought his mouth down her neck, ravaging her flesh along the descent. Clasping her breast, he held her captive while he took the nipple into his mouth and suckled her—soft, then harder, then soft again.

"*Andrew.*" Her deep, but oh so feminine voice cloaked him in desire.

He made love to her breasts in equal measure, using his hands and mouth to taunt and pleasure her. She moved with abandon, and her breathing grew more irregular. He trailed his fingers down her rib cage and glided them over her hip to her thigh. He went slowly to her core, gently stroking her curls and then finding her clitoris, that sweet nub of need that would send her over the edge.

Her legs parted, allowing him easier access, and he was again thrilled and pleased with her fervor, but not surprised. He continued to focus on her breast with his mouth while touching her, softly at first and then with more purpose. She was wet, and he wanted nothing more than to sink into her heat. But he couldn't do that. This was already far more than they ought to be doing.

He pressed his finger into her, and she gasped. He worked at her clitoris, increasing his pressure and speed until her desperate cries filled the room. Her response only intensified his desire.

He left her breast and moved down her body. He pushed her thighs apart and focused on her sex, parting her pink folds and licking her delicious flesh. She bucked up, her fingers threading into his hair.

"What are you *doing*?"

He didn't think she really required an answer, and he didn't need any further encouragement. He thrust his tongue into her and stroked her folds, her clitoris. Her hips moved relentlessly as her hands pulled at his head and shoulders. She began to quiver, her muscles jerking. He moved his mouth up to that most sensitive spot and slid his finger into her, filling her again and again until he felt her sheath contract around him.

His cock twitched, desperate to replace his finger. He'd have to find release, and he didn't think it would take long.

He stroked into her while her orgasm crested, moving more slowly once it subsided. She panted as she lay back, spent, her legs sprawled around him.

"Good Lord, that was a revelation."

He chuckled at her summarization—so matter-of-fact and yet so full of wonder. That was his Lucy.

His?

He sat back on his calves, and her gaze went directly to the tent his cock had created with the bottom of his shirt.

She licked her lower lip, and his cock twitched again. She was going to kill him.

"What about you?" she asked. "Aren't you going

to…" She used her eyes to indicate what she meant—wasn't he going to put his cock inside her?

"I want to, but there are…concerns."

She frowned, her brow furrowing. "Yes. But aren't there precautions? I want to feel that. *You.* Can we do it just a little?"

She wanted to do it just a little? Hell and damnation, that was going to sorely tempt him, but he'd take a little of Lucy if that was all he could have.

"Are you certain?"

She sat up and put her palms flat on his thighs. Her eyes slitted. "Take off your shirt."

Lust snaked through him. He tore off the garment and tossed it viciously aside.

She stared at his cock. "That's, ah, impressive."

"*Lucy.*"

She massaged his heated flesh, her fingertips digging into his hips. "Can I touch it?"

"You can do anything you want to it."

She gave him a saucy look. "Anything?"

God, she was amazing. "*Almost* anything."

She slid her hands up his thighs and clasped his hips. "Mmm."

He worked to keep still lest he thrust toward her. He wanted her so very badly.

"I think I should start up here. You're so muscular." She ran her hands up his sides, her fingers splayed. She came up on her knees in front of him, her gaze connected with his. The more she touched him, the harder it was for him to keep his eyes open and not fall completely under her spell.

She kissed his jaw, his neck, his chest, exploring him as she likely did every other facet of her life.

"You have no fear, do you?" His question came out

raspy and dark, almost broken.

"Not much. But I guess we have that in common." She licked at his nipple. "*Duke of Daring.*" She closed her mouth over him, and he groaned. He twisted his hands in her glorious hair.

"Lucy, I'm ready." He was more than ready.

"Not yet." She inched back and skimmed her hand down the plane of his stomach until she found his shaft. "I haven't done *anything* to this yet. What do you call it? My friend Ivy says that men have names for them."

Good God, they discussed this sort of thing? "It's just my, uh, cock."

"Right. Cock." The word tumbling from her mouth elicited another groan from him. Or maybe it was that her hand had closed around the base and was squeezing him gently. "Am I doing this right?"

"God, yes. You can…move your hand. If you like." He prayed that she would like.

"Show me."

His hand closed over hers, and he demonstrated how to stroke him. She picked up the motion easily and applied a natural pressure that made his balls tighten. "Lucy, you are a bloody gift."

"Hmm. There's liquid. Can I taste it? Never mind, I'm fairly certain that falls in the category of things I can do."

"It's probably at the top, actually."

"I see." She dropped her head and put her mouth on him, and he was quite hopelessly lost.

She suckled him gently, her hand still wrapped around him, but then she moved her mouth as she'd moved her hand, and within seconds, he feared he might come.

"Lucy, I don't think I'm going to be able to put myself inside you. Not now. I'm going to…" *Hell.* She drew him deep into her mouth and sucked while her fingers squeezed him.

His hips moved then; he couldn't help himself. He pulsed into her, his orgasm building. She released him and pulled him deep again, and he was done. He pumped into her mouth, his seed exploding forth. "Lucy!"

She didn't let him go but kept him inside of her until he was finished.

He shouted and yelled and made an absolute bloody racket until he was completely spent. He wanted nothing more than to collapse beside her and take her into his arms.

She sat back, releasing him and wiping her hand over her mouth. She looked uncertain, but also…satisfied. A sheen of pleasure glazed her eyes. "Was that…all right? I don't know if that was normal…" She looked away.

"Lucy, that *wasn't* normal. It was spectacular. I can't imagine how you knew to do that, but I don't like to question such gifts."

She blushed as she returned her gaze to his. "Well, then I shall take that as a compliment."

"Please do." He kissed her hard and deep and long, holding her tight against him and then falling onto the bed with her clutched to his chest.

When they pulled apart, she laughed. "What about the other . . . act?"

"Not tonight," he said. "We haven't even had dinner. I asked Tindall to bring it up later." He looked at the clock on the mantel and realized it was probably nearing that time. "We should get dressed."

She made a face. "I don't want to go through all that

just yet. Can't I wear something of yours if we're eating in here?"

The thought of her donning one of his dressing gowns as her dinner costume was an alluring image. "Absolutely." Common sense, which had been in rather short supply, battered at the back of his mind. "You need to get back to London before you're missed."

"I can send a note to Aquilla. She'll make an excuse for me with my grandmother." She traced her finger along his forehead, gently touching his cut. "Anyway, I'd rather stay here and look after you, if that's all right."

The idea of having her here was tempting, yet also frightening. He hadn't had a visitor here ever. After his family had died, he'd lived here alone with the staff. He'd spent a good deal of his time at school and then in London. This was his home, but it didn't feel like home. Because he didn't want it to. Home was his family, and they were gone.

He closed his eyes briefly as despair pulled at the edges of his mind. He opened his eyes to see her watching him.

"What is it?" she asked. "You look upset."

He didn't want to talk about it. "You can stay." His answer surprised him.

"What about your retainers?"

"I don't have many, and they'll keep your presence a secret."

She studied him, her brows dipped over her eyes with concern. She smoothed her fingertips along his forehead and drew her hand down the side of his face before kissing him softly. "All right."

"We'll dispatch your note shortly and see to your

coach and driver, after I get you something to wear." He started to pull away, but she clasped his shoulders.

She looked into his eyes. "Kiss me again first."

"You're a demanding woman."

She arched a brow as if to silently ask if this was a problem. It was absolutely not. His lips curved up before they met hers.

This was an unprecedented day, and he was going to do his best not to think about why.

Chapter Twelve

LUCY FINISHED THE last of her dinner, surprised at the quantity of food she'd eaten, but then she'd been ravenous. It had been a long day full of astonishing events. She looked over the table at Andrew. He'd donned his shirt and a pair of trousers, but she could barely call him "dressed," with his bare feet and a goodly expanse of his magnificent chest exposed. She had no intention of complaining.

"How's your head?" she asked.

"It aches, but the tonic seemed to help a great deal. I should take another dose." He fetched the bottle from near the bed and returned to where Tindall had set up their meal on a small table in front of the hearth. Andrew brushed a kiss against her temple as he passed her. "Or mayhap it's all due to you and your healing powers."

Lucy rolled her eyes. "If anything, I'll cause you more harm than good."

He sat down opposite her and grinned. "Never."

She thought about what they'd done earlier—it weighed heavy on her mind for so many reasons—and wasn't sure if he wanted to repeat the activity. Or take it further. "You truly wish me to stay?" She'd already written a note to Aquilla, and it was at least halfway to London by now.

"I do." He sipped his wine. "Tell me why you're a wallflower. I don't understand it one bit."

She blinked at him, thinking him mad, then laughed. "I'm not conventionally beautiful." She held up her hand. "You can't argue with me. I didn't say I wasn't beautiful—you're entitled to your opinion. However, I am neither blond nor blue-eyed nor am I adorned with especially feminine curves." She felt odd describing herself that way now. After being with him, she did indeed feel desirable. "Plus, I don't like feminine things such as needlepoint or singing or tittering."

He laughed. "Tittering? Were you taught that as part of your comportment?"

"No, which is probably why I fail." She smiled at him, enjoying his wit and the frank and respectful way he spoke with her. He talked to her as no man ever had, as if he were truly interested and maybe even entranced.

"You're the better for it," he said. "Did you never have a suitor? Not even once?"

"I did in my first Season."

"And what happened with this suitor?"

"He wasn't *really* a suitor, just someone who paid me attention for a short time." She didn't like thinking about Caruthers, let alone discussing him. "That was five years ago. I scarcely remember."

Andrew set his glass on the table and leaned forward, his gaze pensive. "I doubt that, but I'm in favor of forgetting things that trouble us. However, I've decided I don't like this fellow, so if you'd give me his name, I'd be happy to trip him when next I see him, or fleece him over a game of whist."

Now it was Lucy's turn to laugh. Warmth and joy spread through her. She'd never had a champion. She could get used to this. Goodness, that was a sobering thought. She plucked up her wineglass and took a long drink.

"I'm quite serious," he said. "He's an imbecile."

"He married an heiress, and I believe is a terrible spendthrift. I'm rather pleased he didn't pursue me."

"You are the most practical-minded woman I've ever encountered."

She lifted her glass in a toast. "Thank you."

He toasted her in response.

After taking another sip of wine, she broached the subject that had been hovering about her mind since he'd tumbled from the balloon. "Why don't you want people coming to Darent Hall?"

He shrugged as he turned his head to look into the fire. "I don't like to entertain."

It couldn't be that simple, could it? "You were rather angry," she said quietly. "It seemed more important than a question of entertaining."

He gave her a wry look. "I'd just fallen out of a descending balloon after bouncing off the ground several times. By tomorrow, I'll be sporting bruises over half my body."

She couldn't argue his point. She couldn't imagine she'd have her wits about her after going up into the sky, even if the balloon had landed perfectly. "Was it frightening?"

"The falling? Surprising, but I wasn't scared, no." He cocked his head to the side, sending a lock of his dark hair falling over his forehead. "Or did you mean the flight? That was *exhilarating*. Probably the most exciting thing I've ever done." His lids dipped over his eyes as he raked her with a provocative stare. "Perhaps with the exception of disrobing you."

She was growing accustomed to his compliments and his flirtation so that she didn't blush. However, heat and appreciation still filled her every time he made her feel special. And he did that often. "I don't think I would care for it."

He sat forward in the chair, his features growing animated. "Indeed? While I was up there, I thought you'd enjoy it. I considered asking if you'd want to go with me—as Smitty, of course."

He had? She didn't know what to make of that. Were they friends now? She glanced toward the bed. They were rather more than *that.* But what, then, were they?

He continued, his eyes lighting with excitement. "You can see all of London laid out below you. It's astonishing—the dome of St. Paul's, the spires of Westminster Abbey, the masts on the ships in the Thames. You can't imagine the view. Well, you can, but it wouldn't do it justice."

"I'd be too terrified of falling, especially now after seeing you fall."

He shook his head, smiling. "I don't think so. You're not scared of that sort of thing, are you?"

"Not really," she admitted. She was, however, becoming afraid of falling *in love.* With him. That realization sent prickles of unease along her skin, so she shoved the thought away.

"Anyway, the threat of falling isn't anything compared with the ear pain and the cold."

"What ear pain, and what cold?"

"The higher we rose, the more frigid it grew. Sadler warned me—it's why I was wearing a heavy greatcoat—just as he did about the earache. The pain was minimal as we ascended, at least for me. Sadler says it's a bit different for everyone. However, on the descent, it was excruciating. It's due to the change in altitude. The air up high has less pressure, and you sometimes have to work at opening the ear canal to bring everything into alignment."

"How on earth do you do that?"

"By swallowing and yawning, if you can believe that. Although, it didn't work terribly well for me, I must admit."

"You're not encouraging me to try this."

He laughed again. "I'd go again right now."

She loved his enthusiasm. "Whatever gave you this idea to go up in a balloon?"

"My brother always wanted to fly. This is the closest I could come."

"You've never mentioned your brother." And he spoke of him as if he were deceased. "He died?" She realized she knew nothing about his family.

He turned his attention to the fire again. "Yes. A long time ago. When we were young."

"I'm sorry to hear it. And your parents?" She knew his father had to have passed, since Andrew was the earl.

"They're both gone too." He picked up his wineglass and drained it. He didn't look at her as he sat back in the chair.

She longed to ask more, but he didn't seem inclined to talk about them. What was it he'd said earlier? He was in favor of forgetting things that troubled him? She'd wager what she'd lost today on the balloon contest that his family troubled him. Hopefully, she'd find out why. Because no matter what they were—friends, associates, something far more intimate—she cared for him a great deal.

He stood abruptly. "We should go to sleep. My headache is returning, and I'm exhausted."

Lucy looked up at him tentatively. "I should ask Mrs. Alder to prepare a room for me."

"You could. But I would prefer you stay here. With

me." He held his hand out to her.

"It's terribly scandalous, but then I'm a walking scandal about to happen, aren't I?" She laughed, uncaring about her reputation but also realizing she needed to guard it for her grandmother's sake. Indeed, if it weren't for her grandmother, she might have asked Dartford to make her his mistress.

Lucy pushed that thought right out of consideration. She *couldn't.* She could, however, sleep beside him tonight. It would be an experience that she would likely never repeat. She put her hand in his and let him guide her to the bed. The hem of his dressing gown, made of dark blue silk, trailed behind her.

Mrs. Alder had discreetly provided a night rail for her, which she'd donned beneath the dressing gown before dinner. She shrugged out of his gown, and he took it from her shoulders.

She climbed onto the mattress while he laid the garment on a bench at the foot of the bed. He shucked his breeches and slipped in beside her, then drew her against his chest.

"We're just sleeping," he said before kissing her temple.

"I admit I'm a trifle disappointed."

He arched a brow at her. "Just a trifle?"

"More than a trifle." She curled her hand around the back of his neck and pulled his mouth to hers. He tasted of wine and pleasure, and the ache he'd satisfied earlier bloomed anew, pooling in her belly and spreading out until her breasts tingled and her core heated.

He pressed her back into the bed and kissed her deeply, his tongue slicing into her mouth with delicious strokes. She clutched at his neck and shoulders, desperate for more, but he pulled away.

"You are a temptress," he hissed. "Sleep."

He rolled to his back, but held her close against his side. Lucy laid her palm on his chest and fell asleep surprisingly easily.

Until a sound jolted her awake. She opened her eyes, uncertain for a moment of where she was. Everything came back to her—the balloon descent, Andrew's injury, the intimacy that had come after…

Next to her in the bed, Andrew mumbled something. It wasn't loud, and it was absolutely unintelligible. She rolled to her side, and he vocalized again, this time louder, but she still couldn't understand him. He lay on his back, his brow furrowed. He spoke again, "It's cold."

She leaned up on her elbow and with her other hand smoothed her fingers over his forehead. He didn't feel cold at all. He exhaled softly, and the creases over his eyes disappeared. She didn't know how long she watched him, but he slept quietly now.

She settled back against the pillow and realized she wouldn't find sleep again. She climbed out of the bed and padded to the window. Peeking behind the curtain, she saw that it was no longer dark, but neither was it full daylight yet. The clouds were thick and gray, giving everything a muted tone.

Turning, she glanced around the room, looking for something to occupy herself. She didn't see any books. Perhaps she could steal down to the library, assuming he had a library. She probably oughtn't leave the chamber, but it was very early, and she was unlikely to encounter a member of his staff, particularly when he'd said it was rather minimal.

Tiptoeing across the room, she picked up his

dressing robe and wrapped it around herself before leaving. She closed the door softly and made her way along a corridor that opened onto a long gallery. She vaguely remembered passing through it on their way upstairs yesterday, but she hadn't paid much attention in her concern for Andrew.

Andrew.

She liked thinking of him that way and was glad he'd asked her to address him so informally. It, along with everything else that had happened yesterday, introduced a level of intimacy she'd never imagined to share with a man. Honestly, she'd never expected to meet anyone she'd *want* to share that with.

As she strolled the gallery, she looked at the portraits hanging there. She suspected they were former earls and their families, until she came to one that confirmed her theory. It was a family with four children, the oldest of whom was clearly Andrew at around ten years old. He looked a great deal like his father, who stood with his hand on the shoulder of a woman with light blonde hair. A small girl sat on her lap, while another who was slightly older stood next to her, holding her mother's hand. Both girls were blonde and pale with arresting, dark brown eyes. Andrew stood with another boy in front of their father. The other boy was younger, and of all the people in the portrait, he looked the most engaging, with a mischievous smile playing about his lips that the painter, for whatever reason, had decided to include. Lucy's heart twisted, thinking that his parents and brother had died. She wondered what had happened to the girls.

"Excuse me, Miss Parnell?"

The soft query came from Lucy's right, making her jump. She turned abruptly and saw the housekeeper,

Mrs. Alder. "Yes?"

Mrs. Alder smiled gently. "I didn't mean to startle you. I just wanted to make sure it was you." She chuckled. "Though I can't imagine who else it would be. There aren't that many of us to keep track of. I see you're looking at his lordship's family. Such lovely people." The sad tone of her voice revealed the truth—they were *all* gone.

Lucy turned toward the housekeeper. "What happened to them?"

Mrs. Alder's eyes narrowed briefly. "His lordship hasn't told you? Of course he hasn't. He rarely speaks of them. He also rarely comes here." She exhaled and shook her head. "I don't mind sharing the story with you. They all took ill just before the holidays that first year his lordship went to Eton. When he came home, his mother was already near death, and his sisters—Jane and Margaret—weren't far behind. His father went next, and Albert, the sweet boy, tried to hang on until Christmas, but I'm afraid he didn't quite make it."

Lucy's insides chilled, and her skin felt numb. She couldn't imagine shouldering such losses in quick succession. "His lordship wasn't ill?"

Mrs. Alder shook her head. "No. For whatever reason, he was spared. For a long time, he wished he'd gone with them." She looked down at the floor. "Sometimes I wonder if he still does. All those dangerous things he insists on doing." *Like racing and ballooning*, Lucy thought. The housekeeper squeezed her hands together and looked at Lucy. "I beg your pardon. I shouldn't say such things."

Compassion propelled Lucy forward, and she briefly touched the housekeeper's arm. "I hope I'm not too familiar, but please don't regret telling me what happened. It helps me…understand him better." In truth, her mind was spinning from this revelation. She felt as if she ought to have known, which was silly. Their relationship had only just progressed. Perhaps he'd planned on telling her. Except he'd clearly avoided the topic when it had come up.

Mrs. Alder nodded, then tipped her head to the side. "You and he are close, then?"

It didn't make sense to deny it, and she saw no reason to conceal the truth from the housekeeper. "I suppose so, yes."

"You should know there hasn't been a visitor to Darent Hall since they died. Not one." Her gaze was warm and hopeful. "This is an important occasion. My husband and I noted it last night. I hope *you* won't think *me* too forward, but we're rather pleased."

Oh dear. Did they expect something permanent? Despite what had transpired and feeling as if their connection had deepened, Lucy didn't know what it would mean in terms of the future. Neither one of them wanted to marry. Even so, a tiny voice at the back of her mind quietly said that marriage to Andrew wouldn't be bad. And it would be better than ending their association, which she found she didn't really want to do.

Yes, they were close. Closer than she ought to be comfortable with.

"I should go," Lucy said, half turning. She considered trying to explain the realities of her relationship with Andrew but decided it didn't matter. If Mrs. Alder wanted to believe that Andrew might find happiness, who was Lucy to crush her hope? She couldn't help but wonder, however, where Andrew actually found happiness or if he did so at all. She thought of what

Mrs. Alder had said about his dangerous activities. Was that what made him happy? The notion gave her a chill.

"Just let us know when you're ready for breakfast." Mrs. Alder nodded once, then turned and walked toward the stairs.

Lucy stood there for another moment before retracing her steps back to Andrew's bedchamber. As soon as she stepped inside, she heard thrashing and shouting from the bed.

Lifting the front of the dressing gown lest she trip over the hem, she hurried to Andrew's side. He gripped the coverlet in one hand and twisted his body this way and that. His face was contorted with pain or anger or some other sinister emotion or probably many emotions.

She couldn't understand what he was saying, but he had to be suffering a nightmare. Tentatively, she touched his shoulder. "Andrew, wake up."

He knocked her hand away. She locked her jaw with determination and clasped him more forcefully. "Andrew! Wake up!"

He grabbed her forearm and sat upright. His eyes came open. They were dark and wild. "Who are you? Did you come to help them?"

"Help who?" She didn't understand him at all. "Andrew, it's me, Lucy."

The furrows in his brow deepened. He stared at her, and gradually his eyes lost their savage haze. "Lucy."

She relaxed and let her hand settle on his shoulder, her fingertips caressing his heated flesh. He'd somehow lost his shirt, she realized. Which meant he was nude. She tried not to think about that.

"You were having a nightmare."

His breathing was rapid, the muscles of his neck

tense. He pushed her to the side and jumped from the bed, heedless of his nudity. "You need to go." He stalked to his dressing chamber, leaving Lucy to stare after him in confusion.

Was he still in the throes of whatever he'd been dreaming of?

She followed him, slowly, uncertain of what to say or do. He nearly ran into her as he came back into the chamber, now wearing a forest-green dressing gown. His skin was pale, his gaze haunted. He almost looked ill.

He backed away from her. "What are you doing? I told you to go."

She frowned. "Andrew, tell me what's wrong. Were you dreaming of the balloon descent?" It was the only thing she could think of that might have him this upset. It had been quite a tumble, and he'd been agitated afterward. Not quite like this, but similarly.

He lifted his hand to his mouth, and she could see that he was trembling. Apprehension squeezed her lungs. "You're scaring me. Please tell me what's wrong." She stepped toward him, but he evaded her, moving around her entirely.

"I asked you to go. I'll send Tindall and Mrs. Alder to assist you." He went to the door and didn't turn when he spoke. "It was a mistake for you to stay here. I want you to leave. And don't come back."

He left the bedchamber, closing the door firmly behind him.

Lucy stood there and stared, her mouth hanging slightly open for a moment before she snapped it closed. Confusion and hurt ripped through her. Why wouldn't he share with her what had happened? Weren't they…close?

Not really. She thought she knew him, believed they were friends who trusted each other, but she'd clearly been wrong. She hadn't even known about his family.

Her face felt hot, her throat tight. She was such a fool. He'd behaved so differently from other men. She'd let her guard down, and he'd taken advantage, as all men did. Now that he'd gained all he wanted from her, he was tossing her out.

Lucy swallowed and straightened her spine. This was nothing—a hitch in her plan. She didn't need Dartford, and if he came forward to expose her to Grandmama now…well, that would be unfortunate. But Lucy would weather the storm, just as she had every other calamity that had tried to beat her down.

No, she *didn't* need Dartford. What's more, she didn't want him either.

Chapter Thirteen

ANDREW OPENED HIS eyes and blinked at the canopy overhead. For the first morning in a week, his body didn't feel as though it had been beaten to a pulp. Instead, he just felt stiff and sore in a few places. He pulled himself up, eager—also for the first time in a week—to greet the day.

He'd spent the past several days recuperating at Darent Hall. It had ended up being one of his longest visits, which had pleased Mrs. Alder, who clearly thrived when she had someone to fuss over. What hadn't pleased her, however, was Lucy's abrupt departure without sufficient explanation. Andrew had only said she had to get back to town. And when Mrs. Alder had asked about a potential future with Lucy, Andrew had decided it was time to return to London himself.

Lucy.

He'd tried not to think of her too much, but now that he was back in London, he couldn't seem to help it. He'd arrived last night and had actually considered going to the corner of her street to see if she would go out. Had she ventured out in his absence? Hopefully, she hadn't taken the risk. Yet he couldn't blame her if she had—she needed money, and he hadn't been here to help her.

Hell and damnation, he'd botched things badly with her. Having her stay had been a colossal mistake, but he oughtn't have thrown her out like that. He wished he'd behaved differently, but he'd been incapacitated by another one of his attacks. The ones that accompanied his nightmares were particularly devastating, driving him to take to his bed for the rest of the day. He'd blamed his injuries and was actually grateful for the opportunity to hide behind them.

He was such a coward.

"My lord?" Tindall came into his chamber as he did every morning, except the last several because Andrew had sent him back to London so that he could care for his mother.

"How is Mrs. Tindall?" Andrew asked, sitting up.

The valet came inside and closed the door behind him. He stood near the bed, his spine ramrod straight, his features composed. "Quite well, thank you, my lord. The medicine seems to have improved her condition. I can't thank you enough for sending the physician."

Andrew wasn't terribly comfortable with the praise, especially when he was feeling ashamed about the way he'd treated Lucy. "I'm glad to hear it."

Tindall coughed softly. "Now that she's on the mend, I shall take up my search for a new position. I do appreciate your patience."

This news should've filled Andrew with relief, but he felt…odd. He'd missed Tindall while he'd been at Darent Hall. He was an exceptionally fine valet, anticipating Andrew's every need and exceeding his expectations.

He expressed none of this to Tindall.

"Have you set your schedule today, my lord?"

Andrew had a meeting with his secretary later this morning and should visit his club later. No, what he *should* do was call on Lucy. He owed her an apology at least and perhaps even an explanation. He'd go after his appointment.

After sharing his plans with Tindall, he dressed for the day and went down for breakfast. Instead of thinking about his business matters, however, he could think only of Lucy and what to say to her. She had to be terribly angry. And concerned—she needed money, and he'd abandoned her in her time of need. He'd already decided it wouldn't be wise for them to continue visiting gaming hells. Then he'd gone and taken her into his bed, and he wasn't sure how it would be to see her again.

He felt a powerful attraction toward her. Plus, he liked her. What a disastrous combination.

No, they needed to part ways, much as that disappointed him. He'd have to think of another way to help fill her coffers. Perhaps he could sell something for her. In fact, why hadn't he offered that in the first place? Because he'd thought their enterprise would be mildly diverting and quite temporary. Neither of those had proven true.

He could also invest whatever she had left—he winced thinking of her losses over their last few encounters together. How much had she lost with the balloon contest? He hadn't spoken to any of the others who'd been there. A few had sent notes to Darent Hall inquiring after him, but he hadn't responded. He owed several apologies, he realized, feeling distinctly uncomfortable. Why should he apologize? He hadn't invited them, and he didn't care what they thought of his rudeness.

As he ate breakfast, he turned his mind back to Lucy's financial problems. He'd talk to his secretary about investment opportunities with a fast return. And if there were none, he could just fabricate something and give her the money himself. Yes, *that* was what he should have done from the start—given her a nest egg and offered to invest it for her. She probably would have refused, given her independent nature, but she was also practical. She'd come around to the logic of it and accept his offer.

Feeling much better about his ability to help her, he went into his meeting with a sense of optimism toward the rest of his day. He ignored the pang of anticipation he felt at the prospect of seeing her. He'd keep their association focused on business and do his best to forget her lush kisses, her audacious touch, and most of all, her surprisingly delightful concern. He could find the first two anywhere, and he didn't need the last.

The ghost of his family told him he was very wrong. So he did what he did best and ignored them too.

LUCY SCANNED THE advertisements for small cottages near Bath for lease. The money she'd saved would support only a very small one—she'd have to sleep in a closet—and it was farther from Bath than Grandmama would like. She had friends in Town, and the whole reason she wished to retire there was to see them more regularly.

There was no help for it—Lucy was going to have to find employment in Bath. Perhaps she could work at a school or provide secretarial assistance to a widow. Ivy had told her of women doing that.

Once, Lucy might've thrilled to these thoughts. She didn't mind employment and would appreciate the independence it would afford. She imagined feeling a sense of accomplishment and self-worth—things she saw in Ivy and admired immensely.

Instead, these ideas made her feel forlorn and…empty. She blamed Andrew. He'd shown her what Aquilla had always insisted—that good men existed and that Lucy could find one and be happy.

Only Andrew wasn't a good man. He was a selfish, thoughtless blackguard.

"How many times have you danced with Edgecombe, dear?" Grandmama's question jolted Lucy from her reverie, and she was grateful for it.

Lucy had attended two balls in the past week, and she'd danced with Edgecombe at both of them. She'd also danced with a few other gentlemen, including Mr. Greene. She'd panicked when he'd first approached her, wondering if he'd somehow recognized her. But he hadn't, much to her relief.

"Twice, Grandmama." She hid a smile because Grandmama absolutely knew how many times they'd danced. He'd also sent flowers again.

"Three times if you count Lady Colne's. You did dance with him then, didn't you?" She didn't wait for Lucy to confirm this before adding, "And that's twice he's sent flowers. I daresay he'll be calling very soon." She looked up from her knitting. "It's just splendid, isn't it?"

No, but Lucy didn't say so. She only murmured, "Mmm."

"What, you don't like Edgecombe?"

Oh, he was pleasant enough, with an easy smile, and he demonstrated at least a passing interest in Lucy as a person, asking her what she liked and even engaging in a rousing discussion about riding. "I like him fine. That doesn't mean I've changed my mind about marriage, Grandmama. Would it be so terrible if I simply retired with you?"

"No, but that isn't an option, I'm afraid." She exhaled and returned her attention to her knitting.

Lucy didn't think Grandmama had really ever considered the possibility. In her mind, Lucy *had* to marry.

Lucy set her newspaper aside and stood up from her chair. She went to Grandmama and squatted down in front of her. She set her hand on her grandmother's knee and looked into her familiar, beloved face, framed by gray hair topped with a white cap. "Just think of how lovely it would be. Our own little cottage. I would take care of you and make sure you were able to do everything you wished."

Grandmama had lifted her sherry-colored gaze partway through Lucy's plea. Now she smiled. "It would be lovely. But you would grow bored, dear."

"I wouldn't." Lucy shook her head but didn't feel as confident as she had, say, a fortnight ago. Before she'd shared all those experiences with Andrew. Damn it all, he'd ruined *everything.*

Lucy heard movement and conversation from the hall. Someone must be here.

Their butler, Burton, came through their small dining room and into the sitting room. "Lady Parnell, Miss Parnell has a caller."

Grandmama dropped her knitting needles and snapped her attention to Lucy, beaming. "It must be Edgecombe!"

Lucy, her legs starting to protest from her crouched position, stood and smoothed her hand over her skirt. She considered things she might say to Edgecombe to discourage him.

Burton glanced at Lucy briefly before returning his full attention to Grandmama. "It's Lord Dartford, my lady."

Every muscle in Lucy's body tensed. What the devil was he doing here? She looked at Grandmama, who was squinting up at the butler. "Dartford?" She swung her head to look at Lucy. "Why is he calling on you?"

For a moment, Lucy couldn't answer. All she could think to say was a litany of things she could *not* say. At last she found her tongue. "I'm not certain. We danced at Lady Colne's."

Grandmama sat up straight. "I'd forgotten about that." She waved a hand at the butler. "Show him in."

Lucy smoothed a hand over the back of her hair and glanced down at her day dress. Her wardrobe was a bit lacking, and this was one of her older gowns. Ah well, she didn't really care what he thought of her. She tilted her chin up, prepared to send him on his way as soon as possible.

But then he walked into the drawing room, and her knees went weak. She wanted to blame it on having crouched down next to Grandmama, but she knew that wasn't the reason.

He wore a dark blue coat and tawny trousers tucked into glossy black boots. His hair was swept back from his brow, save a solitary lock grazing his forehead in rebellion. His dark eyes found hers, but only briefly. He turned to Grandmama and offered a deep bow.

"I regret that we have not been formally introduced, my lady. Please forgive my intrusion."

Grandmama smiled, her cheeks turning pink, as she regarded him. "It is our pleasure to receive you, even if it is a bit indecorous." She fluttered her eyelids, and if Lucy didn't know better, she'd say her grandmother was flirting.

Andrew grinned in response, and Lucy nearly

groaned. He was far too attractive when he wasn't smiling, and then when he did so, it was as if the sun was shining on you alone. Grandmama would forget all about Edgecombe after this.

Lucy wished he hadn't come. "To what do we owe your visit?" She considered tapping her foot to demonstrate her impatience but decided against it. Grandmama would only ask her to stop and then frown at her in perturbed disappointment.

"I hoped we might take a stroll, perhaps in your garden." He looked past her to the doors leading to the very small patio and garden behind the town house. He could likely see that a walk in their garden would take all of about two minutes. And that was if they moved very slowly. "Or we could just stay here."

"Why don't you walk over to Devonshire House and back?" Grandmama suggested. "Take your maid with you."

Andrew looked at her expectantly. Lucy looked at him with disdain.

"Burton," Grandmama called, "fetch Lucy's maid, and have her bring Lucy a hat and gloves."

There was no avoiding it, apparently. Fine, she'd go on the bloody walk so she could tell him exactly what she thought of him.

Grandmama gestured for Andrew to move farther into the room. "Dartford, I don't believe I've seen you much in Society. What do you do to keep yourself busy?"

"I've quite a number of hobbies, my lady." He glanced toward Lucy, a hint of mischief in his eye. "I've acquired the nickname of the Duke of Daring."

Lucy did groan then, but softly so that Grandmama wouldn't hear her.

Grandmama appeared nonplussed. "But you're not a duke."

He laughed. "That's what I said. Nevertheless, that's what it is."

"What does that even mean, 'daring'?" Grandmama peered up at him. "What are your interests?"

Lucy leapt into the conversation, eager to show Grandmama that he was not the sort of gentleman she ought to champion. "Racing, gambling, swimming, and most recently *ballooning*." She said the last word with an angry edge.

Grandmama blinked at him, her expression rapt. "You ascended in a balloon?"

"I did. Last week."

Grandmama's eyes lit. "How wonderful! If I were twenty years younger, I'd love to fly among the clouds." Her gaze turned wistful.

Andrew chuckled again. "Perhaps you should be the Duchess of Daring."

Another blush stained Grandmama's cheeks. "I'm far too old for you, dear, but I appreciate the sentiment." She winked at him, and Lucy nearly hugged Judith as she entered at precisely that moment, saving her from further torture as Grandmama fell even deeper under Andrew's spell.

Judith, already garbed for their outing, handed Lucy her bonnet and her gloves.

"Thank you," Lucy murmured.

"Have a nice walk," Grandmama said, smiling particularly at Andrew. "It was a pleasure to meet you, Dartford."

He bowed to her again, this time taking her hand and floating a kiss above her knuckles. "I assure you, the pleasure was entirely mine."

Grandmama giggled softly and waved them off.

Lucy rolled her eyes as she preceded him from the room. Burton opened the door, and she left the house, going down the stairs and out along the pavement without waiting for him.

He caught up easily, coming up on her right. "You're quite angry with me."

She glanced at him, her eyes wide. "Why ever would you think that?"

"Because you should be. I was an ass."

Whatever Lucy had expected, and she'd really had no idea, it wasn't that. The ire that had propelled her from the house dissipated and was replaced with an uneasy wariness.

"Yes, you were."

"Good, I'm glad we agree. Now we may move on."

Lucy stopped short and stared at him as he continued for another couple of steps. Did he mean to just forget about everything that had happened at Darent Hall? "I think you owe me an explanation."

He'd turned but didn't meet her eyes. "There's nothing to explain. I fell out of a balloon, and I behaved in a ghastly manner."

He meant to blame it all on his accident? She moved closer so she could lower her voice to a near whisper. "Which part was ghastly, exactly—the part where you seduced me or the part where you evicted me from your house forever?" She delighted in the play of emotions across his face—his eyes widening, his brow furrowing, his jaw dropping for an instant.

"Did I really seduce you? I thought, and perhaps I was fabulously mistaken, that you'd shared in the seduction duties."

"Even if I did, you didn't answer my question, *which*

part was ghastly? Or was it all just a tremendous, horrid mistake?"

He pressed his lips together and looked at her intently. He inched closer, keeping his voice low. "All of it was a tremendous mistake. I wouldn't, however, characterize it as horrid. Would you?"

His gaze dipped briefly, caressing her body before piercing her with heat and desire. Damn him.

She steeled herself against the arousal he was stirring within her. "That morning was absolutely horrid. I was so worried for you, and you cast me out with no concern whatsoever. I think I deserved better than that."

He started to touch her hand, but let go. She wished he hadn't, but they were standing on a public street. She understood why they couldn't do that. Not here. Not anywhere, really. He'd said what she knew in her heart—it had all been a mistake.

"You deserved far better than everything that happened. I mistreated you badly, Lucy, and I'm deeply sorry. Can we walk?"

Overcome by the depth of sincerity in his apology, she couldn't find her voice. She nodded.

He offered her his arm, and she took it. She glanced back at Judith, who'd stopped several paces behind them. They exchanged knowing looks. Judith was well aware of who Andrew was. While Lucy hadn't told her about what had happened at Darent Hall—she hadn't told anyone, not even Ivy and Aquilla, who'd been frustrated by Lucy's lack of disclosure—she knew Andrew was the man who accompanied her to the hells.

As they walked to the corner, Lucy reflected on how strange it was to be traversing this path with him in broad daylight and dressed as a woman. He seemed to be thinking the same thing, because he chuckled softly. "This feels somehow wrong."

Lucy couldn't help but smile. No matter what happened, she had wonderful memories of the time she'd shared with this man.

"Sometimes I have nightmares," he said, surprising her with his candor. Like his heartfelt apology, she didn't quite know how to react to his honesty. "And they leave me somewhat…debilitated. I didn't want you to have to deal with that."

"That didn't mean you had to send me away."

"But I did. You shouldn't have stayed in the first place. You must agree that we both lost our heads."

Yes, they had. "I don't regret staying, however. And if that makes me a scandalous hussy, then so be it."

He threw her a half smile. "How I adore your intrepid streak."

How she adored hearing him say he adored anything about her. She wanted to be angry with him, but he was making it deuced difficult what with his charming apologies, demonstrations of common sense, and willingness to open up to her.

"What are your nightmares about?" she asked.

"Is it enough for me to say they're terrifying and I don't wish to discuss them?" He stared straight ahead. "I hate to admit that even talking about them can threaten to send me into an attack."

She squeezed his arm. "I'm so sorry." She'd thought about that morning a great deal over the past week and thought she'd come up with a reasonable explanation. She only wanted to know if she was right—not for her own edification but because she wanted to know him. "Was it to do with losing your family?"

He snapped his head toward her, but only briefly. "Did Mrs. Alder tell you about them?"

"Yes. Don't be upset with her." She'd fawned all over Lucy when she'd helped her back into her Smitty costume, apologizing for Andrew and saying that he wasn't himself and that she hoped Lucy wouldn't hold his behavior against him. "She cares about you like a mother."

"She's not my mother." The words came fast and hard.

Lucy winced, realizing that had been the absolute wrong thing to say. "No, she's not. But she's still like family, isn't she?"

"No."

They walked in silence for a bit, almost to Devonshire House. He finally said, "I don't have a family, and I like it that way. You and I—we prefer to be alone, independent. I think it's why we formed a…connection."

She agreed, but when you liked being with someone more than you liked being alone, what then? Especially when the person you liked being with more than being alone didn't feel the same. Lucy tugged on his arm, turning them since they'd arrived in front of Devonshire House.

He followed her lead. "I've been thinking about that connection."

She wasn't sure she wanted to hear what was coming. "I have too." He'd occupied too many of her thoughts of late.

"Since you can no longer continue as Smitty—"

"Not since you made him a physician and ruined the entire scheme." It was rude of her to cut him off, but she thought he deserved it.

"I apologize for that as well." Again, he sounded earnest and truly remorseful. Lucy appreciated that, but it didn't change the fact that she now had to readjust everything. "I should like to make amends. I have several ideas about how to provide you the money you need to take your grandmother to Bath."

Provide her? Her skin prickled as she tried to imagine what he was going to propose. "What do you have in mind?"

"First, if you have any items of value, I'd be happy to sell them. Although, you really don't need to. I'd be delighted to give you a sum, which I will invest on your behalf."

She stopped again, her mind processing what he'd said. "You want to just give me money?" There was only one reason a man gave money to a woman who wasn't his wife.

Wife. If she was his wife, he could give her all the money she needed. But she didn't want to be his wife. She didn't want to be anyone's wife.

Liar.

The whispered voice in the back of her mind echoed through her, turning her insides into knots. She could marry him. In fact, she *would*—if he asked. Despite what she'd thought earlier in her anger, he *was* a good man, just troubled. And she could help him work through that. She could be the family he didn't have. She wanted to be.

Oh God, she *was* falling in love with him.

And she didn't want to. She didn't want to marry him. She didn't want to want him, not when he didn't want her.

She let go of his arm and started walking again, passing Judith who'd stopped when they'd turned at

Devonshire House.

He walked beside her. "What are you thinking?"

"That I don't want your money. It's offensive that you would even make the offer."

"I realize it's scandalous, but no one has to know. We're rather good at keeping secrets."

From each other too. He never would've told her what had happened to his family and how it had affected him, she realized. She still didn't really understand the latter.

She didn't want a man she couldn't trust—not after her father. "I don't want a man managing my life. I'll find something you can sell. That's the only offer I'll accept." She tried to think of what she might give him. All she had was a pearl necklace and matching pair of earrings that had belonged to her mother. She wouldn't ask Grandmama for anything of hers.

She kept up a brisk pace, and they turned onto Bolton Street.

"You're angry with me again," he said.

"No, just thinking," she lied. She *was* angry, but at herself as much as at him. "If you wait outside, I'll send my maid down with the items you can sell."

"What about investing the funds?" he asked. "Will you let me do that?"

That would only tie them together, and she wanted him out of her life. "No, thank you. I expect you to obtain a decent sum. Please deliver it at your earliest convenience." They arrived in front of the town house. "I thank you for your acquaintance and wish you all the best in the future. Good day, my lord." She turned quickly and motioned for Judith to come with her.

At the door, Lucy threw him a brief glance. His lips were pursed, and his forehead had formed deep grooves. Good. Let him be confused or upset or whatever he was. She was sure it would fade. Unlike her, he would be able to disentangle himself from their connection with barely any bother. She suspected Andrew would remain with her for a long time, and of course the memories she had of him would last forever.

She ran upstairs to her room to fetch the jewelry. She didn't want to become sentimental or change her mind. Quickly, she wrapped them in a handkerchief and gave them to Judith. "Give these to his lordship."

Judith's hand closed around the pearls. "What am I to say?"

"Nothing." There were no more words that needed to be said.

Chapter Fourteen

ANDREW WALKED INTO Boodle's and made his way to the parlor where he typically met his friends. He hadn't thought overmuch about how they might react to seeing him, but now that he was here, he wondered if any of them harbored anger toward him at the way he'd behaved following the balloon descent.

"Dart!" Beaumont grinned widely at him as he entered. "Come and join us."

The table was quite populated—Charles, Thursby, and Greene were there, as well as two other gentlemen.

"It's about time you showed up," Thursby said. "We've been wondering about your recuperation."

Andrew couldn't recall everyone who'd been at Darent Hall beyond Greene, Beaumont, and Charles—he remembered them. He assumed Thursby had been one of them. "I'm quite recovered, thank you. It was a hell of a fall."

Charles shuddered. "Indeed. You won't catch me trying that. I daresay you won't be doing it again either."

"Actually, I'll be going up again soon. This time I plan to parachute."

Charles gaped at him. "Did the fall injure your head?"

Andrew laughed. "Well, yes, but not permanently."

"Then you've gone mad."

"He's always been a little mad," Beaumont said. "Who else would jump nude into the Thames in the middle of the night?"

"Or scale the dome of St. Paul's?" Charles added.

"You actually did those things?" Greene asked before sipping from his whiskey.

That had been, what, three years ago? Before Greene had come onto their scene. "At least once." Andrew was glad that there was no awkwardness and that no one seemed to care to ask him about his behavior at Darent Hall. The disintegration of his relationship with Lucy had been bothersome enough, especially since he hated that they'd even grown close enough for him to care.

But their association was finished. He'd taken her jewelry to a pawnbroker that afternoon and would send over what they were worth tomorrow. He'd also include a little extra because he didn't think she'd notice. His chest tightened at the thought of never spending time alone with her again.

A footman brought Andrew a glass of his favorite gin, and Beaumont indicated the empty chair next to him. Andrew dropped into it and sipped his liquor before setting the glass on the table.

Greene, who was seated across from him, glanced around. "No Smitty? We realized he must not be a member since you don't meet him here."

Next to Greene, Charles nodded in agreement. "It makes further sense because he's a physician. How did we not know that before?"

"I'm sure I must've told you," Andrew lied. He'd thought about how best to conceal or at least minimize the fact that he *hadn't* told them. "Anyway, he's taken a post in Edinburgh, so I'm afraid you've seen the last of him."

"That's a shame," Beaumont said. "I enjoyed his company."

"I did as well. Very much. I'm disappointed I didn't get to see him shoot." Greene picked up his whiskey and swirled the amber liquid in the glass. He looked over at Andrew, his gaze enigmatic. "Did he leave an address? I should like to correspond with him and perhaps call on him when I visit my uncle in Edinburgh in the fall."

Andrew had lifted his glass to take a drink, but stopped midmotion. What could he say to discourage Greene? Nothing without drawing attention to the matter, and he couldn't do that. No, he'd let Greene look for Smitty, and when he couldn't find him… Well, Andrew wouldn't know what happened to him. "I'm afraid I don't have an address."

Greene, who'd watched Andrew closely during his response, lifted a shoulder. "I'm certain he won't be difficult to find."

Impossible, Andrew thought, but he remained silent. He hoped Greene wouldn't bother. Perhaps he should create a story in which Smitty was besieged by highwaymen on his way north and sadly never arrived…

The conversation turned to the balloon descent and Andrew's plan to parachute. Most of the table thought him insane, but a few, including Greene, were intrigued and asked if Sadler would take them up too.

"For a fee," Andrew said.

Greene sat forward, his dark blue eyes gleaming with excitement. "I'd be willing to pay."

Andrew finished his gin and signaled the footman for another. "You should write to him."

"I will. Would you put in a word on my behalf?"

"Certainly, but truly it's just about paying a fee. Sadler loves ballooning—you don't have to persuade him to go."

Thursby stood. "I'm afraid I must take my leave. Time to make an appearance at the Goodwin ball. Anyone else going?"

One other gentleman nodded, but the rest, including Andrew, shook their heads. He idly wondered if Lucy would be there and for a moment reconsidered. But what would he do? Watch her from afar? He doubted she'd accept an invitation to dance. There was no delaying their separation. Best to cut her out completely and immediately.

"Not you, Greene?" Charles asked. "You seemed to have quite a good time the other night."

Beaumont chuckled. "Indeed. I daresay you may have set a record for dancing with the most misses." He shook his head. "I don't know how you did it. I would have gone mad with the insipidity of it."

Greene rolled his eyes. "It wasn't terrible. In fact, I danced with a rather engaging young woman—Miss Parnell."

The footman was just handing Andrew his second glass. It slipped from his fingers, splashing gin on his sleeve and on Beaumont as well as it tumbled to the floor.

"How clumsy of me," he murmured.

"The fault is mine, my lord." The footman plucked up the glass. "I'll just fetch some napkins."

Beaumont brushed at his sleeve. "I'm fine."

"I am too, thank you. Truly, it was my mistake." Andrew hated that the footman felt responsible when the blame was entirely Andrew's. Greene's mention of Lucy had jarred him. "Are you looking for a wife?" Andrew hoped his question sounded casual, but a jealousy he shouldn't feel ate at his insides.

"Not particularly. I attend a ball periodically and dance as much as possible to appease my parents. They would *like* me to look for a wife." He surveyed the table in question, and everyone nodded in commiseration. Greene looked at Andrew directly. "Miss Parnell just caught my eye."

Andrew's mind began to whirl. At Darent Hall, after the balloon descent, he'd mistakenly referred to Lucy as "her." He'd covered for his error, but he now recalled Greene studying her too closely. He also remembered Greene asking about a woman's laugh after the phaeton race. Now, tonight he'd displayed a candid interest in "Smitty" *and* Miss Parnell. Had he somehow puzzled out their secret? Andrew's replacement gin arrived, and he eagerly took a long drink.

Beaumont waggled his brows at Greene. "She's attractive, eh?"

Greene lifted his shoulder again. "Not traditionally. Her wit and her intelligence are her better features, I'd say."

Andrew wanted to argue. No, he wanted to plant his fist in Greene's face for saying she wasn't attractive. She was stunningly beautiful. At least the imbecile had recognized her other attributes.

Greene glanced at Andrew. Did he seem overly interested in Andrew's reactions to his discussion of Lucy? Or was Andrew simply seeing things that weren't there? Hell, he didn't like this one bit. If Greene had put things together and knew that Smitty and Lucy were one and the same, what would he do with that information? There was a chance he meant to do nothing, but Andrew wasn't sure he wanted to wait to find out. Neither, however, did he want to address the subject with Greene directly. It was probably best if he did nothing and simply kept an eye on the situation. He had to be overthinking this.

"I'm off, then," Thursby said, taking his leave.

Andrew had been invited to the Goodwin ball. Perhaps he should go on the chance that Lucy would be there. That way he could warn her about Greene.

Why? So she could worry about something that was only a suspicion? No, he'd already decided it was best to make their break as clean as possible, before he contemplated a future he never intended to have.

•ɛ•ɜ•

LUCY SIPPED HER tea as she listened to Aquilla tell her and Ivy about the Goodwin ball last night. Aquilla had danced once, which might have sounded inadequate, but since it was precisely once more than the previous ball she'd attended, Aquilla counted it as a success. Lucy heard the disappointment lurking behind her friend's cheerful disposition. For some time now, she'd been waiting for something to break within Aquilla—for her to lose her perpetually pleasant outlook. But Aquilla was still, for now at least, Aquilla.

Ivy asked Aquilla about her dancing partner, Lord Linley, and as they conversed, Lucy's mind turned to the money that Andrew had obtained for her mother's pearls, which had been delivered just before Aquilla and Ivy arrived for tea. It was a decent sum, and Lucy was considering how she might invest it. No, that wasn't entirely true. She'd been wondering if Andrew was as sorry to see their association over as she was.

Likely not, since she was frustratingly in love with him, and he could apparently turn away from her without a second thought.

"I can't tell if you liked Linley or not," Ivy said. "Never mind, you like everyone."

"That's not true," Aquilla responded. "I don't at all care for Lady Abercrombie."

"No one cares for her," Ivy said. "She's tedious and loud."

"Some people say I'm loud."

"Don't compare yourself to her. You are *not* loud. If anything, you have an excess of charm, and that can't be bad. Isn't that right, Lucy?"

Lucy sat up straight at the sound of her name. "That Aquilla's charming? Of course."

Ivy regarded her over the edge of her teacup. "You *were* listening. Here I thought you were off in some daydream."

She *had* been.

Aquilla looked at her shrewdly, her gaze narrowing. "She's been like that since she went to Darent Hall. I should love to know what transpired there, but she won't say."

"And that is her right." Ivy looked at Lucy in sympathy.

Lucy appreciated her support. While Aquilla longed to know what had happened, Ivy had said it was none of their business. She had, however, privately—and in a most dire tone—told Lucy that if she ever wanted to discuss what had happened, she would be happy to listen.

Lucy looked at her friends, wondering why she was bothering to keep it from them. Because it had felt incredibly intimate—something just between her and Andrew. Now that they'd gone their separate ways, it seemed like a dream. She was removed from the entire experience somehow.

"You know that he was injured in the landing." Lucy had said that in her note to Aquilla, citing her need to look after him as the reason for staying at Darent Hall. "And I'm sure you wonder why it was necessary for me to remain to care for him when he likely has a house full of retainers."

Both Ivy and Aquilla watched her intently. "We did wonder," Ivy admitted.

Lucy wasn't surprised—or annoyed—to learn they'd discussed the situation. "Andrew and I developed a rather close association through our gaming hell excursions."

Aquilla's eyes widened. "*Andrew?*"

Lucy pursed her lips. "Yes, Andrew. As I said, we became rather close. He asked me to stay." She'd thrilled at his specific request that she remain while demanding everyone else leave. Except she hadn't fared any better the following morning. "So I stayed."

"I see." Ivy sipped her tea.

"You say you cared for him," Aquilla said. "Is that all that happened?" She pressed her lips together. "My apologies. I don't mean to pry."

"It's all right. I've decided I don't mind if you do. I've nothing to hide when it comes to him—at least not from you. Our association is at an end anyhow."

Aquilla leaned forward, her expression one of distress. "What happened?"

"We, ah, shared his bed for the evening, and he asked me to leave in the morning." She didn't want to disclose the specifics of his behavior. Those were *his* secrets, not hers. She also saw no benefit in describing the horrid way he'd treated her or the crushing disappointment she'd felt, just as she didn't plan to share the unexpectedly lovely apology he'd given her.

None of it mattered.

"You *didn't*." Ivy's hand had arrested with her teacup partway to her mouth. Her tone was low and deep—wounded almost.

"We didn't do *that*," Lucy clarified. "We were…intimate in other ways." She wasn't quite certain how to describe it. She knew Aquilla had never done those things, but she honestly wouldn't be surprised to learn that Ivy had. She was older than both of them by a few years and had lived an independent life for nearly a decade.

Aquilla was rapt, her blue eyes wide with curiosity. "How was it?"

"It doesn't matter," Ivy snapped. "He threw her out when he was done with her."

That was precisely what Lucy had thought at the time, but now she believed she understood. "Andrew had his reasons for asking me to leave."

Ivy set her cup down with a clack. "He's a scoundrel. That's reason enough. He should be marrying you."

For some bizarre reason, Lucy felt the need to defend him. "How do you know he didn't ask? You know I don't want to marry."

"He asked you to marry him?" Aquilla sounded incredulous. "And you said no?"

"He did not, actually." Lucy threw Ivy a quelling glance. "We shared a lovely evening together—one that I shall never forget *or* regret."

Aquilla sat back and studied Lucy for a long moment. So long that Lucy shifted and wondered if she maybe had a crumb on her face from one of the cakes she'd eaten.

"I'm not sure I believe you," Aquilla said at last. "You were quick to defend him, you call him Andrew, and watching you talk about him…your eyes light up. And you almost smile, even as you're talking. I think you *would* marry him if he asked."

Aquilla, her dear and charming friend, had done what she did best—she'd cut right to the heart of a matter and astutely comprehended what was really happening.

Lucy looked from Aquilla to Ivy, who wore an expression of concern, back to Aquilla. She whispered what she never thought she'd say, "I *would.* If he asked. But he won't." Her insides twisted. "I'm sure you don't approve or understand, Ivy."

Ivy exhaled. "Approval has nothing to do with it, but no, I don't understand. He misused you horribly."

Lucy arched a brow at her. "I was a willing participant. No, he didn't handle things well, but it's my own fault. We were very clear early on—neither one of us desired marriage."

"Does he know you've changed your mind?" Aquilla asked.

"No, and I don't plan to tell him."

"Why is he so adamantly against it? He's an earl. Surely he understands the need to beget an heir."

That was a valid point and one Lucy hadn't pressed with him. She was curious about that now. But she wouldn't have the opportunity to ask him about it. "I believe it's because he lost his entire family when he was young. They all died of winter fever." Mrs. Alder had confirmed the illness when she'd helped Lucy preparc to leave.

Aquilla brought her hand to her mouth. "How terrible. My family is awful, but I wouldn't wish them dead."

"I would," Ivy muttered.

"My family?" Aquilla asked, her eyes round with

shock. "I know you don't care for them, but that's rather cruel."

Ivy looked down at her lap. "I wasn't speaking of your family but mine." She flicked a glance at Lucy. "He doesn't wish to have a family of his own because he's still mourning the one he lost?"

Lucy longed to ask Ivy about her family—whom she never talked about—but could tell she wasn't ready to reveal more than she already had. "Something like that, yes." Lucy reached over and stroked Ivy's arm briefly. "We're your family, you know."

Ivy smiled at her and then Aquilla. "I do know, and I love you both for it. I know I'm not always the easiest person to like, and that you've both become the dearest people in my life means the world to me."

"Oh, Ivy." Aquilla jumped up and went to hug her.

Lucy joined them, and soon they were in a heap on the settee, laughing.

When they'd composed themselves and returned to their respective seats, Aquilla looked at Lucy. "What do you plan to do now?"

"As I said, my association with Andrew—Dartford—is over." She'd do well to stop first-naming him. He was nothing more than a memory now. "I sold some jewelry. Between that and my winnings, I have enough to invest. We'll need to live frugally for a bit, but I think it will work out. I've been looking for cottages near Bath."

"Is your grandmother happy?" Ivy asked. "I imagine she must be."

"Or not," Aquilla said. "She's been clear about her wish for Lucy to marry."

"What Aquilla says is true, but I think she would like for me to be with her. I'm acclimating her to the idea."

Lucy turned to Ivy. "I may also seek employment, so I'd be keen to be introduced to your contacts in Bath."

"I'll send letters when you're ready to move."

Aquilla crossed her arms over her chest, frowning. "I'm going to miss you terribly. Is there no way we can persuade Dartford to marry? He clearly felt something for you, yes?"

Something, yes. But Lucy didn't think it went anywhere near as deep as the way she felt about him now. He treated her like an equal—appreciating her talent and her mind and, yes, even her beauty, which she'd thought was nonexistent. He made her feel special. Admired. Hadn't he even said he'd admired her once?

She didn't want to think about this, about him, anymore. It was too painful.

Lucy summoned a hearty smile and looked at Aquilla. "It doesn't matter what he might have felt or what I feel, our association is over, and I'm making plans for the future that don't include him."

Aquilla's frown deepened. "I'm still disappointed. I suppose we must make the best of the time we have left together, then. You're still coming to Lady Morecott's ball tonight, aren't you?"

"Yes, Grandmama has been looking forward to it." Lucy even had a new gown—at Grandmama's insistence that she needed it to snare Edgecombe. However, since Andrew's visit yesterday, Grandmama had begun talking of him instead of Edgecombe, much to Lucy's chagrin.

"Excellent, we'll play name that Untouchable." Aquilla grinned as she uncrossed her arms and straightened.

"Haven't we named them all?" Ivy asked.

"Probably, but perhaps we should change some of their names. I think I'd like to rename Dartford the Duke of Disdain."

Ivy laughed. "Perfect. I don't like him at all anymore. Sorry, Lucy."

Lucy wished she didn't like him anymore either. Instead, she loved him. And it hurt.

Chapter Fifteen

ANDREW STROLLED INTO the ballroom at Morecott House. Even though it was one of the largest, most opulent homes in Grosvenor Square, the event was still a crush. He doubted his ability to find Lucy in the crowd.

He'd regretted his decision not to seek her out at the Goodwin ball last night. He wanted to share with her his suspicions about Greene. Or maybe he just wanted to see her.

He should just have called on her that afternoon, but he imagined she wouldn't receive him. Perhaps he should've sent a note. Except he wondered if she would've tossed it in the fire without opening it.

Since she hadn't acknowledged the money he'd given her, he assumed she didn't wish to have any communication with him. And their parting yesterday had been stiff and…strange. Her words had been clipped, and though she'd said she wasn't angry, he was fairly certain she had been.

But there was nothing he could do about any of that. What he *could* do, however, was warn her about Greene.

He scanned the ballroom, but it was a confusing jumble of people. He supposed touring the wall might be his best chance of finding her.

That annoyed him. She shouldn't be a wallflower. She should be the most sought-after woman here. Men were idiots, he decided. They'd marry an insipid beauty with rocks in her head over a smart, stunning woman who would engage him every single day with her vitality and wit.

A nagging voice in his mind said that if he felt that way, *he* should marry her, but Andrew ignored it. Marriage and family weren't for him.

Andrew moved closer to the wall and began a circuit of the ballroom. After a few minutes of plodding movement, his gaze caught a familiar face—Lucy's friend whom he'd met.

Mustering his most charming smile, he stopped in front of her. She stood with another young woman who was taller, with reddish-blonde hair and a rather severe look. "Good evening, Miss Knox. I'm looking for your friend, Miss Parnell."

Miss Knox had a bright smile and lively eyes. "Ah yes, Dartford. Allow me to introduce Miss Ivy Breckenridge."

The tall blonde glared at him. He nearly recoiled at the disgust in her gaze. "I'm certain Miss Parnell has no interest in speaking with you."

Miss Knox clearly elbowed her friend in the side and whispered something Andrew couldn't hear but was fairly certain was "Be quiet!"

The two women could not be more different in their reception of him. Miss Knox had seemed quite welcoming, even pleased to see him. Miss Breckenridge, on the other hand, looked as if she might cheerfully lead him to his execution. His neck prickled. He directed his attention to the friendlier Miss Knox. "Is Miss Parnell here this evening? It's rather important that I speak with her."

"She is, in fact."

Now Miss Breckenridge elbowed Miss Knox. Andrew stifled a smile. They seemed like the perfect friends for Lucy—not the typical diffident young women who populated these sorts of events.

"Might I inquire where she is?" he asked.

Miss Breckenridge scowled. "No."

Miss Knox threw her a chiding glance. "She's dancing. And it's a rather long set, I think."

Damn. Andrew turned his head to look at the dance floor but couldn't see her. He looked back at the two women and smiled. "Thank you for your time."

He spun around and found a place where he could better survey the dance floor. It was a reel, and he scanned the dancers until he found her group. Seeing her… It was as if the breath had been sucked out of him.

He'd just seen her yesterday, but it was as if he'd forgotten how stunning she was. She wore a vibrant green gown with gold trim, and a gold band encircled her upswept dark hair. She looked elegant and beautiful, utterly feminine. And he wanted to pummel her dance partner. He craned his neck to see who it was. They were in a group, so he supposed it could be any of them.

Hell and the devil.

Greene was there. Was he her partner? Probably. Andrew circuited the dance floor, waiting impatiently for the set to end. He ended up near the doors leading to the terrace where he stood seething.

"My lord."

The feminine voice came from his left. He turned his head to see Miss Breckenridge eyeing him disdainfully.

"Miss Breckenridge, to what do I owe this…pleasure?" He wasn't in the mood to charm her. Besides, he had the distinct sense that she was immune.

"Let us walk to a more private location—closer to

the wall, if you please."

Andrew looked out at the dance floor and at potential places along the wall. His sight line might be impaired.

Her green eyes pierced him with their intensity. "My lord, *if you please.* This is a conversation I insist on having, and I won't do it here."

Resigned, he walked to the left of the terrace doors, near a potted tree. He turned, putting his back to the wall and made sure he could still see Lucy. "Will this do?"

She moved closer, taking a position beside him. "I came to ask you to leave Lucy alone." She kept her voice low, just above a whisper.

That she referred to her friend as Lucy drew his attention. Miss Breckenridge didn't mean this to be a formal, rule-abiding conversation.

"I came to speak with her about a matter of importance," he said. He inwardly flinched as Greene took Lucy's hand in the dance.

"Is it important enough that you would cause her distress in the delivery?"

He snapped his gaze to hers. "Perhaps you should progress directly to your point. You don't strike me as a woman to mince words."

She smiled, but he doubted it was prompted by humor or any sense of pleasantry. "You are very astute, my lord. Lucy is my very dear friend, and I don't wish to see her hurt by the likes of you. She deserves far better."

He agreed. "Yes, she does." Miss Breckenridge blinked, and he knew he'd caught her off guard. "*Is* she hurt, or are you protecting her from the potential?" He thought of how their walk had ended the day before, and while he knew she'd been angry, he hadn't considered that it might be more than that. He didn't *want* to consider it.

Miss Breckenridge's eyes narrowed, and there was a fire in their depths. "You used her and tossed her aside."

Bloody, bloody hell.

Was that how she felt—that he'd used her? "She told you that?" He looked out at the dance floor and saw Lucy laughing, her face glowing with pleasure. His chest tightened. He hated thinking that he'd hurt her.

"She told us enough. She doesn't deserve that kind of treatment."

No, she didn't. But he hadn't used her. He'd wanted her, and, yes, he'd probably taken advantage, but he hadn't used her. He had, however, tossed her aside—he wouldn't have put it quite so inelegantly, but there it was.

He'd thought she'd agreed that nothing had changed, that they were both still committed to independent lives. Except things *had* changed. He felt a dangerous connection to her. A connection that could threaten the carefully constructed wall of protection he'd built after his family had died.

His throat constricted, and he fought to take a deep breath. "I have nothing but the utmost esteem and admiration for Miss Parnell. Please excuse me."

He wanted to talk to Lucy, but he couldn't do it here. Had he hurt her? He needed to know. He also needed to warn her about Greene. He cut his way through the crowd, his mind made up.

He directed his driver to drop him at Bolton Street.

LUCY WATCHED HER grandmother begin to nod off as they rode home in the carriage from the ball. They'd stayed later than normal, and Lucy wondered if Grandmama would even make it upstairs without assistance.

"That was quite a successful evening." Grandmama's sudden declaration surprised Lucy, making her twitch.

"Did you have a good time?" Lucy asked.

"Oh yes, of course. But I meant you. You danced so much! I daresay this might finally be your year. Yes, I'll be shocked if Edgecombe doesn't come up to scratch."

Lucy had danced with him again, and while he was charming and pleasant, he wasn't Andrew. Unfortunately, she compared everyone to him.

"Who was the young gentleman you danced with—the tall one?"

Greene. Lucy had grown suspicious when he'd asked her to dance again. He still hadn't seemed to recognize her, but she'd gone out of her way to act incredibly feminine to be sure. She'd actually *simpered.* Or at least she'd tried. As with tittering, she didn't count simpering as one of her skills. "Mr. Greene," she belatedly answered.

"He's very attractive. You may inspire a battle." Grandmama's eyes gleamed with satisfaction in the lamplight.

Lucy didn't want a battle. She didn't want Edgecombe or Greene or anyone who wasn't Andrew. And she couldn't have him.

The coach stopped in front of the town house, and the footman helped Grandmama down. Lucy stepped out and took her grandmother's arm as they walked up to the door. The butler let them in, and Lucy escorted

Grandmama to her chamber where her maid was waiting to take over.

"She'll be asleep in a trice," Lucy whispered. The maid nodded.

Lucy yawned, thinking that she'd fall asleep quickly too. Good, she didn't want to lie awake thinking of Andrew.

She went to her chamber, closing the door behind her and immediately pulling the band from her hair. As she crossed the carpet to pass her bed on the way to her dressing area, she stopped short.

There, reclining on the bed, his cravat loosened and his coat nowhere to be seen—wait, it was on the back of a chair—was Andrew. His gaze connected with hers, and a fervent longing stabbed through her chest and spread heat lower.

She clutched the band with her fingertips and stared at him in shock. "What are you doing here?"

He uncrossed his legs and jumped up. "I came to see you."

She tried to ignore her attraction to him. It was incredibly difficult because he was almost unbearably handsome. His cravat was loose, exposing more of his neck than was appropriate. But then she supposed they'd moved quite past propriety, especially since he was standing in her bedroom. "How did you get in here?"

He gave a light shrug. "I'm sneaky. I saw your maid, but I convinced her I was here with your permission."

"You aren't."

"No." He came toward her slowly. "I saw you dancing with Greene."

"You were at the ball?" Her voice sounded a bit high to her ears.

"Yes. I went to find you."

He'd gone to the ball, and now he was here. Awareness danced along her flesh and flutters of desire careened in her belly. She turned from him and dropped her headband on her dressing table. "What's wrong?"

He'd moved close behind her—she could feel his proximity like a fire heating her back. "I believe Greene knows you're Smitty. I wanted you to be aware."

She turned. He was very close. She pressed her thighs back against the dressing table. "He told you?"

"No, but he's been acting odd." He scowled. "I nearly ruined everything at Darent Hall when I called you 'her'."

She arched a brow at him. "You ruined everything when you told them I was a physician."

His scowl deepened. "I apologized for that."

"Did you?" She honestly couldn't remember. "Anyway, it doesn't matter. What's done is done. I appreciate you sharing your suspicion. I shall take it under advisement."

His brows formed a V over his eyes. "What does that mean?"

She shrugged, perversely enjoying his agitation. "It means that I'll assess the situation for myself when I next see Greene." She ought to tell him she agreed with his assessment, that she'd wondered if Greene had seen through her disguise, but didn't want to give him the satisfaction.

He blinked. "You have plans to see him?"

Was he jealous? "Not specifically, no. Is there another reason you came to my bedchamber? You could just as easily have sent me a note about Greene."

"I could have, but I didn't wish to write it down."

She appreciated that.

They looked at each other without speaking. He seemed to be trying to determine what to say. Lucy, meanwhile, was trying not to throw her arms around his neck and kiss him.

At last he said, "I didn't like how our conversation ended yesterday."

Her breath stuttered in her chest. "How was that?"

"It was very…formal. Businesslike. And final."

Yes, it had been all those things—on purpose. "Should it have been something else?"

He edged closer. "Perhaps. Lucy… Did I hurt you?"

"No." She'd enjoyed every moment of their encounter at Darent Hall. She realized, stupidly, that he didn't mean it like that. He wanted to know if she was upset about the dissolution of their association. "We had a temporary arrangement. Things…progressed beyond what we would have imagined." She lifted her chin. "On the contrary, I'm grateful to you for the experiences we shared. Particularly since I doubt I'll be able to repeat them in the future."

"*Lucy.* I don't like thinking about you…alone. Never…" He didn't finish his statement, but she knew what he meant. She'd die a virgin, never knowing what it was like to truly lie with a man. The notion hadn't plagued her before, but now that she'd tasted pleasure with Andrew, she had to admit she didn't like thinking of that—being alone forever—either.

"Andrew, what are you doing here? Did you come to seduce me?" She prayed he didn't hear the hope in her voice. God help her, she wanted him, even if it was just for one night. One night that would provide the fodder for a lifetime of dreams.

He stroked the side of her face and gently tugged a

lock of her hair as he stroked it between his fingertips. "I didn't. But now that I am here, I am utterly captivated. I thought that maybe things had changed. Your friend Ivy, she approached me at the ball and told me to leave you alone."

Lucy thrilled to his touch, even if it was just her hair, and longed for him to cup the side of her face or pull her against him. Delicious anticipation stretched and grew between them.

"Ivy doesn't like men. I told her what happened, and she was horrified. She doesn't speak for me."

"I see." His Adam's apple bobbed as he swallowed. "In that case, I *could* seduce you. Even though I shouldn't."

Emboldened by his response, she laid her palm against his waistcoat over his heart. "Mayhap I'll seduce you."

His lips curved into a toe-curling smile. "I would expect nothing less from you, Lucy. You're the most extraordinary woman I've ever met."

His words heated every part of her. She pulled her gloves off in quick succession, never breaking eye contact. When her hands were bare, she curled them around his neck. "No one will bother us. You did tell my maid that you were here at my request?"

"I think I told her that her mistress said I should call on her at any time of day if I had something important to share."

Lucy stood on her toes and pulled his head down to hers. "This is very, very important."

"Very." His lips captured hers in a searing kiss, and his arms came around her, pulling her tight against his chest.

He felt like heat and man. He felt like home. She

kissed him with abandon, thrusting away all the reasons she shouldn't be doing this. Rules, she decided, weren't for her. She didn't need to preserve her reputation, not when she had no intention of marrying Edgecombe or anyone else. If she couldn't have Andrew, she didn't want anyone. But right now, Andrew was hers. And she meant to hold on to every moment that he was.

Lucy tugged at his cravat, loosening the knot until it gave way. She wound her hands in the ends of the silk, holding his neck down while he kissed her. His hands moved down her back and cupped her behind through her garments. He pulled her up against his groin. His cock pressed between her thighs, sending pulses of desire outward from her core.

She tossed his cravat away and unbuttoned his waistcoat, eager to feel his bare skin. Once she had the buttons free, she pushed the garment over his shoulders. A moment later, she felt his fingers along her back, plucking at the fastening of her gown.

He drew away from her with a groan. "Lucy. Are you certain?"

She nodded. "Never more."

She went to lock the door and when she returned his gaze raked her from her feet to the top of her head. "I'm so glad you're dressed as a woman. As much as I enjoyed disrobing you the other day—I'll admit there was something rather erotic about it—your feminine beauty takes my breath away."

His words enflamed her. She reached out and pulled his shirt from his waistband.

"You're so far ahead of me. It isn't fair." He picked her up and bore her to the bed, where he laid her carefully on the coverlet where he'd reclined earlier. Removing first one shoe and then the other, he tossed them to the floor. "I think I did that wrong," he said, frowning. "Stand up again." He helped her up, her stocking feet hitting the carpet beneath her bed.

"How do I take your dress off?"

"Over my head." She helped him pull the garment off, raising her hands while he swept the fabric over her head. This left her in a petticoat and stays, with her chemise and stockings beneath. "I think men's clothing is far easier."

He laughed. "You may be right. Still, this is incredibly arousing." He leaned forward and kissed the side of her neck, his lips and tongue devouring her flesh as he moved down along her collarbone.

Lucy curled her fingers around his head, holding him to her as sensation rushed to her breasts and far lower. He untied her petticoat and let it fall to the floor.

His hand came up and cupped her breast. She closed her eyes on a moan but jerked them back open before she completely lost herself. She turned, presenting her back so that he could unlace her stays.

He pulled at the cord, tugging and loosening until she felt it fall away from her back. He shoved the corset down, and she wriggled her hips until it slid down her legs, and she kicked it away.

"Do that again," he rasped, his mouth at the back of her neck.

"What?"

He clasped her hips and pulled her back against him. "Move like that."

She twitched her backside, and he groaned.

"God, Lucy." He kissed the back of her neck, his mouth open and hot, his tongue licking and enticing her. He wrapped his arm around her hips, holding her snug to his arousal. His other hand came up to cup her breast through her chemise. He squeezed and stroked her, his fingers pulling on her nipple.

His hand stole beneath the hem of her chemise and caressed her thigh, then her hip until his fingertips settled over her mound. "Open your legs." He spoke low and rough against her ear, his teeth tugged at the lobe.

She widened her stance, giving him access to her heated core. He swept his fingers against her, coaxing her, stirring her, driving her mad with need.

"You are so wet for me." He slipped a finger inside her, going slow and then pumping in and out.

She bent forward, clutching the coverlet for something to hold on to.

With his other hand, he pushed the back of the chemise up, exposing her spine. He tugged it off her completely, forcing her off balance as she lifted her arms. He caught her before she fell forward, wrapping his arm around her beneath her breasts. His hand continued its delicious assault on her womanhood, stroking her folds and thrusting inside her.

He caressed her breast, still supporting her, drawing on her nipple so that every bit of her was focused on his touch. She panted with need as her hips moved to the rhythm of his hand.

"If it wasn't your first time, I'd take you like this." His groin moved against her, sparking a flood of lust. He'd said she was wet, and now she felt even wetter. "*Lucy.*"

He kissed along her spine, his tongue tracing her flesh and making her shiver with need. He pumped his finger into her faster and tugged her nipple. His lips were at her ear once more. "Come, Lucy. Do you know what that means? Orgasm. Let go. Fall to pieces. I will pick every one of them up and put you back together again."

He suckled her neck and found that place that seemed to be the center of every sensation between her legs, and she did precisely what he asked. She fell utterly and completely into a thousand pieces.

He didn't leave her but kept his hand on her until her shudders slowed and the world came back to her. And what a world it was. Everything was warm and golden and replete.

"On the bed," he urged, his hand moving to her backside as she scrambled up onto the bed. "And take your hair down. I meant to do that before I was swept away."

He'd been swept away? Heat suffused her again. Her bones felt like liquid, but she plucked the pins from her hair and put them in a pile on the table next to the bed.

He perched on the edge of the mattress and pulled his boots and stockings off. She watched him as he worked, loving the play of muscles along his back, evident even beneath the lawn of his shirt.

Next, he removed his trousers and swiped his shirt over his head, exposing the smooth plane of his back. She sat up and brushed her fingers over him, unable to resist touching him.

He turned, coming over her and kissing her soundly, his tongue tangling with hers. She thrust her fingers into his hair, surprised that desire was once again pulsing through her. Was this normal? She'd felt utterly satisfied moments ago, and yet now she was desperate to feel him again. And she wanted to feel all of him. Inside her.

She broke the kiss and looked into his eyes. "You're not going to stop, are you?"

"Do you want me to?"

"No. If you try, I'll shoot you. And you know I won't miss."

"No, you won't." His eyes gleamed with admiration and promise. "I'm not stopping unless you tell me to."

"Good. What do I need to do?"

"Whatever you want. But I can't last much longer. You remember what happened before?"

She thought he was talking about what she'd done with her mouth and what he'd done with his…cock. "You…came?"

"Yes. I'm not going to do that inside you, though."

Because of a pregnancy. She nodded in understanding.

He knelt between her legs and thrust his hand into her hair, spreading it over the pillows. "I love your hair. It might be your best feature. Except for your eyes. They're so enchanting—full of intelligence and utterly provocative. No, maybe your lips. Whether they're arguing a fair point or locked with mine, I am captive." His gaze dropped to her chest, and his hands stroked downward until they cupped her breasts, kneading and stroking them. "These must be considered." He leaned down and suckled her, first one and then the other. She moaned, unable to help herself. "So lovely. There's also the curve of your stomach and the arc of your hip." His fingertip traced over her and then moved between her thighs again, brushing against her gently. "And this. I find I just can't decide."

"If I tell you that you can have all of it, will you stop this torture?"

He arched a brow at her. "You'd bribe me?"

"I'm a desperate woman." She was joking but serious at the same time. She wanted him with a power that almost frightened her. Why? Because she felt exposed. Vulnerable. Things she hated feeling but didn't seem to mind with him.

"No more so than I." He fell on her, kissing her savagely, his hand working her flesh, pushing her back up the mountain of pleasure. He settled between her thighs, and his cock nudged her opening.

She reached between them and touched him, stroking the smooth softness of his shaft. She wanted to feel him inside her. She was more than ready.

His hand grazed hers as he positioned himself. Slowly, he pressed inside, all the while kissing her. She moaned into his mouth, and he stopped.

"Are you all right?" he asked, looking down at her with concern.

"I'm fine. Can you…go faster?"

He grinned. "I could, but I was trying to be gentle."

She reached around and clasped his backside, pulling him down. "I appreciate that, but I *need* you. All of you. Please."

"Lucy, you astonish me." He smoothed her hair back from her face as he slid completely inside her, his eyes never leaving hers.

She felt full and wonderful, but it wasn't enough. "Move."

"This is why I adore you, Lucy. You ask for what you want." He pulled back briefly before thrusting forward again. "Hold on to me."

She did as he bade, clutching at his back as he moved between her legs. He went slowly at first and then more quickly, creating an exquisite friction that was similar to what she'd felt earlier but intensified. Pleasure and need mingled and built. She closed her eyes and gave herself over to the sensations.

"Shhh." He took her mouth in a blistering kiss. Had she been making noise? Probably. She was absolutely senseless.

Pressure built in her core, she squeezed her legs tight around his waist, and her muscles began to contract. Bliss washed over her as she crested the mountain.

"*Lucy.*" He gripped her thighs and pulled out of her, leaving her bereft.

She clutched at his shoulders. "Come back."

Wetness spilled on her stomach.

"I can't." He spoke between pants, the words coming hard and rough. "I told you."

Yes, he had. He'd just failed to mention that it would be a trifle disappointing.

He sat up. "I need a…cloth."

Yes, they did. "Over in that cabinet with the ewer." Where she washed up.

He found the cloths and gave one to her while he tidied himself. "And I should put this…"

She stood up from the bed, her muscles feeling delightfully lethargic. "I'll take it." She stashed them back in the cabinet and made a mental note to launder them herself.

His gaze was a bit uncertain as he regarded her. She took his hand and led him back to the bed, pulling back the coverlet in invitation.

"Will you stay, just for a little while?" she asked.

She slipped into the bed nude, marveling at how scandalous yet wonderful it felt. When he joined her, he pulled her against him and kissed her temple. She couldn't help but think of their night together at Darent Hall and recall how much she'd enjoyed sleeping next to someone. Next to him.

Her lids were heavy, and she let them close. "I fear

I'm going to fall asleep."

"I won't, don't worry."

She nuzzled his chest. "Will you sneak away, or will you give me the satisfaction of throwing you out?"

He chuckled, and she felt the slight rumble against her cheek. "I'll give you any satisfaction you desire. I promise I won't leave without waking you."

She yawned, losing her thread on consciousness. The last thought she had before falling asleep was about how lovely it was to feel his heart beating right next to her.

Chapter Sixteen

ANDREW WASN'T SURE how long he dozed, but it was still dark when he woke up with Lucy curled against him, her back flush to his chest. He inhaled the scent of her—flowers and spice, clove to be exact. He buried his face in her hair. He really did love it.

She was warm and soft against him, and he didn't want to leave. But he had to. Soon. He could hold her a little longer.

What the hell was he doing? He'd come to ensure she was all right after their encounter at Darent Hall and to tell her about Greene. He'd never meant to make love to her. Hell and damnation, he'd never taken a woman's virginity before. He was a cad. A reprobate. An absolute beast.

And yet he couldn't bring himself to regret it. She'd been very clear about wanting him to stay, and he didn't think she'd regret it either. Particularly since she'd also clearly stated that nothing had changed between them. She was content to move forward as she'd intended—alone.

Was he?

Contentment wasn't an emotion he remembered feeling. Consequently, he wasn't sure if he'd recognize it if it came along. He definitely, however, preferred to remain alone.

He looked down at her sleeping face, her dark lashes curled against her cheek. He said he'd wake her, but he didn't want to disturb such loveliness. He'd just kiss her good-bye, and if she woke up, well…

He brushed her hair back from her temple and kissed her there. Then he kissed the outer shell of her ear. Then he kissed her jaw. She snuggled back against him, and he went from half-erect to completely hard.

Yes, he should go.

Instead, he kissed her neck, using his teeth and tongue to nip and lick her. He cupped her breast and stroked the nipple, pulling and caressing.

She wriggled her backside against him—just as she'd done earlier. He closed his eyes in ecstasy and sighed her name.

"It's not my first time," she said, her voice even deeper and raspier than usual, but not at all like Smitty. "Do what you wanted to before."

Take her from behind? His cock grew as he envisioned himself thrusting into her as the muscles of her back flexed. "Are you sure?"

She looked at him over her shoulder, her lids heavy, her eyes dusky with sleep and desire. "Have I ever given you cause to find me indecisive?"

He chuckled. "No."

She reached back and stroked his thigh. "Tell me what to do."

"For now, just feel." He lowered his hand from her breast and found her sweetest spot, teasing her flesh into arousal. He worked relentlessly until she was panting with pleasure.

"Please."

Her soft plea fired his senses. He clasped her thigh and guided it up, pushing her knee toward her chest and opening her legs. He moved his hand to caress her from behind, slowly at first, to acclimate her. She wriggled her backside again, and he smiled to himself. Then he plunged his finger inside her and relished her answering gasp. He thrust into her as he rose up on his elbow and kissed her neck. He sucked her flesh, loving the taste of her.

She jerked her hips back, seeking more of him. He gave her two fingers, and she lifted her backside. He kept up his pace until she cried out, her muscles tensing around him.

"On your knees, love." He helped her rise up and palmed his cock, more than ready to claim her.

Her hair fell over her shoulder and fanned across her upper back as she came up on all fours. "Is this right?" she asked huskily.

"It's perfect. You're perfect." He caressed her back, dragging his fingertips from her nape to the base of her spine.

Gripping his cock, he positioned himself at her entrance. He reached around and fondled her breast before clasping her hip and easing into her. He intended to go slow, but she thrust back, taking him fully inside. She was so wet and tight. He closed his eyes and tried very hard not to come.

She moved her backside again in that damnably provocative way that was even more stimulating when he was filling her. Then she moved, sliding forward and then pushing back. Good God, she was impossibly wonderful.

"Lucy. You're going to kill me."

"I hope it's a pleasant death."

He couldn't help but grin. This woman was more than he dared dream. More than he dared risk.

She rocked forward and back, driving him to the brink of madness. He lost rational thought and leaned forward, winding his hand in her hair and twisting her head so that he could kiss her, his tongue spearing into her mouth with savage need. She kissed him back as long as she could until another orgasm racked her body and she had to pull away, gasping for breath and moaning in the most delicious way.

Hellfire, he was so close. He had to get out now before he completely lost his mind. But she felt so good…*he'd* never felt this good…

He held her hips and snapped his pelvis, driving into her with a staccato rhythm. His balls tightened and his orgasm rushed over him. He managed to pull out of her and turn, spilling himself into his hand and onto the bed. Damn, he was making a mess.

When he was finished and his body had come back to a semblance of normalcy, he clambered off the bed and went to the cabinet to fetch another towel. He only had himself to tidy this time. He stashed the cloth back where she'd put the others.

He watched her roll over and took in the satiated expression on her face. Her eyes were half-closed, her lips curved into a smile. She looked content.

There was that word again. That sensation he wasn't sure he'd ever felt. Or maybe he had. It had just been so long that he didn't remember. Like love. He wasn't sure he recalled the emotion, just the pain and longing he'd felt in the aftermath of losing it. The pain and longing he still felt.

His chest tightening, he went to find his clothing and began to dress.

"You're leaving now?" She'd slipped under the covers and held them to her chest.

He could still see a good portion of one breast, however. He was grateful for the view. "Yes, before I decide not to leave at all."

She smiled. "You could stay—for at least an hour.

You seemed to be sleeping well. No nightmares."

No, no nightmares. But then he didn't have them often anymore. Except when he was at Darent Hall. The first night he stayed there on a visit, he always had one. Which was why he rarely went there. He couldn't believe he hadn't thought of that before he'd invited her to stay. He'd either been too shaken up by the accident or too overcome with desire for her. The latter, he decided. Definitely.

"I don't have them very often," he said.

"What happened in the morning…you looked…haunted. Is that typical after you have a nightmare?"

"No," he lied. And he didn't even need a nightmare to feel like that. In fact, those bleak emotions were creeping over him right now. He had his trousers on and pulled on his shirt. Locating his stockings and boots, he sat on a chair to don them.

She climbed out of bed and walked, nude, to an armoire. He tried not to stare at the alluring sweep of her back and the tantalizing curve of her backside and failed miserably. She pulled out a pale yellow dressing gown and wrapped it around herself, shielding her from his hungry gaze.

He forced himself back to putting on his footwear.

She walked over to stand near him. "I'm not sure I believe you," she said softly. "Mrs. Alder cares about you. She said you deserve to be happy, that you need to forget about the past."

He pulled on his boots and didn't look at her. "I don't think about it." He *tried* not to think about it. He started to shake, his flesh feeling chilled. Jumping to his feet, he tucked in his shirt and sought out his waistcoat.

"Maybe you should? Maybe talking about them

would help you move past the tragedy so that it doesn't haunt you."

He shrugged into his waistcoat. "There's nothing to talk about."

Her gaze was full of concern and pity. He didn't want her pity. "Your entire family died within a span of a few weeks. You were young. There's plenty to talk about. I'm here to listen if you'll let me."

Ice coated his spine, and his vision tunneled for a moment. He plucked his cravat from the floor and wound it around his neck but didn't tie it. He had to walk past her to get his coat and hat. "Please leave it alone."

He moved toward his coat, and she clasped his forearm—gently but firmly. "Tell me about them. Your mother, your father, your brother."

The thought of Bertie nearly drove him to his knees. His brother had been so scared, but then he'd tried to be brave for Andrew. Andrew had sat there, helpless, while they'd all died. But Bertie, more than the others, cut him to the bone. He'd looked up to Andrew, and Andrew had said he'd always protect him. He'd told him that just before he'd died—*"I'll save you, Bertie."* Even though he'd known it was too late. Logically he knew that no one blamed him, but he still felt such immeasurable guilt.

"Tonight," he rasped into the cool, nearly dark room. "My brother will never have a night like this. My sisters will never have children to love. Why was I blessed? What did I do to deserve to live while they died?"

She wound her fingers through his. Her eyes were wide and so rich with emotion. "Nothing. There's no reason. Will you let me help you make peace with this?"

"I can't. There's no peace. And there shouldn't be. I can't…I can't let them go. I'm all they have left." He pulled his hand from hers and snatched his coat and hat from the chair. He didn't look at her as he swept past. He stopped at the door but didn't turn to face her. "You can't help me, Lucy. No one can."

He left, closing the door behind him.

Taking deep, gulping breaths, Andrew stole down the back stairs, the way he'd come in earlier with a bit of assistance from Lucy's maid. Now it was dark and quiet, just the way he preferred things when he was feeling like this—as if a great weight pressed upon his chest and might crush him into oblivion. But wasn't that what he wanted? Hadn't he wished for a way to bury his thoughts and be free of the guilt because he'd lived?

He walked briskly through the bowels of the town house to the front, where he let himself out and climbed up to the street. It was very late or maybe terribly early. Whatever it was, he wouldn't find a hack. It was cold and damp, having rained earlier. He pulled the collar of his coat up and tugged his hat lower over his brow.

It seemed as though his episodes were growing worse. He thought he'd conquered the debilitating terror that came over him when he thought of his family too closely. He'd learned to keep them at bay, to occupy his time with activity and the pursuit of adventure.

He'd done such a good job that he had trouble conjuring his brother's face and voice. They were hazy, growing hazier by the year. And his sisters were all but lost to him now, their singsong voices indeterminate in his memory. The panic seized him again, that helpless feeling that he was chained to a rock while water rushed in, drowning him.

Stop thinking about them. Think about something jolly. Think about what you're doing next. Parachuting.

Yes, parachuting. He'd be going up with Sadler again in a few days, and if the conditions were favorable, he'd parachute. He'd meet with him the day after tomorrow and review the procedure. *Yes, parachuting.*

With each step, the darkness seeped away, leaving him numb and hollow. Later, when he was finally abed as the dawn began creeping over the horizon, he relaxed. His body felt like lead, deliciously heavy and without feeling. As he closed his eyes, his mind was blissfully blank. But as he drifted to sleep, he smelled flowers and clove and tasted heaven on his lips.

AS HE TYPICALLY did after a nightmare, Andrew slept rather late. He hadn't, however, had a nightmare. He'd suffered an attack, but once he'd fallen asleep, he'd dreamed. Of his family and Lucy, and it hadn't ended badly with cold and darkness and that horrible pain that left him feeling hollow.

Tindall brought him something to eat along with his mail. Andrew ate ravenously and then picked through his correspondence. The third letter he opened made his blood run cold.

Dartford,
I know that Smitty is really Miss Parnell. If you'd like this to remain a secret, deliver five thousand pounds in a package addressed to Mr. Black to the head footman at Boodle's by five o'clock. I should

hate for her to be ruined by your inaction.
Yours,
Mr. Black

The ice in Andrew's veins melted as hot anger poured through him. How dare this man threaten Lucy? And demand money from him? He crumpled the paper in his fist.

Black.

Andrew didn't know anyone named Black. He did, however, know someone named Greene. It seemed to be too much of a coincidence—both names being colors—but perhaps it wasn't.

He stood up and bellowed for Tindall. He didn't know where Greene would be at this hour, but he'd run him to ground.

It took him well over an hour, but Andrew finally caught up with Greene at a coffee shop on St James's. He sat with two other gentlemen at a table and looked up when Andrew approached.

"Dart, what a pleasure to see you here. Join us."

Andrew barely kept his temper in check. "I need a word. Privately."

Greene's brow tipped low. He flicked a glance at his tablemates. "Please excuse me." He rose and motioned for Andrew to follow him to the back of the shop, where he led him into a small chamber that looked to be some sort of retiring room.

Without preamble, Andrew glared at him, his lip curling. "I received your letter. You'll extort no money from me, nor will you expose Miss Parnell. Give me your word right now, or I'll summon a second."

Greene stared at him, his gaze…confused? "I didn't send you a letter about Miss Parnell. What are you talking about?"

He seemed genuinely perplexed, which sucked the vitriol right out of Andrew. "I thought…that is, you didn't send me a letter?"

He looked offended, his eyes narrowing. "No. Nor would I extort money from you. I'm aghast—and outraged on your behalf—that someone would. I'm doubly angry that anyone would target Miss Parnell. I hold her in high esteem."

Greene spoke of her as if he didn't realize she was also Smitty. Or else he was an exceptionally good actor.

Andrew narrowed his eyes at Greene. "You don't know what this is about?"

"I'm unaware of anything to do with Miss Parnell that would be worth exposing, but judging from your behavior, there clearly is." Greene's brow furrowed. "I don't wish to pry, but if there's any way I can help, I should like to do so. As I said, I hold Miss Parnell in high regard, and I consider you a friend."

A friend.

The word made Andrew mildly uncomfortable. Yes, he had friends, but he kept them at a distance. And he didn't ask them for help. This felt too close—too much like something he could look forward to and miss if it were gone.

Like Lucy.

A knot formed in his throat. He swallowed. He coughed. He didn't know what to say about their friendship, so he addressed Greene's other comment instead. "You say you hold Miss Parnell in high esteem. Do you wish to…court her?"

Greene blinked. "I, ah, no." Then Greene laughed, and Andrew was suddenly confused. "Because you are my friend, I'll tell you *my* secret. As I told you and the others, I go to balls and dance with an array of misses to please my parents. Miss Parnell is charming in a way most of those misses are not, and that is why I sought her out last night. I am not interested in pursuing a romantic relationship with her. I was, *however*, interested in Smitty, and I'm disappointed he moved away."

Andrew felt like an ass for at least the second time that week. "I didn't realize."

Not only had Greene not penned the letter, he didn't even know that Lucy and Smitty were one and the same.

"Of course you didn't," Greene said. "I don't advertise my preference for men." He tipped his head to the side with a thoughtful expression. "If you thought I'd written the letter, you decided it had to be someone you know. Is it possible they're from our set?"

Their *set.* It was like the word friend. It made Andrew feel connected, and the sensation was odd. It wasn't, however, distasteful, which was both shocking and frustrating. He liked his isolation. Things were much simpler, and there was less potential for loss.

He forced himself back to the conversation and the fact that Greene had made an excellent point. Andrew had assumed that Greene was the extortionist based on his behavior, but now that he understood Greene's interest in Smitty, he was fully satisfied that Greene was innocent. Which meant it was another of Andrew's "friends." But who? He considered sharing the letter with Greene, but then Lucy's secret would be out, and he couldn't do that.

"You're correct," Andrew said. "It has to be one of our…set."

Greene exhaled. "I'll be honest, Dart. When I think

of who might resort to extortion, Charles immediately comes to mind. I don't know him as well as you, but his gambling seems to be a problem."

It was, but Andrew didn't want to think Charles would do that. Beaumont? Andrew didn't want to think it was him either. Thursby? Again, Andrew would be surprised…and disappointed. Why, because they were friends? Hell, how had he let any of this happen? He didn't want to care about people. He'd promised himself all those years ago that he'd remain stoic and alone.

Only he wasn't stoic, and it seemed he wasn't alone. He had these *friends*. And Lucy. He'd thought he could push her away and guard himself from further heartache. But when he thought of her being hurt by this person who would expose her secrets, he realized it was too late. He already cared far too much.

"Dart?" Greene prompted. "What are you going to do?"

His mind was racing, and at the same time, he was fighting to take a breath. "I won't be extorted." But neither could he allow Lucy's secret to be exposed.

"If I might offer an opinion—and do tell me if I've interpreted this wrong. This secret, whatever it is, has to do with Miss Parnell, and you are clearly regarded as someone who can protect her. Given your query about my interest in her, I think I can deduce that you *are* interested in courting her. Or perhaps you're considering the ultimate protection. Perhaps you should ask her to be your wife."

Andrew's vision tunneled briefly. "I don't…I don't know if that would be an acceptable solution." For her or for him.

Greene straightened, his gaze direct. "Is there some

reason you can't marry her?"

There were many. Or maybe just one rather large reason: fear. Andrew swallowed, his throat feeling raw. "You've given me something to think about. Thank you."

He turned and made his way from the coffee shop, his mind reeling from what seemed an obvious solution. If he married her, he'd be able to protect her from whatever this Mr. Black might say, and he'd ensure her future—and that of her grandmother—was secure.

A part of him thrilled to the idea. He loved being with her, and the thought of sharing adventures with her, including in the bedchamber, filled him with anticipation. The rest of him was paralyzed with the fear of losing her.

He didn't know if it was a risk he could take.

Chapter Seventeen

LUCY SPENT THE day in a bit of a haze. She'd slept later than usual, waking to a feeling of utter contentment and languor. Until she'd recalled how Andrew had left. It had been the reverse of what had happened at Darent Hall, but it felt the same.

No, it felt worse because now she knew she loved him.

She pulled on her gloves as she waited for Grandmama to come down. They were going to the park because it was perhaps the nicest day in what had so far been a rather wretched spring.

For the hundredth time, she told herself she'd been a fool to succumb to Andrew's charms last night, and for the hundredth time, she argued that she hadn't succumbed to anything but her own heart's desire. And she refused to regret it.

She tied her bonnet beneath her chin with determination. Nothing had changed. She was not some pathetic miss who would crumble to pieces over a man.

Grandmama came down the stairs outfitted for their ride in the park. Lucy smiled at her, glad for the opportunity to put Andrew from her mind. "You look lovely, Grandmama. I've always admired that hat." It sported a gorgeous violet ribbon as well as a cluster of faux violets that appeared absolutely real.

"Thank you, dear." She stepped into the hall and looked Lucy over from head to foot. "You'll do, but I do wish you had a new walking dress." She shook her head and made a clucking sound with her tongue. "I'll be much happier when you are wed and have a man to take care of you as you deserve."

Lucy appreciated that her grandmother wanted the best for her—they just disagreed about what that was. "A new dress will not make me happy."

Grandmama pursed her lips. "So you say. I cannot understand your independent ideas. I know you haven't been raised with the best example of manliness." She exhaled. "Your father, God rest his soul, allowed his vices to take control of him. You won't marry a man like him." She gave Lucy an earnest look. "You do realize not all men are like him—or like your grandfather?"

She did, but as she'd learned from her experience with Andrew, they likely had some problem or another. The question was whether she wanted to deal with them. Damn, there she went thinking about him again.

"I know, Grandmama. Are you ready?" Lucy hoped the conversation would die a swift death.

"Yes, let's be on our way."

Burton opened the door, and a footman helped them into their coach, an ancient contraption—ancient being at least twenty years old—that creaked and wobbled excessively. The footman had tried to repair it, but the mechanics were beyond his expertise. He wasn't even a coachman, but they couldn't afford one of those.

Once they were ensconced inside and the vehicle had lurched forward, Grandmama angled toward her. "Who do you hope to see this afternoon? Edgecombe? Or maybe Dartford? I like him."

It seemed Lucy wouldn't be able to forget about him today. She ought to have known better. Even without Grandmama asking about him, he was clearly hovering about her head.

"I'd prefer to just walk with my friends." Lucy expected she'd see Aquilla but never knew when Ivy might be there. She and Lady Dunn kept a less predictable schedule, much like Lucy and her grandmother.

Grandmama sighed. "It's no wonder you aren't married. You must engage with these gentlemen, or you'll be a spinster."

Lucy bit her tongue lest she point out that she already *was* a spinster. "I don't need to marry, nor do I want to. I have an excellent plan to move us to Bath. I found a charming cottage today, and I've already written to the owner."

Grandmama frowned. "How can we possibly afford that? I've already told you that I don't have enough to support you."

"I know, but I've saved up enough of my own money, and I'm going to invest a small sum. I won't be buying any walking dresses, but I don't have need of them anyway."

Grandmama leaned back on the seat, her hand fluttering to her chest. "My dear, I can't believe you'd choose that over a future with a man like Dartford. Sometimes I wonder how we are related, but then I remember who your mother was."

Lucy knew her grandmother meant no insult. Grandmama and her mother hadn't been close, but Grandmama had respected her son's choice in wife, and she'd even remarked that it had been good for him to marry such a strong woman. Indeed, she and Lucy had discussed on a few occasions that if Lucy's mother hadn't died, gambling might not have consumed her father. It was tragic how death could alter a person's course in life. Such as how it had affected Andrew. If he hadn't lost his family, he might not have pushed Lucy away. Twice.

Forever.

Her throat felt tight as they drove into the park. She didn't want to think about him, but she couldn't seem to help it. She supposed that was what happened when one was in love.

The footman drove them to where the carriages stood. Lucy looked for her friends, eager to disembark and take a brisk walk to ease the turmoil inside her. Grandmama would stay in the coach and visit with passing acquaintances.

Though she didn't see Aquilla or Ivy, Lucy stepped from the vehicle. They'd be along presently, she was certain. She pivoted toward the gate to watch for their arrival.

"Look, Lucy," Grandmama said from inside the coach, pointing behind Lucy. "Here comes Dartford."

Lucy turned and saw that Andrew was coming straight for her. What the devil was he about *now*? Anger and frustration welled with hurt and longing. She didn't want to see him. Especially not here, in a rather public setting, where she couldn't tell him to leave her alone.

Well, she *could*, just not in the volume she might have desired.

As he came toward her, she thought of that morning in the park with him, when they'd raced in his phaeton. How glorious and exhilarating it had been. She nearly smiled at the memory, until she remembered that she wanted to be irritated at him.

"Miss Parnell," he said, stopping before her. He looked toward the coach with a wide, handsome smile.

"Lady Parnell. It's surely too fine a day to remain inside?"

Grandmama wave her hand at him, chuckling. "Don't you bother with me. Take my granddaughter for a promenade."

"I shall be honored." He offered his hand to Lucy and looked down at her. "May I?"

Lucy wanted to say no, but if she went with him, she could tell him to leave her alone—for good. Then she could tell Grandmama to stop pairing them off.

"Yes." She hissed the word at him and reluctantly took his arm.

Once they were on their way, he said, "You're angry with me again."

"I'm not angry with you. I *dislike* you. There's a difference."

"You dislike me now?" He sounded surprised.

"Is there a reason I shouldn't?"

He seemed to ponder this for a moment as they took several steps along the path. They passed another couple and nodded at them.

"Not that I can think of, unfortunately. I suppose it's too much to ask for us to be friends?"

"Andrew—*Dartford*—what do you want?" It no longer signified. "Never mind. I don't care what you want. I'd like you to leave me alone. Don't ask me to promenade. Don't ask me to dance. And *don't* show up in my bedchamber uninvited." She felt him flinch as she said the last.

"You regret last night." He didn't frame it as a question.

"I don't, but I should regret a repeat occurrence." She longed to rail at him. With every step, she was reminded of how much she enjoyed being with him, how she was willing to take a chance on a future she didn't expect to want, how painfully she loved him.

And how he shared none of those sentiments.

He drew her off the path so that they were away from people but not out of sight. He turned to her and looked into her eyes. If she didn't know better, she'd say he looked nervous. Or unsettled. Or anxious.

"Lucy, what would you say if I asked you to marry me?"

She stared at him, unable to summon a thought. Or a word. Or any kind of reaction.

She had to have misheard him. "I beg your pardon?"

"I know you said you didn't wish to marry, but it seems you might have changed your mind."

He was right, but she didn't want to admit it. His question had been odd. She tried to discern what was going on behind his dark eyes. She withdrew her hand from his arm. "Is that a proposal?" She wasn't at all sure that it was.

He hesitated, but only a moment. "Yes." He clasped her fingers in his. "I want you to be my countess."

She suffered another moment of shock when words and thought utterly deserted her again. Her breath caught, and then her heart sped as joy spilled through her. Her brain, however, remained detached. She simply didn't comprehend why he was asking this now. "Why? If it's because of what happened last night, there's no need for us to marry."

"What if there's a child?"

Now it was her turn to feel anxious. "You took precautions."

"Nothing's foolproof."

She relinquished the sensation of anxiety in favor of annoyance. "You're asking because of a very small possibility that I'm with child. No, thank you."

He exhaled. He squeezed her fingers. "I'm asking because I want to. I've never met anyone who made me think twice about marriage. Until you." His eyes darted to the right and left. "If there weren't so many damn people here, I'd take you in my arms and kiss you until you agreed."

Heat suffused her, and now her ire gave way to something far hotter—desire. He wanted to marry her. She honestly didn't know what to say.

"You're killing me." His words came out as a near growl. "Are you going to leave me wondering?"

"I should. You deserve that and more."

His thumb stroked the back of her hand. "I do. You could spend the rest of our lives making me suffer."

She couldn't help it. She smiled. Until her cheeks hurt. She loved him so much. He hadn't said he loved her, but she knew he at least liked and admired her. An echo from the past warned her to be careful—that he could hurt her as her father had—but she silenced the dissenting voice. The future she never imagined was in front of her now, and she wanted it.

"I'll marry you." As soon as she said the words, giddy happiness swelled in her chest. She never thought to say those words, let alone to a man she loved.

He brought her hand to his lips and kissed the inside of her wrist. "Thank you."

He sounded relieved. Was he as happy as she was? A shadow crept over her jubilation.

"Dartford!"

They both turned their heads at the sound of his name. It was Charles, his long strides devouring the path and then veering away from it as he came toward them.

"Good afternoon, Charles," Andrew said. He still held Lucy's hand. "Do you know Miss Parnell?"

Charles inclined his head toward her. He looked a trifle unkempt—his hair, usually teased and styled, was rather flat, and his cravat was askew. "We met a few years ago. I'm not sure Miss Parnell remembers."

She hadn't before, but now that he mentioned it, she recalled being introduced at a house party she'd attended with Aquilla and her family. In fact, she thought he'd invited her to play Blind Man's Bluff, and she'd declined in favor of riding. In retrospect, she was glad he hadn't recognized her while she'd been dressed as a man. "I do remember, Mr. Charles. How lovely to see you again."

He frowned at her before turning his attention to Andrew. "I hate to have this conversation in front of her, but I'm afraid I'm rather desperate. Did you receive the note from Mr. Black?"

Andrew's hand went tense in hers. "Yes. What do you know of it?" The question was razor-sharp.

Charles's mouth was drawn tight, his posture stiff. "I regret to say that I am Mr. Black. I need that money, Dart." He twisted his hands together. "Why didn't you send it to the club as I asked?"

Andrew let go of her hand and took a step forward. He grabbed Charles's lapel. "*You're* Black? *You* threatened her? I ought to call you out, you miserable piece of offal."

Lucy clasped Andrew's forearm—the one that wasn't gripping Charles. "Andrew, stop! You can't do that here."

"You don't know what he's done." He didn't take his eyes from Charles. "I'm not giving you a shilling."

Charles's gaze flicked to Lucy for just a moment.

"Dart, please. I don't want to expose her."

Lucy froze. She stared at Andrew, unable to look at Charles. "What is he talking about?"

Andrew spared her only the briefest of glances. "He threatened to expose you as Smitty unless I gave him five thousand pounds." He snarled at Charles and tightened his grip. "You won't say anything. She's going to be my countess—no one will believe what you say. Good God, man, are you really in such dire straits? I thought we were friends."

Charles's pallor took on a grayish tinge, and he seemed to shrink. Andrew finally let go of him, shoving at his chest as he did so.

After stumbling backward, Charles regained his footing. "I'm a dead man, then," he whispered.

Lucy watched the light go out of Charles's eyes, and she felt a surge of pity. His excessive gambling had led her to dislike him, but now she regretted that. He was deeply troubled—as her father had been. She thought of all the times her father had been in debt and of the things he'd had to sell to keep himself out of prison.

She looked at Charles. "Will you be arrested?"

"Worse. I borrowed money from a dangerous fellow. Apparently, he works for Gin Jimmy."

Andrew shook his head. "Hellfire, Charles."

Lucy looked between them before settling on Andrew. "Who's that?"

"A notorious criminal. I saw him once when I ventured into St. Giles. It was another of my daring adventures."

"That's one of the most dangerous places in London." Lucy hadn't realized the extent of his activities. She'd thought climbing the dome of St. Paul's or ballooning was risky enough, but entering St.

Giles was positively deadly. Or it could have been. "You're mad," she breathed, momentarily losing track of the current conversation.

"He's going to kill me," Charles said. "If I don't give him the money tomorrow."

Andrew wiped a hand over his eye and moved toward Charles. "We'll work this out. Meet me at my town house."

Charles nodded, then looked at Lucy. "My apologies, Miss Parnell. I'm not proud of what I did. I liked you. Rather, I liked Smitty." He hung his head as he turned and walked away.

Andrew touched her hand, but she drew it away. "Where will you be tonight? I'll come find you."

Cold realization knifed through her. There *had* been something off with his proposal. "No. Please don't."

He looked momentarily perplexed. "All right. Tomorrow, then?"

As much as she appreciated what he was trying to do, she couldn't continue with the ruse. Not when she knew he was haunted. He didn't want a family, not after losing one. And given how averse she'd been to a potential husband who was no better than her father—not that Andrew was necessarily that man—she understood. "No. You don't really want to marry me. You did it because of that threat. Don't deny it, because I know it's true."

The muscles along his jaw tightened. "I thought it would solve a great many things, including our mutual attraction. I meant it when I said I didn't like thinking of you alone."

Sadness engulfed her, and for the first time, she fully comprehended what that meant. Now that she'd had a glimpse of what it might have been like to share her life with someone she loved, alone seemed a far worse fate than it had before. Still, she had to let him go.

"Yet, alone is a state that's perfect for you, isn't it? You've made that more than clear. I do appreciate you trying to protect me." She allowed a small smile as the last of her hope slipped into the past. "I'm glad you're going to help Charles. It will be good for you. Maybe you can start to heal."

His forehead pleated as his brows slashed over his eyes. He looked as though he might speak, but in the end, he said nothing.

"Good-bye, Andrew."

She turned and left him in the park, along with the greatest happiness she'd ever known.

ANDREW WATCHED HER go, unable to find the words to ask her to stay. He ought to feel relieved that he didn't need to marry her. Instead, he felt numb.

Numb was good, wasn't it? It was certainly better than the agony of loss.

He strode across the park, ignoring the paths so that he could avoid talking to people, and made his way to his town house. He'd deal with Charles first. Then he'd think about Lucy. Maybe. A part of him didn't want to. The part of him that said it was better to go on without her. Alone. As he'd planned.

His gait slowed as he approached his house. Was he really alone? He'd worked so hard to keep people from getting too close, to keep relationships simple and easy. In school, he hadn't attached to any particular group of friends, and he'd tried to do the same in adulthood. He even went so far as to hire a new valet periodically.

How, then, had he ended up with a group of friends and with Lucy?

Because maybe it was time. Maybe he'd suffered with the guilt and the fear long enough.

Probably. But his attacks had only grown worse recently, which would lead him to believe the opposite. He needed to evict all these people from his life.

Andrew's butler, Roland, opened the door. "My lord. Mr. Charles is in the drawing room."

Andrew nodded as he stalked to the stairs and walked up to the first floor. Charles stood in front of the window, staring down at the street. He turned as Andrew came into the room.

"You look terrible," Andrew said as he went to the sideboard and poured two glasses of whiskey. He went to Charles and handed him one.

Charles glanced down at Andrew's glass. "Not gin?"

Andrew shrugged. "I felt like something different." He wanted to embrace change and starting with his choice of liquor seemed a step in the right direction. He'd grown too comfortable with people, allowing them too close, and he blamed the recent severity and frequency of his attacks on his complacency.

Charles threw back the entire pour. "Thank you. I really am sorry about Miss Parnell." He looked pained. Haunted, even.

Andrew sipped the whiskey. It was fine, but he missed his gin. "How did you get yourself into this predicament?"

"You know me." He gave a half smile. "I can't seem to say no to a wager."

"Was this at a hell?"

He nodded. "I was in deep one night, and a fellow offered to spot me. Somehow it grew to five thousand." He looked toward the windows, his cheeks turning red.

Andrew resisted the urge to throttle him. How many times had he tried to steer Charles down the right path? "Your father has no idea, I take it."

"No, and I can't ask him. He'll cut me off entirely. Then he'll marry me off to some chit in a backward hamlet so far from London that I'll perish of boredom."

"Wouldn't that be better than actually dying, which I believe is a risk given what you said at the park and given what you dared to do? To *me*." Andrew didn't bother masking his scorn. "Your purported friend."

Charles winced. "I was desperate. You've been nothing but kind and supportive—a true friend."

"So if you don't pay this money, one of Gin Jimmy's ruffians will kill you."

"That is what he said, yes. 'He' being the man who loaned me the money." Charles looked down at the empty glass in his hand. "I'm doomed."

Andrew didn't want Charles to die. Yes, he'd allowed the fool too close to him, and he couldn't let him die. "I'm going to give you the money, but you're going to leave London. Tell your father you need to rehabilitate yourself—he'll admire that."

Charles blinked at him. "You'd do that? But where am I to go?"

Andrew steeled himself against the emotions in Charles's voice—happy disbelief at Andrew's offer and despondency at what he likely saw as banishment. Yes, that was a fair characterization, Andrew decided. "That's up to you and your father. I'm not paying for that, but I daresay he will if it means you'll put your life in order. Gain some perspective, and don't come back until you can withstand temptation."

"You're right of course." He sounded resigned but also determined. "My father will be relieved. And pleased, I think."

"I'm certain of it." Andrew felt a pang of envy. What he wouldn't give to know what his father would think of him now. Yes, he tempted fate from time to time, but overall he was responsible and behaved with honor and decorum. His mother, he knew, would be proud. She wouldn't, however, like to know that he kept himself apart. Mrs. Alder had told him that many times.

Andrew finished his whiskey. "I'll have the money sent over in the morning. I just need the direction."

Charles nodded. "I'll write it down for you before I go. I owe you a belated congratulations on your marriage. I'm astonished to hear you're taking a wife."

"As it happens, I am not." Andrew tightened his grip on the glass. "We decided we wouldn't suit after all."

Charles looked stricken. "Is this because of me? You were betrothed an hour ago."

"No." Andrew didn't want to speak of her. "You should go and talk with your father, and you should leave tomorrow. The sooner you depart London, the better, I think."

"You're right, I'm sure." He clapped a hand on Andrew's shoulder for a brief moment. "I can't thank you enough for what you're doing. You're a true friend."

Andrew didn't want his friendship. He wanted him out of his life. And he'd do the same with Beaumont and Greene and anyone else who might consider themselves his friend. He took Charles's glass and deposited it on the sideboard along with his own. "Come to my office on your way out."

Andrew took down the direction of where to send the money, and Charles left. Suddenly weary, Andrew sank into the chair behind his desk and stared at his inkwell for some indeterminate, but likely lengthy, amount of time. He was interrupted only by the arrival of Tindall.

"My lord?" the valet inquired as he stepped over the threshold.

Andrew looked up. "Yes?"

"I wanted to inform you that I received an offer of a new position today. For Lord Clare."

The Duke of Clare needed a new valet? "Have you any idea what you're getting yourself into?" Clare was a notorious philanderer.

Tindall blinked. "Perhaps a bit of it will rub off on me, my lord."

Andrew wasn't sure he'd heard him correctly, but then laughed when he realized he had. "Perhaps. An added benefit of the position."

"Indeed, my lord."

Put like that, it seemed an excellent opportunity, and an improvement over his current employment situation. Andrew was suddenly sad to see him go. Hell and damnation, what was wrong with him? All this melancholy feeling about friends and retainers and women, and *damn it.*

He nodded. "When will you be leaving?"

"A fortnight, if it's convenient for you to find a replacement before then."

It wouldn't be convenient, but it was necessary. "Yes, thank you. And congratulations."

"Thank you, my lord. I'll prepare your clothing for this evening." He began to turn.

"Don't bother," Andrew said, halting Tindall's

movements. "I won't be going out." He planned to curl up with a bottle of gin instead. Change, it seemed, was going to take some work.

Tindall nodded and left.

Andrew's insides curdled. He was losing Tindall and Charles. He'd excise Beaumont and the others. And he'd already lost Lucy. The dark despair that had choked him for so long after his family had died washed over him, signaling another attack. Damn it, he was tired of losing himself to the pain. It was his own fault for opening himself up as he had with these people.

His eye caught the last missive he'd received from Sadler about the parachuting excursion the day after tomorrow. Thinking about that offered a modicum of relief, of hope. He reread the letter, letting thoughts of flying high and conquering another adventure soothe him.

The memory of his last balloon ascent invaded his thoughts, and his traitorous mind turned to Lucy—her face providing solace when he'd regained consciousness, her care as she'd helped him to the house, her passion when he'd invited her to stay.

He gulped for air, suddenly breathless, as panic surged through him.

Stop it, he told himself. *She isn't dead. She will live on and enjoy a happy life. Just not with you.*

He bolted from the chair and dashed straight to the gin bottle sitting on the table in the corner. If he had to spend the next week drunk, he'd banish her from his mind. He had to.

Chapter Eighteen

LUCY STARED BLEAKLY at the bustling street as the coach made its way to Lady Satterfield's for tea with Aquilla and Ivy. She'd allowed herself a day to grieve the loss of Andrew, silly as that was, but here it was the second day, and she still felt heartbroken, damn him.

Grandmama had been greatly disappointed to hear that he wouldn't be calling again. But this morning she was back to championing Edgecombe and looking forward to perchance seeing him at the ball they planned to attend that night.

Lucy didn't want to go. She'd had enough of Society events, of pretending to care about finding a husband, of comporting herself as everyone expected. She wanted to don trousers, race in Hyde Park, and shoot at Manton's. She wanted to go to Andrew's town house and shake him until his head rolled off. This vision gave her a moment's perverse satisfaction until sadness overtook her emotions.

The coach stopped in front of Lady Satterfield's, and the footman helped her out. She went inside, and the butler showed her up to the drawing room, where Aquilla and Ivy were already seated.

Aquilla jumped up and hugged her. "How are you?"

They'd heard of her promenade with Andrew the other day. Apparently it had been a choice piece of gossip that evening, particularly after Andrew had appeared to be angry with his friend Charles. Both Ivy and Aquilla had sent notes to Lucy, but with varying tones, of course. Aquilla wanted to know what had happened and hoped things with Andrew were perhaps progressing. Ivy, on the other hand, had hoped that Lucy would continue with her plan and that Andrew would have no part of it because she didn't need him. Neither of them knew what had transpired after the ball the other night. She hadn't seen them since then, but even if she had, she wasn't sure she would tell them.

She felt like a fool for continuing her association with Andrew, especially in a sexual manner, and blamed herself for the anger and hurt she now felt. He'd been clear from the start and all along the way. It was her feelings that had taken a detour and thrown her entire plan off course.

She did, however, blame him for giving her hope. His proposal had been surprising, but when she'd had a moment to let it sink in, she'd been thrilled. Delighted. Overcome with joy. Until Charles had shown up and revealed the true nature of Andrew's intent.

"I'm fine," she answered, forcing a smile. She sat in a chair and pulled off her gloves.

Aquilla sank down on the settee next to Ivy, exchanging a worried look with her. Lucy braced herself.

"You don't look fine," Aquilla said. "That was a feeble attempt at a smile."

"Actually, it was a rather Herculean attempt, if you must know." Lucy wished she could take that back. She didn't want to be maudlin or focus any more energy on Andrew. He didn't deserve it.

Ivy grinned. "How I adore your wit."

The comment reminded her of something Andrew had said once. Would everything remind her of him? This business of falling in love was horrid. She hoped falling out of love happened just as quickly and with far more success.

Aquilla peered intently at Lucy. "I am, of course, dying to know what happened in the park. Were you and Dartford merely planning your next excursion, or was there more to it?"

Lucy had been a fool to think she could avoid discussing him today, but she had to at least try. "There is nothing between us any longer."

Aquilla blinked. "Nothing?" She sounded disappointed.

Contrariwise, Ivy appeared relieved. "He was looking for you at the ball the other night. I told him to leave you alone. I'm sorry he didn't listen to me, but it sounds as though you set him straight."

Lucy snapped her head toward Ivy. "What did he say?"

"That he didn't deserve you. I quite agree, but then I did say it first, and he merely agreed."

If he thought that, why would he propose? Because he'd wanted to protect her from scandal. When that threat had passed, he'd been free to let her go. Only, he hadn't initiated that—she had. He'd said no one had made him think twice about marriage until her. He'd also said it would solve many problems, including their mutual attraction. No, he hadn't mentioned love, but when she thought of what she knew of him, she wondered if that emotion wouldn't frighten him to death.

Death.

What a perfectly awful choice of words.

"Lucy, what's wrong?" Aquilla asked. "You look pale."

She held her hand to her mouth briefly before

dropping it and allowing her friends to come into focus. "I fear I've made a terrible mistake."

Ivy's eyes narrowed. "What?"

Lucy surrendered to the emotions catapulting through her. She didn't want to be sad. She wanted to be happy. After everything she'd been through, she deserved that. And so did Andrew. "I love him. Lord help me, but I do. And, *I think*, he loves me too."

Aquilla's eyes brightened as she grinned. "How wonderful!"

"Why would you think that?" Ivy sounded skeptical and predictably pessimistic.

"He asked me to marry him."

Aquilla gasped and brought her hand to her chest. "I can't believe you didn't tell us!"

Ivy looked at her sharply. "Because she said no. At least, that's my assumption since you came in here declaring your association was finished. For the second time, I might add."

Aquilla rolled her eyes and threw up her hands. "Goodness, Ivy, must you be so very negative?"

Lucy smiled. "It's all right. Ivy has her reasons for being guarded. Just as Andrew has his reasons for being tentative. I told you he lost his entire family. He suffers nightmares and distressing bouts of—" She looked around as if she could find the word she wanted sitting on a table or hanging on the wall. "Anxiety, I would say. Or despondency. Probably both and much more. He holds himself back from relationships, I think."

"Fascinating," Aquilla said. "What are you going to do?"

Lucy's mind was racing, along with her pulse. There was every chance he wouldn't want her—that he really *had* only proposed to protect her reputation and that he'd been relieved when she'd turned him down. "I'm not sure. But I have to talk to him."

"You have a kind heart, Lucy," Ivy said quietly. "I hope he realizes what a treasure he has in you."

Lucy smiled at her friend. "Thank you. I think he might." She hoped so.

She stood abruptly, drawing on her gloves. Now that she knew what she wanted, she was eager to make it happen. "I have to go."

Aquilla looked up at her. "Where? You can't just show up at his town house."

No, she couldn't, not if she wanted to maintain her reputation. What did she care if she was to be married? Because maybe she *wouldn't* be married. A chill raced up her spine as she contemplated a future without him. She thought she'd resolved herself to that but realized she'd still nurtured a bit of hope. It had just taken her friends to fan it into action.

"Send him a note and ask him to meet you in the park later," Ivy said, surprising Lucy with her advice.

Aquilla looked at her and blinked. "Ivy, are you in support of this? I can scarcely believe it."

"I'm in support of whatever makes Lucy happy. Even if it is a man." Her lips spread into a smile that made her eyes sparkle.

"You should do that more," Aquilla said. "You really are beautiful."

Ivy rolled her eyes. "Please."

Lucy was already thinking ahead to meeting Andrew at the park. How could she ensure that he came? If he was concerned about her reputation, she'd threaten to go to his house. That ought to provoke him to meet her. "Can I send the note from here?" she asked.

"Of course." Aquilla jumped up from the settee. "We can go downstairs to the library. Lord and Lady Satterfield have gone to the balloon ascension."

Lucy froze. She'd completely forgotten that was today. Andrew would be going up. And then he would be coming down. Via parachute. Her heart twisted as she thought of him falling to the earth. That hadn't ended too well for him the other day. He was fine, but would he be today?

"Do you know what time the ascension is?" Lucy asked, her heart thundering.

"At three, I think," Aquilla said.

Lucy glanced at the clock on the mantel. That was in less than half an hour. With the crowd, they might not make it in time. "We need to get to Burlington House right away."

Ivy rose. "Why?"

"Because Andrew is going to parachute out of a balloon, and I should like to give him a reason not to risk his life." She only hoped it would be a good enough one.

Aquilla immediately strode toward the door. "I'll have the coach brought around posthaste."

"Thank you," Lucy called after her. She turned to Ivy. "I hope we're not too late."

"You won't be," Ivy said, smiling. "You'll save him."

She only prayed he wanted to be saved.

ANDREW STOOD WITH Sadler amidst the roaring crowd at Burlington House. The parachute device, consisting of a framed canopy with a small basket, was affixed to the balloon. Once they were at the proper altitude, Andrew would climb into the basket from the balloon's gondola, and Sadler would cut the parachute free.

The feelings of anticipation and excitement that he'd felt before his first ascension were there, but strikingly diminished in comparison. It wasn't that he didn't want to go up. It was that there were matters holding him down.

He'd done an excellent job of drinking himself into oblivion the night before last. So much so, that he'd spent most of yesterday cursing his very existence. Last night he'd found sleep, but he'd also dreamed. Vividly.

Erotic encounters, and every single one of them with Lucy. Until the darkness had crept in and served him another nightmare. It had been different, however. He typically saw each of his family die as he stood there, helpless and alone, the hollowness inside of him growing with each death until he was certain it must swallow him whole.

Instead, he'd seen Lucy. She was sick, and he'd held her hand while life slipped from her body. He'd woken in a cold sweat, a desperate fear gripping him and leaving him breathless. Despite the horror of it, he hadn't felt as terrified as after his other nightmares. He'd pondered it for a great while—it wasn't as if he'd been able to sleep again.

The only conclusion he'd reached was that Lucy was still alive. Whereas he'd always come out of the nightmares about his family knowing they were lost to him forever, Lucy was still here. She was still a dream that could come true. If he let himself pursue it.

That meant confronting his fear and acknowledging the fact that he *could* lose her. There were no promises in life, save those they made to each other.

He thought of the promises he'd made to Bertie. Before he'd died, he'd sworn to protect him, and he'd failed. Afterwards, in more recent years, he'd promised Bertie that he would fly for him. Today was about that—flying for Bertie. Carrying out the promise he'd made and doing the only thing he could for his long-dead brother.

But what of the living?

He thought of Charles, who was on his way to northern England. He'd written Andrew a letter thanking him for his kindness and generosity. He'd said, *"You saved my life, and not just because you prevented Gin Jimmy from killing me."*

Andrew had understood. He hadn't saved Bertie, but maybe, just maybe, he'd lived so that he could save Charles.

He also thought of Tindall and his mother, who'd made a full recovery. Tindall credited Andrew's intervention, thanking him for his kindness and his generosity. He'd said, *"You saved her life—I believe that."*

For the first time, Andrew had been grateful that he'd survived, instead of feeling guilty.

Which in turn made him feel less guilty for being glad that he hadn't died. Since he'd met Lucy, he'd begun to think of a future of love and contentment—a future he hadn't thought he deserved or wanted. To admit that he wanted to live—to love—somehow seemed to dishonor his family. But that was foolish. His mother, his father, and especially Bertie would want him to be happy.

"Are you ready?" Sadler asked, his dark gray brows arching high on his forehead beneath the brim of his hat.

Andrew looked at the balloon and saw Bertie's face.

The sound of the crowd faded, and in his mind, he heard the voice of his brother, clear again as if Bertie was beside him. He told him to go—but not into the air.

Angling toward Sadler, Andrew shook his head. "No. I'm not going. My apologies. I need to do something."

Sadler looked surprised. "If you're certain. There won't be another chance. At least not with me."

Andrew knew that. Sadler was past sixty now, and didn't ascend as often as he used to. His sons, however, went up, and Andrew could probably go with one of them. He didn't think that he would.

"I know." He clasped Sadler's hand and shook it firmly. "I thank you. You've given me the experience of a lifetime. And prompted me to pursue the adventure I really want."

Lucy. She would be his greatest risk, and his most fulfilling reward. *If* she accepted him. He'd botched things quite badly and wouldn't be surprised if she refused him completely.

He stepped away from the balloon and started into the crowd. Beaumont stood near the front. He grabbed Andrew's arm as he went past. "What's wrong? Aren't you going up?"

Andrew shook his head amidst the cacophony of noise around them. "No. Why don't you go?" He grinned at his friend and clapped him on the shoulder. Yes, they were friends. "See you later."

As he picked his way through the throng, the anticipation and excitement that he *should* have felt about parachuting coursed through him, driving him to move more urgently. He couldn't wait to get to Lucy.

The crowd surged, and the noise grew. He turned his head and saw the balloon ascend. His task became harder as he now sought to go against the wave of the throng. They moved forward as he tried to reach the back.

Finally, he broke free and stopped dead in his tracks. Standing there, with her head tipped back, staring at the sky, was Lucy.

He strode toward her and saw the look of anguish on her face. "Lucy!" he called and started to run.

Her two friends stood on either side of her, but he barely registered them. She lowered her head, and her gaze found his just before he came to a stop in front of her.

He worked to catch his breath but decided he didn't need to. She made his heart race and his chest constrict, and he prayed he felt that way for the rest of their—hopefully, very long—lives.

"Andrew."

"Lucy." He cupped her face, eager to kiss her, heedless of anyone who might see. "If you tell me to go, I will, but I want to stay. With you. Forever."

She reached under his arms and clutched his back. "Kiss me."

He claimed her mouth and kissed her fiercely. That she kissed him back with equal fervor heated his body and fired his soul. He pulled his lips from hers but didn't move away. "I love you, Lucy. I was an idiot."

"Yes, you were. But I understand why."

Now he pulled back and looked at her in wonder. "You do?"

She nodded. "I think so. You're still deeply wounded by your family's death. And, *I think*, you're scared to allow yourself to love anyone."

He stared at her in wonder. "How is it you understand me so completely?"

"Because for a long time I felt the same way. I was afraid I'd marry someone like my father, so I thought it was best to not marry at all." She touched his face, her gloved fingers running over his temples and caressing his jaw. "I was so afraid you'd gone up in the balloon. Why didn't you?"

"I didn't need to. I wanted to fly—for my brother—but I think he'd understand that I want you more. I've spent over half my life running from ghosts and protecting myself from a hurt that you can't really escape. Loving someone is accepting that you might lose them. I don't ever want to lose you, Lucy, but that's a risk I have to take."

She smiled at him, her eyes full of love. At least he thought they were full of love. She hadn't said it. "I'm so glad. I came here to convince you that you should. I'm so glad that you realized you love me. You've made my task so much easier. In fact, you've saved me from it entirely."

"Does that mean you love me too?"

She laughed, and the sound was a glorious balm to his wounded soul. "Could you doubt it? I think I started falling in love with you the minute you took me to shoot at Manton's. How could I not? You've always treated me with respect and admiration. No one, especially no man, has ever made me feel so special. So cherished. Of course I love you. With all my heart."

He kissed her again, holding her close against him.

"The crowd is starting to look," one of her friends—if he had to guess, he'd wager it was Miss Breckenridge—said urgently.

Reluctantly, he pulled away from Lucy, but he snatched her hand in his, bringing it to his lips. "Does this mean you'll marry me?"

"As soon as possible."

"I don't know if I can get a special license, but I'll do my best."

She looked at him confidently. "You're the Duke of Daring. No one expects you to have a conventional wedding."

He chuckled. "No, I suppose they don't. But does anyone really call me that besides you three?"

She exchanged looks with her friends, both of whom were smiling, even Miss Breckenridge. "Probably not."

"Actually, I'm fairly certain Nora does," Miss Knox said. She looked at Andrew. "Lady Kendal. She's our mentor. Of sorts."

"I see." He saw that the crowd was beginning to dissipate. "Shall we go?"

Lucy took his arm, her eyes shining. "Yes. Let's go on our next adventure."

He put his hand over hers and squeezed her fingers. "I can't wait."

Epilogue

Lucy eyed the target, her farthest yet, and steadied her arm before she squeezed the trigger. The ball fired and hit the target square, knocking the block off the post to the ground. She yelped with glee, turning to Andrew, who was grinning at her work.

"You are incredible," he said, shaking his head. "My turn."

She stepped to the side as he loaded his pistol on the table. She watched his hands work and wondered if it was odd that she could've stood there and stared at him all day.

He lifted the weapon and took aim. His ball hit the target next to the one she'd knocked down, but he only grazed it.

He lowered his arm and let his shoulders slump. "You trounced me again. Clearly it's the shooter, not the weapon."

She'd beat him the other day using his Purdey, but today she had her new Manton—his wedding gift to her along with her mother's jewelry, which he hadn't sold but had only had appraised so that he could settle on a sum. She grinned at him, unable to contain her joy. "I didn't win by much."

He arched a brow at her. "I will demand a rematch."

Lucy caressed her pistol. "I'll look forward to it." She laughed as she set the weapon on the table.

He shook his head again and swooped down to kiss her. "Perhaps I was foolish to marry such a strong woman."

She pulled back in mock affront. "Perhaps I was the fool if you can't see how lucky you are."

He snaked his arms around her and held her against him. "I see quite well, thank you. Although not as well as you if that target is to be believed."

"Oh, now it's my eyesight that's to be given credit?"

"You talk too much," he growled before kissing her soundly.

Lucy sighed into his mouth, loving this man and feeling luckier than anyone had a right to be.

A fat drop of rain found its way to her cheek, splashing against her and making her jump.

Andrew blinked. "What? I was only teasing."

She pointed up. "It's starting to rain."

He tilted his head back and grabbed her hand. "It's about to pour, I fear."

She snatched up her pistol, and they took off running for the house. By the time they reached the terrace, they were quite wet but laughing.

Mrs. Alder greeted them, looking in horror as they dripped on the carpet. "Why are you laughing?"

Andrew sent Lucy a provocative glance. "Why not?"

Why not indeed. Lucy's body heated at the promise in that brief look he'd sent her. "I think I need to go upstairs and change."

"Yes, me too." Andrew squeezed her hand as they made to move past Mrs. Alder.

The housekeeper chuckled. "Go on, then." She smiled to herself and hummed.

She and her husband and the rest of the staff had been overjoyed at their marriage a fortnight ago. It had happened quickly after Lord Kendal—the Forbidden Duke—had helped Andrew procure a special license. All their friends had come to their wedding breakfast, but no one had been happier than Grandmama. She'd said she'd always known that Lucy would break the husband curse and marry a man who was both worthy and reliable. That she was also benefiting from Lucy's match—by way of a lovely town house in the heart of Bath—was an unexpected boon. Lucy was grateful to see Grandmama settled and happy.

Tindall met them as they entered their bedchamber. "My lord, I understand you were caught in a downpour."

Andrew gestured toward his damp clothing. "Yes, as you can see."

"I'll just lay out a fresh set of clothes." He turned to Lucy. "I believe Judith is already doing the same for you."

Lucy looked at Andrew and sighed. "Such brilliant efficiency. I'm almost afraid to tell them we won't be needing their services just now."

"I'm not," Andrew said. He glanced at Tindall but didn't really take his attention from Lucy. "Please excuse us, Tindall."

"Just so, my lord." The valet departed quickly.

"Thank God I convinced him to decline Clare's offer," Andrew said as he sent his hat sailing into the corner.

Lucy untied her bonnet just as Andrew swept it from her head. "He's quite a good valet. I can't believe you were going to let him go. And to the Duke of Desire, no less."

"The Duke of what? Never mind, it suits him perfectly." Andrew spun her around and began to disrobe her. "Although I might've gone with Debauchery."

"Ivy calls him that sometimes. But back to your

point, I'm so glad you asked Tindall to stay."

"As you know, I worked very hard to keep everyone from becoming too important to me. It's precisely because he was so indispensable that he had to go."

She understood. They'd talked at length about his fears and the nightmares and attacks that had plagued him since his family had died. Their first night back at Darent Hall, he'd had another nightmare, but instead of retreating from her, he'd talked about what he'd seen and what he'd felt. Then she'd made love to him, and they'd both agreed that it was an excellent way to deal with things.

"Just think, if I hadn't dressed up as a man and gone to a gaming hell, we'd both be living our sad, lonely lives."

He removed her dress and started on her corset. When that was on the floor, he turned her around. "I've become rather impatient. You do the rest." He began stripping his own clothes away.

She arched a brow at him. "First person naked gets to be on top."

He goggled at her, then laughed. "No fair! You have a head start, thanks to me."

She shrugged as she kicked her shoes off.

He swore and tried to remove his boot without sitting down, nearly falling down in the process.

"Don't hurt yourself!" She tossed her petticoat aside. "I need you to be able to function."

He sat on a chair and worked his boots and stockings off. "Oh, I can function, or don't you remember how I *functioned* after the balloon descent?"

"I remember everything about that night. Shall I demonstrate?"

His eyes darkened, and the muscle in his jaw flexed

as he swallowed. "Yes, *please*."

He tore the rest of his clothes off as if they were aflame, and Lucy had to rush to beat him. In the end, she won, and he prowled toward her, scooping her up and tossing her on the bed.

She giggled, but sobered at the look of stark desire in his eyes. She knelt up and reached for his chest, stroking the now-familiar flesh. "On your back, my lord."

"Whatever you command, my lady." He kissed her first, hard and deep, his tongue sweeping against hers in delicious, arousing strokes.

He lay on his back, and she straddled him, caressing his cock as she held him to her entrance. Her breath was coming fast, and her anticipation was fever hot. "I'm quite ready," she rasped.

"Take me," he said, piercing her with his hungry gaze.

She did, riding him until they were both gasping for breath and completely sated.

Falling on top of him, she kissed him before sliding to the bed and snuggling against his side.

After a few minutes, when they'd both regained their breath, he stroked her back and kissed her forehead. "I take back what I said. Every man should marry an independent woman. Too bad, men are mostly stupid."

"That's true. We just need to find one—for Aquilla."

"What about Ivy?"

"She won't ever marry." Lucy traced her fingertips over his chest. "A pity since it's such a wonderful estate."

"You say that *now*."

"As do you."

"Indeed." He abruptly rolled to face her and smiled.

"Thank you for coming after me that day."

"I realized you loved me—you just needed a little help working it out for yourself." She smoothed his hair back from his forehead. "As it happened, you got there all on your own."

"I worked so hard to fill my life with adventure and distraction in order to keep love out. You, however, finagled your way in, and there was no distraction in the world—not even jumping out of a balloon—that could compare." He kissed her, his lips lingering against hers. "I love you, Lucy, my wonderful, exciting, sharpshooting Duchess of Daring."

A happiness Lucy had never imagined threatened to burst through her chest. "And I love you."

The end

Thank You!

Thank you so much for reading *The Duke of Daring*. I hope you enjoyed it!

Would you like to know when my next book is available? You can sign up for my newsletter, at http://www.darcyburke.com/newsletter/, like my Facebook page at http://www.facebook.com/DarcyBurkeFans, or follow me on Twitter at @darcyburke.

Reviews help others find a book that's right for them. I appreciate all reviews, whether positive or negative. I hope you'll consider leaving a review at your favorite online vendor or networking site.

The Duke of Daring is the second book in The Untouchables series. The next book in the series is *The Duke of Deception*. Watch for more information! In the meantime, catch up with my other historical series: Secrets and Scandals and League of Rogues. If you like contemporary romance, I hope you'll check out my Ribbon Ridge series available from Avon Impulse.

I appreciate my readers so much. Thank you, thank you, *thank you*.

Books by Darcy Burke

Historical Romance

The Untouchables

The Forbidden Duke
The Duke of Daring
The Duke of Deception
The Duke of Desire

Secrets and Scandals

Her Wicked Ways
His Wicked Heart
To Seduce a Scoundrel
To Love a Thief (a novella)
Never Love a Scoundrel
Scoundrel Ever After

League of Rogues

Lady of Desire
Romancing the Earl

Contemporary Romance

Ribbon Ridge

Where the Heart Is (a prequel novella)
Only in My Dreams
Yours to Hold
When Love Happens
The Idea of You
When We Kiss
You're Still the One

Acknowledgments

First and foremost I want to thank my readers for embracing this series. I'm so thrilled you found *The Forbidden Duke* and hope you enjoyed *The Duke of Daring*.

I couldn't do anything without my amazing team, which includes my fabulous cover designer, Carrie Divine and the spectacular editing team of Linda and Toni. You all make my job easier and more fun! Thank you also to Danielle Gorman who is so often a voice of sanity in my crazy schedule. I appreciate your assistance so much.

Other critically important members of my team include my writing friends and partners Elisabeth Naughton, Joan, Swan, Erica Ridley, and Rachel Grant. You make me laugh, share my frustrations, and inspire me every single day. Thank you for being such wonderful co-workers and awesome friends.

The biggest thank you of all goes to the team members I simply can't live without—my beloved family. I love you unconditionally and with the power of a million goat screams.

Praise for Darcy Burke's Secrets & Scandals Series

HER WICKED WAYS

"A bad girl heroine steals both the show and a highwayman's heart in Darcy Burke's deliciously wicked debut."

–Courtney Milan, *NYT* Bestselling Author

"...fast paced, very sexy, with engaging characters."

–Smexybooks

HIS WICKED HEART

"Intense and intriguing. Cinderella meets *Fight Club* in a historical romance packed with passion, action and secrets."

–Anna Campbell, *Seven Nights in a Rogue's Bed*

"A romance...to make you smile and sigh...a wonderful read!"

–Rogues Under the Covers

TO SEDUCE A SCOUNDREL

"Darcy Burke pulls no punches with this sexy, romantic page-turner. Sevrin and Philippa's story grabs you from the first scene and doesn't let go. To Seduce a Scoundrel is simply delicious!"

–Tessa Dare, *NYT* Bestselling Author

"I was captivated on the first page and didn't let go until this glorious book was finished!"

–Romancing the Book

TO LOVE A THIEF

"With refreshing circumstances surrounding both the hero and the heroine, a nice little mystery, and a touch of heat, this novella was a perfect way to pass the day."

–The Romanceaholic

"A refreshing read with a dash of danger and a little heat. For fans of honorable heroes and fun heroines who know what they want and take it."

-The Luv NV

NEVER LOVE A SCOUNDREL

"I loved the story of these two misfits thumbing their noses at society and finding love." Five stars.

–A Lust for Reading

"A nice mix of intrigue and passion...wonderfully complex characters, with flaws and quirks that will draw you in and steal your heart."

–BookTrib

SCOUNDREL EVER AFTER

"There is something so delicious about a bad boy, no matter what era he is from, and Ethan was definitely delicious."

-A Lust for Reading

"I loved the chemistry between the two main characters...Jagger/Ethan is not what he seems at all and neither is sweet society Miss Audrey. They are believably compatible."

-Confessions of a College Angel

League of Rogues Series

LADY of DESIRE

"A fast-paced mixture of adventure and romance, very much in the mould of *Romancing the Stone* or *Indiana Jones*."

-All About Romance

"This book gave me a little of everything...adventure and mystery laced with a healthy dose of heat...to say that I loved it is an understatement.

-A Lust for Reading

"...gave me such a book hangover! ...addictive...one of the most entertaining stories I've read this year!"

-Adria's Romance Reviews

ROMANCING the EARL

"Once again Darcy Burke takes an interesting story and...turns it into magic. An exceptionally well-written book."

-Bodice Rippers, Femme Fatale, and Fantasy

"...A fast paced story that was exciting and interesting. This is a definite must add to your book lists!"

-Kilts and Swords

"I would recommend this book to anyone who enjoys a good mystery and a great romance!"

-The Ardent Reader

Ribbon Ridge Series

A contemporary family saga featuring the Archer family of sextuplets who return to their small Oregon wine country town to confront tragedy and find love...

The "multilayered plot keeps readers invested in the story line, and the explicit sensuality adds to the excitement that will have readers craving the next Ribbon Ridge offering."

-Library Journal Starred Review on YOURS TO HOLD

"Darcy Burke writes a uniquely touching and heart-warming series about the love, pain, and joys of family as well as the love that feeds your soul when you meet "the one."

-The Many Faces of Romance

I can't tell you how much I love this series. Each book gets better and better.

-Romancing the Readers

"Darcy Burke's Ribbon Ridge series is one of my all-time favorites. Fall in love with the Archer family, I know I did."

-Forever Book Lover

About the Author

Darcy Burke is the USA Today Bestselling Author of hot, action-packed historical and sexy, emotional contemporary romance. Darcy wrote her first book at age 11, a happily ever after about a swan addicted to magic and the female swan who loved him, with exceedingly poor illustrations.

A native Oregonian, Darcy lives on the edge of wine country with her guitar-strumming husband, their two hilarious kids who seem to have inherited the writing gene, and three Bengal cats. In her "spare" time Darcy is a serial volunteer enrolled in a 12-step program where one learns to say "no," but she keeps having to start over. She's also a fair-weather runner, and her happy places are Disneyland and Labor Day weekend at the Gorge. Visit Darcy online at http://www.darcyburke.com and sign up for her new releases newsletter, follow her on Twitter at http://twitter.com/darcyburke, or like her Facebook page, http://www.facebook.com/darcyburkefans.

Manufactured by Amazon.ca
Bolton, ON

16588060R00176